MEMORIES AND REMORSE

MEMORIES AND REMORSE

A WARRENTON NOVEL

CHAD SPRADLEY

THE PAPER HOUSE
PUBLISHING

To my wife Jennifer for all her love and support over the years.

CONTENTS

Chapter 1	1
Chapter 2	7
Chapter 3	17
Chapter 4	23
Chapter 5	29
Chapter 6	35
Chapter 7	43
Chapter 8	47
Chapter 9	53
Chapter 10	57
Chapter 11	61
Chapter 12	67
Chapter 13	75
Chapter 14	81
Chapter 15	87
Chapter 16	91
Chapter 17	95
Chapter 18	101
Chapter 19	105
Chapter 20	109
Chapter 21	115
Chapter 22	121
Chapter 23	127
Chapter 24	135
Chapter 25	139
Chapter 26	143
Chapter 27	151
Chapter 28	157
Chapter 29	163
Chapter 30	167
Chapter 31	177

Chapter 32   183
Chapter 33   189
Chapter 34   195
Chapter 35   201
Chapter 36   209
Chapter 37   217
Chapter 38   221
Chapter 39   227
Chapter 40   233
Chapter 41   239
Chapter 42   243
Chapter 43   247
Chapter 44   251
Chapter 45   255
Chapter 46   257
Chapter 47   263
Chapter 48   269
Chapter 49   273
Epilogue   277

About the Author   281

CHAPTER
ONE

It has all the makings of a good night. One of the kinds of nights that came around so few times. His daughter Lauren was at a friend's house, and his wife Rebecca finally had a night off from the hospital where she worked as a nurse. So far, things have gone exactly the way Randall Morris planned.

The last several months were one struggle after another for the couple when it came to making time to be a family. He worked nearly non-stop at his remodeling business. One of the jobs proved far more complex than he had planned, putting him far behind schedule. Hardly a weekend passed since early summer when he and his crew were not putting in tremendous amounts of overtime. All the overtime caused conflict at home. Just his luck after an abnormally busy winter also kept him away from home.

Another source of conflict with Rebecca was the sunporch. The project started a few months ago and still needed to be finished. He worked on it during the weekends when he did not have more significant projects that needed his attention. Part of the problem of owning your own business was that if things needed to be done, you were usually the one to do them. Sure, he had guys who worked for him, but his reputation was on the line, and he prided himself on a well-done job. So, the restoration of the sunporch continued to drag on longer than it would have if he were a client. Still, it was coming along, and he would finally get back to work on it this weekend.

He checked his watch and saw it was close to the time for Rebecca to arrive home. Quickly, he picked out his best shirt and ran the iron over it several times. He moved to the bathroom and combed his hair. His beard was beginning to show more gray than brown lately, as was the hair on his head. At least he could still say the thickness of his hair had not changed. Satisfied that he was properly attired, he retrieved the small bouquet of flowers he had bought for Rebecca on his way home from lunch.

Rebecca got home at her usual time, not expecting what he planned for them to do this evening. He met her at the door with the flowers.

"Hey," he said, "These are for you. I hope you like them."

"They're beautiful," Rebecca said. "What's the occasion?"

"Well, I made reservations at Anderson's for us tonight."

"Anderson's? I've been wanting to go there for a while. I guess I should get ready then."

"You've got time; our reservations are at six-thirty."

"Okay then, looks like you've thought of everything. I'll get ready."

Randall sat on the sofa and turned on the television while he waited for Rebecca to get ready. Almost an hour passed as he watched the local news. He checked his watch, and tried to reassure himself that they had plenty of time. Tension coursed through him no matter how much he tried to relax. He wanted he night to be perfect.

When she finally emerged from their bedroom, he again shot a quick look at his watch. To his relief it was not quite six. It was only a ten minute ride to the restaurant.

"You look lovely,' he said. Randall stood and took her hand and kissed it. "Shall we?" he asked.

"Thank you. Lead the way."

When they arrived, there was a delay of several minutes before their table was ready. The hostess apologized, telling them she would do her best to have the table prepared as soon as possible. It didn't matter to him; the delay allowed him more time to be with the lovely lady he had married six years ago. That's what tonight was supposed to be about, reconnecting with her and their marriage. Besides, the food here was well worth the wait.

When the meal came, they were not disappointed. They ordered shrimp and steak, a nice bottle of wine, and even shared a dessert of chocolate cake. As they dined, they talked about the things in their lives and chatted about little things of interest to them. It probably seemed to anyone observing them that they were more like two young people dating than a married couple of six years. It felt nice to have an evening where they did more than pass each other in the hallway before settling into bed. There were nights when they barely spoke a word to each other, and he wanted to change that, starting right here and now.

Rebecca seemed to be enjoying herself. She worked extra hours at the hospital so often that she felt like family time was a memory. She told him a few days ago that she was tired of never seeing him and that he was neglecting his duties around the house. It had been stressful for her, and he knew he did not often make it any easier on her. Later she apologized to him, saying the stress of her job was bringing out the worst in her. He knew she was right. He promised her that things would change. He vowed to be the attentive husband she deserved.

Leaving the restaurant, Rebecca told him she needed to stop by the grocery store to pick up several items to make a dessert for the community bake sale. From the look on his face, Rebecca could tell he was disappointed in the change of plan. She smiled at him, took his hand, and lightly kissed him. She softly whispered, "Relax. Some things are worth waiting for." He chuckled lightly and drove to a nearby grocery store.

The trip inside the store ended up giving them another opportunity to be together as a couple. Aisle by aisle they collected the things they needed. The whole time Rebecca played with her long brown hair, glancing slyly at him, smiling at just the right time. *Oh my god, she's flirting with me*, he thought as their eyes met, causing her to smile at him again. He could feel his desire for her grow with each passing glance, each movement of her body, and every blink of her eyes. Her flirtations made him want her as they eventually made their way to the checkout aisle. *Maybe this was not such a bad idea*, he thought as the cashier scanned their items.

The drive home seemed to last forever. They lived in a small subdivision outside of Warrenton on Fountain Street. Their house might not have been much, but they made it a lovely home. *A happy home*, he thought. *I'm the luckiest man on the face of the Earth.*

After the divorce from his first wife, he had all but given up on finding love again. He had joint custody of his daughter Lauren, and for a time, that was enough. But Lauren was a teenager, and spending a lot of time with Dad was not a big priority to her. So, when he met Rebecca, it was a godsend. It was odd at first. Rebecca was several years younger, and he worried she and Lauren would not get along. Their relationship was a bit rocky initially, but Lauren seemed to accept Rebecca, even telling him she wanted her dad to be happy.

The romance didn't happen all at once, but the two began seeing each other more and more over time. Before Randall knew it, they were in love and planning on spending their lives together. They got married, and like every married couple, they had differences, spats, big arguments, and disagreements. Yet he never went to bed mad at her, at least not that he could remember. Despite all their problems, they were happy and still very much in love. She was his dream come true.

Finally, they arrived home. They carried in their groceries and put away the things that needed to be refrigerated. As Rebecca stood up from putting the heavy cream into the refrigerator, he took her by her waist and began kissing her neck. She giggled and turned to place her arms around him. She pressed her lips to his, and the rest began to happen naturally. Soon they were in their bedroom, undressed, bodies intertwined in the heat of passion. Every movement built upon the next one until the inevitable release. They lay gazing into each other's eyes, whispering lovers' words, wishing they could hold onto the moment forever.

After several more minutes, they partially dressed and returned to the kitchen. Rebecca began putting the ingredients together with his help. She looked around and got a distressed look on her face. "Where is the vanilla extract we bought?" she asked him as she looked through the cabinets.

"I don't know. It should be on the island. Did you put it in the cabinet?"

"I looked, and it's not there. Did we leave it off?"

"Don't think so. Where's the receipt?" They looked over the receipt, and sure enough, they had left it out of the cart. Rebecca was beside herself with embarrassment. She ran her hand through her hair and shifted on her feet.

"Well, I have to go back to the store," she said, exhaling a frustrated breath.

"Can't it wait until tomorrow?" he asked.

"No, it can't. I don't want to go back to the store, but I have to. I have to deliver it to the bake sale by eight in the morning. Okay, I'll run back to the store and be right back."

"I'll go with you," Randall said. "Just let me get my jeans on real quick."

"No, don't worry about it. I'll go. It's not that big of a deal, I guess."

"You sure? I don't mind," he said, trying to be helpful.

"Really, no. I'm a big girl. I'll be fine. Besides, we may start over again when we get the cake in the oven."

"Oh well, okay, Mrs. Morris, if that's what you want."

She put on a pair of jeans and a t-shirt, slipped on a pair of shoes, grabbed her purse, and left for the store. She promised to be gone only a short time. He watched her drive away and then shut the door. He decided to check on the remodeling job on the sunporch while she was gone.

He walked to the back and inspected the work he had completed. Everything seemed to be coming together nicely. This weekend he would finish sanding the drywall along the seams he mudded a couple of weeks ago. By Sunday evening, he could have the first coat of paint on the walls and, maybe next weekend, finally finish this project. Randall, in his mind, began to plan a Super Bowl party, not that the Rams would make it that far. He always wanted a man cave, and soon he thought his hide-away would finally be ready. This would be his refuge from the worries of the world. A place he could relax.

Suddenly something knocked him to the floor. At first, he thought something had fallen from the ceiling and knocked his breath out. As he tried to rise, he saw the blood on the floor and felt weakness in his left arm. His breathing became short and erratic as he realized this wasn't an accident. He never knew what happened next. His attacker fired three more shots, and while only two found their mark, it was enough. His last vision was of the floor and the quickly massing pool of blood. Two breaths later, the world faded away forever.

CHAPTER
TWO

Roger Taylor sat alone at the bar of a place that was all too familiar. It was the same place where he and Shelia used to meet. She tried her best to elicit information from him on cases he was working on while she was looking for a story. They usually sat at a small table near the back of the place, just out of earshot from most people but not too far away to arouse suspicion. Tonight, as many nights since she died, he could not bring himself to sit there or even look at the place they used to share.

They were not a couple before her death. Years before, though, when he was a young cop, recently discharged from the Army, and she was a rookie reporter right out of college, they had met and fallen in love. They went as far as to get engaged, but when a Sacramento television station called her for a job, she jumped at the chance. He stayed in Warrenton, and they promised to make it work. One day she stopped answering the phone, and he eventually stopped calling.

She offered to return the ring one day in an email of all things, but he did not want it. He always thought that one day, when they weren't married to their jobs, they would get back together. Just over a year ago, the dream died forever.

Whether guilt or remorse kept him here, he could not say anymore. The truth was it was probably both. He failed her. That much was true. Granted, she knew the risks of taking on someone like Leonard Pierson. He reminded himself of that fact over and over. Maybe one day, he would even start to believe it.

His mind kept replaying the moment her body was found. When Roger arrived on the scene, he did not know who the victim was. The crime scene detectives rolled over the body, he saw her, eyes wide open, seeming to focus on him. Her eyes seemed to accuse him, "You failed me, Roger. You were supposed to protect me, but you didn't."

The thought of failing Shelia haunted him. Now his usual routine was to go to work, then to his apartment, and try not to fall asleep. About three times a week, he ended up at the bar inside Tavern on the Corner. Anything to keep him from sleep because that brought the dreams that haunted him. He was tormented by the look frozen on her face and the lifeless eyes that pierced into his soul. Drinks helped, but only for a while. It was his fault Shelia was gone, and he had to live with that.

Knowing he never got to settle the score with Leonard Pierson was worse. To see the look in his eyes as his world collapsed around him. True, Pierson didn't pull the trigger, but he did order the hits on Shelia, Sidney Lewis, Luke Brady, and himself. Instead of bringing Leonard Pierson to justice, the man committed suicide with a pistol hidden in his office as Taylor and the police raced up the stairs to Pierson's office. Death by his own hand was one final act of defiance in a long story between Pierson and Taylor. Instead, Taylor had to be content with killing the hitman responsible for Shelia's death. Taylor succeeded in killing the hitman on the day he planned to kill Sidney Lewis as she walked out of prison.

Most nights were like this one. Roger Taylor is sitting here trying to chase away a memory of someone he let down. At first, people tried to talk to him, bring him into their conversations, or interest him in some romance. By now, though, most people left him alone to try and drown in his misery. There was so much left to say, so much left undone. Perhaps that was what bothered him the most.

As it happened often, his cell phone rang. Looking at the screen, he saw it was newly minted Detective Laura Barnes. She passed her detective's exam several months ago and gave Warrenton's police a much-needed boost. Knowing he couldn't send this call to voice-mail, he answered, "Yeah?" He listened to what Barnes had to say on the other end before responding, "Yeah, fine. Send a car for me. Usual place." He hung up and reached for his wallet. He flung a $20 bill on the bar and waved at the bartender, who waved back before returning to serving drinks.

Taylor walked out into the warm September night, still full of the melancholy feelings he felt inside. He waited several minutes, thinking he was sober enough to drive, but why chance it? The marked car arrived and pulled to the sidewalk. He tried to remember the officer's name. *Davis? Phil Davis?* He walked around to the passenger door and got into the car.

According to the nameplate on his uniform, the African American male officer's name was McClendon. Dominic McClendon. There were so many new faces these days that ordinarily, he could be forgiven for not knowing the name of someone who had only been there a few months.

These were not ordinary times, though. He could feel the chill in the car as McClendon drove him to the scene to meet Barnes. He felt it even more as he arrived at the small house in a subdivision outside Warrenton. As Taylor walked toward the well-maintained house, he could feel the icy stares of the uniformed officers outside the home. He knew why they felt this way. Roger had broken the unwritten rule of police work and turned on his fellow officers. Eleven officers were fired or arrested in the aftermath of the Leonard Pierson case. No matter how guilty they were, it was never acceptable to cross the blue line and he had ratted on almost a dozen of them. An uneasy thought flashed into his mind. Eleven were how many they could prove colluded with Pierson, but how many others remained on the force?

In some ways, he wanted to scream at those officers who now seemed to hate and resent his presence. He wanted to tell them those men made their choices. They chose to back a man who was nothing more than a common criminal, no matter how much money he had. They supported a man who pushed drugs, guns, prostitutes, and who knows what else all over the country. Still, they blamed Taylor for what happened. What if he had just left well enough alone? Everything would have been so much better. Taylor broke the rule, and there was a price to pay.

Making his way into the house, he was directed to where Barnes and the crime scene techs were inspecting the body. He found her in a sunporch at the rear of the home. Barnes was looking over the body that lay on the floor in a pool of his own blood. She caught sight of him and rose to her feet.

"Barnes, what have we got?"

"A future hangover by your looks, but I think you'll survive."

"I'm not drunk, nor am I in the mood. Tell me what we have," Taylor responded more shortly than he intended.

"White male, 49 years old. His name is Randall Morris; owns a business here in town. Three gunshots in the back. Got a miss by his left ear. By the pattern of the shots, whoever pulled the trigger doesn't know how to handle a gun."

"How do you know that?"

"Well, the shots are placed all over his back, not in a generalized area. Like whoever shot him just pointed and pulled the trigger."

Roger thought about her analysis of the shooter's accuracy, which seemed logical enough. She could be wrong, and whoever it was could be trying to cover up the fact that they were familiar with weapons. He decided to let it slide. "Any family or witnesses?"

"Wife is Rebecca Morris. A daughter, Lauren Morris, neither was home at the time. We're still trying to contact the daughter, but she's not answering her phone. His wife is outside. She was pretty hysterical. She apparently walked in on someone burglarizing the home. Guy took a couple of shots at her as she entered the door. Another reason I don't think he knew how to handle a gun."

"Which door did she come in when she returned from the store?" Taylor did not notice bullet holes by the front door when he came in.

"The side door walking into the kitchen. Mrs. Morris told me that she jumped into the flowerbed outside when the guy shot at her," Barnes responded.

"Any shell casings?" he asked as he surveyed the scene.

"None so far. Pretty sure the perp used a revolver. I don't think our killer would have had the presence of mind to pick up loose shell casings," Barnes said as she made a few more notes in her notebook.

Taylor had to admit that in the cases she was assigned to so far, Barnes was very meticulous in how she documented a scene. It then crossed his mind this was one of the few murder cases she had worked on since becoming a detective. Warrenton did not have many murders in a year, but they were not unheard of. So far, she seemed to be handling the investigation well. "Probably won't find any prints either. The wife said she thought she saw the man was wearing gloves."

At least the thief, now the killer, knew to wear gloves. Whoever teaches these criminals how to ply their trade should also teach them basic firearms techniques. *Nice to know my sarcasm is still working, he thought.*

Taylor looked around the crime scene for any details they might have missed. "Did the wife get a good look at the guy? Anything helpful at all?"

"No, she said he was masked. She said he might have been about six feet tall but couldn't say for certain."

"Wait, you said she walked in on the guy, so where was she before her husband was killed?"

"She said they had gone to the store after having dinner. Apparently, they forgot an item she needed, so she returned to the store to get it. Said she might have been gone forty-five minutes to an hour." Barnes put her notebook away and looked down at the body. "You think someone might have been staking the place out? Maybe waiting for them to leave, thinking no one was home?"

Taylor thought for a minute. "Maybe. It could be something random. The perp could have been looking for a target of opportunity. But why here? If he saw Mrs. Morris drive off, he might have thought no one was home. Or, maybe this was someone that knew the Morris family and held a grudge or had it out for him. Like maybe a business rival or unsatisfied customer."

He looked outside into the backyard and spotted who he assumed was Rebecca Morris. Carefully he made his way out to where she stood. From the looks of her, she was an emotional wreck. His training told him not to sympathize too much with the victims because it tended to cloud judgment and objectivity. It was tough sometime, especially when it was someone sympathetic. Taylor had to admit this was one of those times. In almost every case, the spouse was the prime suspect, and just because she was not home didn't mean she couldn't have put someone else up for the murder. He tried to remember that as he walked toward her.

Rebecca was wrapped in a blanket, her face streamed with tears. She was noticeably shaking. T Her long brown hair was disheveled. Her clothes were covered in dirt from her dive into the flowerbed. In short, she looked like one would expect from someone with a brush with death. It was safe to say that Rebecca Morris had the worst night of her life. Taylor couldn't help but think that was how he met most people.

"Mrs. Morris, I'm Detective Roger Taylor," he said,. "I want to say I'm sorry for your loss. I understand you were also attacked, is that right?"

Rebecca Morris didn't make immediate eye contact. She seemed far off as if things were moving too fast for her to comprehend. The whole experience seemed to have left her empty and hollow. "I...I, yes, yes I was...I was..." she trailed off. Her breathing accelerated, and she seemed off balance.

Try as he might, Taylor had a hard time being objective. This poor lady had just been through hell, and now he was trying to pry into her most horrifying experience. "Mrs. Morris, I know this is tough, you've been through a lot, and I'm sorry to do this now, but time is of the essence." There was never a good way to do this. Victims wanted and needed time to process what they'd been through. Still, there was always the chance that if they acted fast, the police could catch whoever did this if the witness could help. "Can you think of anything, any reason someone would want to do this?"

She hardly moved. "No, my husband is a..." she paused, "was a good man." The tears started flowing again. "Who would want to do this to him? He never hurt anyone and always looked after others before himself."

"I don't know, Mrs. Morris, but we will do our best to find out." He knew not to make too many promises because, at the end of it all, this could become a case that dragged on for a very long time. It wasn't like on TV, where everything got wrapped up in a single episode. Actual investigations took time, and now the clock was ticking. "Look, I know this is tough, but did he have any recent customers, contractors, or anyone who didn't approve of a job or had some kind of dispute with him?"

"No, I don't know of anyone. Randall was such a good person. He shouldn't be gone, not like this," she said as she started to lose what little composure she had.

Taylor could see he would get nowhere with her. The investigator part of him wanted to press for more, but his human side said to back off. It is always a delicate balance between the two sides. Taylor, the man, wanted to let the family grieve and deal with their loss, but the cop wanted to know more. Most people knew more than they let on to the police. Even if they thought what they had to say was not important, the slightest clue could break a case wide open. It wasn't easy, but he decided the human side would win this time.

"Mrs. Morris, here's my card. I want to speak with you in person at the station in the morning. I know this is hard, but the sooner we talk, the better for everyone. Again, sorry for your loss."

She muttered thank you, and Taylor turned to go. In his mind, something kept bothering him other than the obvious question of why someone would do something like kill a man while his back was turned in his own home.

It didn't seem like a thief had been taken by surprise, not if Morris was shot in the back. No, this seemed more like something more deliberate. Taylor could not escape the feeling that this was somehow planned. Granted, if a thief walked in and found the homeowner in the same room, it was possible to make a snap decision and kill him.

Then there was the wife. She walked in, and the killer fired two shots at her before running off. Certainly, seems to support Barnes' theory of a revolver. Her observation of the shot pattern made sense as well. That meant whoever did this was not a gun expert, to say the least. That could explain why he missed Rebecca Morris when she walked in.

Barnes was compiling a list of missing things. The victim's wallet was gone, as was the jewelry he wore. It would still be a while before they knew what was missing from the house. Until then, he could still say this was a robbery gone wrong. Still, there was this nagging feeling like there was more to it. Could the thief have been looking for something specific? Or was it a business rival trying to gain an advantage and then deciding to end the competition permanently. A lot of possibilities but no real answers for now.

Not knowing was the part of the job he hated, the uncertainty in the early stage of a case like this. He had to admit getting to the truth and putting the pieces together as they came was exciting. It was what drove him as a detective. It caused him to take down Leonard Pierson just over a year ago.

Pierson was one of the most significant drug runners on the west coast. For years he managed to slip out of Taylor's grasp, at least until his son, Lawson Pierson, got sloppy. He placed some sensitive information on a flash drive and left it at his fiancée's apartment. Sidney Lewis found it and was horrified to see that Lawson had recorded their intimate moments.

When she confronted him, Lawson lost it and tried to kill her. Sidney hit him over the head with a scuba tank. In his drunken and disoriented state, he fell, hitting his head. He died. To make matters worse, he had recorded himself with several other women while on business trips.

It should have been a clear case of self-defense. Only Sidney made a couple of bad decisions in her panic. Then there was the setup by George Sullivan, a fellow detective Taylor had known and trusted for years. He falsified and tampered with evidence and arrested Sidney for murder. She was sent to prison for six years before Taylor, her attorney, Luke Brady, and Shelia could get her released, all thanks to the flash drive and Sidney's information. Yet it cost Shelia her life.

That last part made it hard to focus. Taylor never wanted her involved in the investigation. Still, once Shelia decided to do something, there was no talking her out of it. He loved that about her, how she kept on time after time. Even as one lead dried up, she started to chase another. Ultimately that was what drove them apart. Yet there they were after all the time that passed, buried up to their necks in an investigation. At least for Taylor's part, he hoped that maybe this would lead them back together. He believed that was what Shelia wanted as well.

Angry at himself for his moment of self-pity, Taylor forced the memory into the back of his mind. This wasn't Leonard Pierson. That creep is dead. It was time to pull himself together and do what he did best. Find who killed an innocent man, and that was what he would do.

CHAPTER
THREE

Taylor surveyed the scene more closely after speaking with Rebecca Morris. She left home for the Reed family residence in the Stillman's Trail neighborhood a few miles away. Lauren was supposed scheduled to spend the night there anyway. When they heard what happened, the Reeds invited them both to stay until the scene was processed.

Randall Morris's body lay face down on the sunporch floor. Looking at the blood splatter on the unpainted wall, he must have been evaluating his work when the killer shot him. A closer look revealed a newly made hole where the bullet went through his shoulder. At least, that was Taylor's initial guess. Donning a pair of gloves, he took out the small knife he carried and dug out the projectile. He placed it in a plastic bag and sealed it.

He believed the other shots were delivered while Morris lay on the ground. Because of the concrete floor, it was possible they could retrieve the other projectiles either from the body or from the floor. Taylor started snapping pictures of the body and the surrounding area with his phone's camera. He walked his pattern around the scene, taking pictures as he moved slowly and methodically.

Taylor began taking photos of the sunporch. He noticed a window near the wall was still partially open. Taylor zoomed his camera in and snapped a picture. Flipping on his phone's flashlight, Taylor walked outside to examine the other side of the window. Looking at the base of the window, he could see scuff marks that looked like someone had forced open the window. Snapping a couple of photos, Taylor returned inside. A quick check of the other windows revealed that many were unlocked, just like the one he inspected. He made a note and continued processing the scene.

Barnes came down the steps and found Taylor examining the scene.

"Hey, you need to come see this," she said, her words waking him from his trance-like focus. Barnes led him to the main bedroom at the end of a hallway. Stepping inside, she drew his attention to a nightstand beside the bed. "See that?" She pointed to the top of the stand. "The jewelry box has been moved. Looks like our guy took what was inside and tossed it over there." Barnes directed his attention to the jewelry box on the floor next to the wall.

"Looks like our guy dumped the contents into a bag and headed back out of the bedroom?" Taylor said as he looked around the room. "What about the daughter's bedroom? Anything out of place there?"

"Doesn't look like it," Barnes said. "I don't think he made it to her bedroom before rushing out." Barnes thought for a moment. "He just killed the homeowner. Why would he risk coming up here? Why not get out as fast as he could?"

"My guess is he wanted to get something out of his efforts. You just killed a man, so run in and get what you can, and get out," Taylor said as he looked around the room. He turned and walked back out into the hallway. From there, Taylor could clearly see the side door to the house. Walking down the hallway through the kitchen, he found where the two other shots landed.

Looking outside the door, he could see a small flowerbed. The plants looked trampled. Thinking back, he remembered seeing dirt on Rebecca Morris's hands and pants legs. He took pictures of the outside and the two bullet holes in the door jamb.

Taylor stood at the intersection of the hallway and the dining room. To his left was the sunporch entrance with the small steps leading into the room. Initially, the sunporch was simply an outside area without any walls, unattached to the house. The homeowners decided to enclose the area into a sunporch years ago. When the Morrises bought the home several years back, Randall decided to remodel it into a man cave. The problem was for a small business owner, personal projects often took second place to customers' demands. The remodeling job was repeatedly pushed back. At least, that was what Rebecca Morris told Barnes in her initial statement.

"Our killer must have been standing right around this area when he took the shots at Mrs. Morris. Probably on his way out of the house," Taylor said.

"Makes sense. You're thinking when the killer made his way out of the bedroom, he heard her keys as she opened the door, so he decided to cover his exit? Why didn't he try to finish her off then? Why just run out knowing she could call the police."

"Good question. He'd already fired four shots, so maybe he didn't have any extra ammo. If he had a revolver, he would have to release the cylinder, eject all the spent bullets, and then reload. By then, Mrs. Morris would have probably gotten away. Or maybe he just decided the body count was high enough and fled."

Out of the corner of his eye, he spotted a tall, lanky man carrying a case and wearing a lab coat. "Hey, Meeks is here," he said to Barnes, motioning for her to follow him.

Dr. Brian Meeks was the chief medical examiner for the county. Generally, at crime scenes, he did most of the coroner's work. It was an arrangement that suited both the coroner and ME well. As they approached him, he turned his balding head with thick, black-rimmed glasses toward the two detectives. "It's about time you showed up. Was beginning to think it was your off day," Taylor said as he offered his hand to Meeks.

Dr. Meeks shook his hand and asked, "Do you know how long I had to wait to get those dinner reservations at the country club? I'm not talking about the cafe upstairs, oh no. The really nice place on the ground floor."

"You mean Paterro's? Wow, probably took you what a month?"

"That's right, a month. Next time would you please schedule your murder investigations better?"

"I'll try, no promises, though. The body is downstairs in the sunporch."

"Please tell me your rookie detective there didn't move or otherwise do anything to mess up the deceased," he said nodding his balding head toward Barnes.

"Are you kidding? The way you handle a body, it's a wonder why your wife stays with you," Barnes quickly shot back at him.

Meeks and Taylor looked at each other in shock. "I like her, Taylor. Tell me she's going to stay around for a while." With an amused smile, he made his way down to the sunporch to examine the body of Randall Morris.

"I think he likes you, Barnes."

"I'm touched," she said.

Meeks looked over the body, processing what he saw, taking notes, and taking pictures with a large camera. Taylor often teased that his "1940's" vintage camera belonged in a museum. Still, Meeks quickly reminded him it was one of the best cameras on the market. At least, it was back in 2000. As hard as the film was getting to find, Meeks knew sooner or later he would have to upgrade to digital photography. Whether Meeks was old-fashioned or not, technology would eventually force him to change or retire.

"Well, there's always next month," Meeks said as he shrugged his shoulders. "Detective Barnes, I hope you make a better detective than a traffic cop," he said as he walked back toward the front door.

Taylor gave his famous half smile to Barnes. "Oh yeah, he definitely likes you."

CHAPTER
FOUR

Taylor arrived at his sparsely decorated apartment just after midnight. He walked in, placing his jacket on a chair next to the door. His keys, wallet, and badge went on a coffee table beside an open beer bottle. He picked up the bottle on his way to the kitchen, discovering that it was still mostly full. He poured the remainder of the contents down the drain in the kitchen sink, tossed the bottle in the trash, then chastised himself for not putting the bottle in the recycling.

Opening the refrigerator, he saw the remains of the pizza he ordered last night. It was a thin-crust supreme, so he grabbed a large piece and started eating it without warming it in the microwave. He took the second beer bottle out of the six-pack he bought last night on his way back from the pizza place. Placing the slice in his mouth, he twisted off the top, snapping it with his fingers toward the trash can. The top missed and bounced across the linoleum floor. Shaking his head, he picked up the top and flipped it into the can.

Satisfied, he carried the pizza and beer to his couch and sat in front of his television. He sat the bottle on the coffee table in front of him and flipped channels for a few minutes before deciding there was nothing worth watching. Sitting the remote next to the bottle, he sat back and finished the pizza slice.

Leaving the mostly full bottle on the coffee table, he went into his bedroom. He sat on the bed for a few minutes in the darkroom. Before he stood to change his clothes, Taylor turned on a small brass lamp on a nightstand beside his bed. After he undressed and put on his night clothes, he lay down and flipped off the light next to his bed.

Sleep came surprisingly fast in contrast to most nights since Shelia died. His dreams did not bother him; he could barely remember them anyway. What did bother him was the quiet. The darkness was broken only by the glare from a streetlight, which cast long shadows onto his bed. Try as he might, he could not find a place for his bed where he wasn't bothered.

His bed felt empty as it had been long since Shelia first left him for her job in Sacramento. He continued to hang on, hoping she would return to him one day. After she died, Roger tried dating several times, but no one ever measured up to Shelia. It was in these moments when he felt her loss all the more.

The alarm on his phone blared at 6:00 am. Switching off the alarm, he got to his feet and went to the shower. Roger never hit the snooze button. He got used to getting up early in the Army and never got out of the habit. Taylor showered quickly, trying to get done in about ten minutes or less, another practice picked up in the Army. When he finished, he dried off and went to the kitchen.

He ate a quick breakfast of a microwave sausage biscuit, a glass of orange juice, and a cup of coffee. Taylor rushed out the door, finishing the last of his microwaved meal as he made his way to his car. Within fifteen minutes he was on his way to the station. The Charger roared to life as he situated himself behind the wheel.

The morning roll call went as usual. Sargent Nichols briefed the patrol officers on their assignments for the day and sent them on their way. Taylor noticed that McClendon, who picked him up at the bar last night, was among the assembled officers. He made a mental note to pull up his personnel file and try to get to know the man better. The way he saw it, he owed the man.

Barnes entered Taylor's office and took a seat across from him. Considering their late night at the crime scene, she seemed in a good mood. "Morning," she said. "I guess you passed a peaceful night, right?"

"Peaceful enough. Probably shouldn't have eaten leftover pizza so late at night."

"You sound like my mother, Taylor. Please tell me you're not getting old before your time."

"Old enough to know not to comment," he said. "The Morris family is supposed to come in this morning. I'll handle the questioning this time around. I don't think two of us in there will be necessary. We can handle it if we need to follow up later, but I'll take the lead for now."

"Sounds good. I can run down some of Morris's business associates and former employees. Maybe call a few of his former customers to see if there are any issues we should know about."

"Good idea. We'll head over to Morris's office later. See if you can get in touch with any of his office staff. Try to see if they would be willing to come down before Monday morning."

"So, about the wife, she's still a suspect, right?" Barnes asked. "I mean, it's usually the wife or someone close to the victim."

"We treat everyone like a suspect until they're not. We can't completely rule her out, but it seems unlikely she is the culprit. Still, we'll follow the evidence where ever it leads."

"But you don't think she had anything to do with it," Barnes said.

Secretly, Barnes wondered if his mind was in the right place. She knew the last several months had been difficult for him. Barnes wondered if he was taking the case a little too personally because of what happened with Shelia.

It was not a subject they talked about often. During the Pierson investigation, Barnes had been more or less a bystander and did not have much to do with the case. Granted, she was the one who took Sidney Lewis into custody, but aside from that, she really was not involved much. In fact, Barnes could not remember ever meeting Shelia.

Her mind drifted back to a conversation that Taylor had with her not long after joining the Investigations Unit. He said she tended to sympathize too much with some of the people she met in the line of duty. It was true. There were some people she hated having to arrest. Taylor told her that a good detective had to separate personal feelings from the job duties. She wondered if that was what he was doing now with the Morris family?

"My gut instinct says no. True, I've been wrong before, but it makes sense. Think about it. First, Mrs. Morris leaves to go to the store. The husband stays at home to work on the project downstairs. Our thief breaks in and finds the husband alone unexpectedly. Kills him and starts to take items from the house. The wife comes home and surprises the thief, who takes a couple of shots at her and then runs off. It matches the story she told us at the scene."

"You don't think it sounds a little too coincidental, do you?" she asked. "Just asking."

"You should ask, and that's why we want them to come in today. See if the story changes. Is she adding or purposely leaving things out from the first time we talked to her? This is a way of finding out more information about the crime and trying to rule her out as a suspect."

"I'll check and see if any other houses in the neighborhood have been burglarized recently. Could be the same people," Barnes said.

"Don't bother. I can already tell you that there have been. The neighborhood had two burglaries in the last month. We've been so understaffed lately that I haven't had time to investigate them. Another reason I tend to believe Rebecca Morris's story."

"Speaking of which, when will we get some more help around here?" Barnes asked. "No offense, but this is getting ridiculous. I mean, we've gone through how many people recently?"

"Look, the new chief is trying to get the department in order. I'm sure she'll be ready to make some new hires soon. Some patrol officers have done a good job and shown real potential as investigators. Just give it some time."

"Yeah, well, a lot of us think you should have gotten the job as chief. You were up for it, and they should have hired you."

"Well, they didn't. So that's that. Besides, I'm not really sure I wanted the job anyway." He took a deep breath and let it out, hoping he didn't come across too harshly. "Don't worry; everything will work out. We can keep using some of the guys from patrol when needed. Now I need to get ready for the Morris family."

CHAPTER
FIVE

The Morris family was at the Warrenton Police Department by nine. Taylor had arrived at the station at seven and used the time to review case facts. Pictures, statements, details both he and Barnes wrote down the night before, trying to find anything useful. He learned the gun was a .38 caliber, most likely a revolver, as Barnes had guessed. The placement of those two rounds lets Taylor know that Mrs. Morris was lucky to be alive.

Lauren, Rebecca's stepdaughter, was with her today. His police training told him everyone was a suspect until they were not. Even so, there was always the possibility they might be again, but Lauren had an airtight alibi. Lauren and a friend had gone to a movie and silenced their phones during the show. When officers eventually found Lauren, she was returning to her friend's house. That's when she first heard the news her father was dead. A brutal way to find out bad news.

No one was home on the night of the murder except the victim. That meant the house was being watched, the thief believed no one was there, or the killer was targeting Randall Morris. Taylor was not sure which it was just yet. He also was not sure exactly why someone would want Morris dead. Everything seemed to point to a robbery gone wrong. Maybe that was why Taylor believed there had to be more to the case.

He walked across the station office area to meet the family. He greeted them and escorted them to an interview room. Both women seemed calm, but he knew they were mourning a husband's and father's death.

"Thank you both for coming in this morning," he began as he sat across from them at the small table in the room. "I know this has been a tough time for you both, and again I am sorry for your loss." Rebecca Morris thanked him quietly.

He decided to proceed slowly and with a small amount of compassion. "Mrs. Morris, can you please tell me one more time where you were at the time of the murder?"

She looked at him with disbelief. Taylor could tell the question frustrated her. "It's standard procedure to ask again. It helps us establish a record of your responses and to keep you thinking about your actions. It may reveal small details over time, although I admit it is repetitive." His explanation seemed to put her more at ease.

"My husband and I went out last night to dinner and stopped by the grocery store on the way home. When we returned, I realized we had left an item off our list. I decided to go back to the store." She paused for a few seconds as her emotions started to take over again. "He wanted to go with me, but I told him I could go alone. I should have let him come with me," she said as sobs began again. "Why didn't I let him come with me?"

"Mrs. Morris, do you remember how long you were gone?" Taylor asked, trying to keep her talking.

"I don't know, forty-five minutes, maybe. I got what I needed, plus a few extra items. Then I came home. When I walked in, I saw that man, and he shot at me."

"Are you sure it was a man," Taylor asked her.

"Pretty sure. I didn't really get that good of a look at whoever it was, but he seemed to have the build of a man."

"When he shot at you, where did you hide?" Taylor continued.

"I dropped the grocery sacks and fell into our flower bed. I crawled along the house and ran to the neighbors for help."

"Why didn't you use your cellphone to call for help?"

"I dropped my purse, and my phone was inside it."

Taylor thought for a second and decided to change his questions. "Mrs. Morris, exactly what did your husband do for a living?"

"He was a home remodeler. He contracted jobs through home builders, individual references, cabinet makers, etc. Randall hung the drywall, painted, and arranged for flooring, cabinets, and other parts of the remodel job. He also built additions to houses. He built things like decks, sunrooms, gazebos, you name it. He's such a good…was so good at building things with his hands."

"Is that what he was doing at your home?"

"Yes, he started that project about six months ago. He stayed so busy with other people's projects he didn't have time to work on our home. That's what he was going to do this weekend. He finally had the time." The irony of the statement was not lost on anyone in the room. Taylor thought how strange it was to believe you had time only to find out that time had run out.

He fought back an image of Shelia that popped into his mind. *It's a distraction to think of her right now. These people need answers, and they cannot get them if I'm distracted by regrets.* Shelia would not want that either. She would tell him to focus his attention and that she did not need him watching over her. Still, the thought echoed in his mind.

"I guess that caused some friction between you two, didn't it. I mean, six months, that's a pretty long time." Taylor tried to be as unchallenging as possible. Though he did not yet consider her a suspect, he had to explore all possibilities. Taylor was not ready to rule her out as a suspect, but nothing raised his suspicions about her. So, he thought her response might help rule her out.

"I can't lie. Yeah, I was getting frustrated. That sunporch was a mess, and he promised to finish it. He stayed so busy. I wanted him to finish it, so we argued about it. Randall kept promising me he would take care of it. That's why he was out there last night."

"You didn't work with him?" Taylor asked.

"Not full-time, no. I'm a nurse at the hospital. I would do some clerical work on my days off, get work permits, and go to the bank. Things like that. Help out where I could in my spare time. I mean, he had a couple of people at the office that did stuff like that full-time, but I didn't mind helping."

"What are the names of his office personnel?" Taylor asked.

"Jennifer Douglas is his secretary, and Brenda Eaton is his interior designer. They run the office. Robert Safford works sales for him part-time. He spends most of his time working for an insurance company. Robert recommends us to some of his customers. I told Randal that he probably shouldn't be doing that. Still, he said it was fine if the company didn't tell people it was mandatory to use our company."

"Mrs. Morris, did he have any rivals, enemies, maybe some jobs that didn't go so well?"

"Sure, we had a few unsatisfied customers; everyone does. We had competitors too, but no one got angry enough to kill him."

"You sure about that? You can't think of anyone who would want to harm your husband? Do you know anyone who may have had a grudge over a job or business competition? Anything?"

"No, if Randal couldn't do a job, he had no problem recommending someone else."

Taylor decided to turn his attention to the daughter. "Miss Lauren, remind me where you were last night."

"I was with Marcy Reed at the movies. I was supposed to spend the night with her and watch a movie. We didn't really care which one; we just wanted out of the house for a while. We had our phones off, so I didn't find out what happened until I got back to Marcy's."

"You're seventeen, right?"

"Yes, but I don't have my driver's license, so Marcy drove us. I turn eighteen on January 18, and I plan to get my license before I go to college next fall."

"How would you describe your relationship with your father?"

"We got along mostly. We argued some, but I loved my Dad." She started fighting back the tears. "I didn't know when he dropped me off at school that would be the last time I'd see him."

"Do you remember hearing your Dad saying anything about someone who might want to hurt him? Did he ever tell you to be on the lookout for anyone? Maybe someone you know might want to hurt your Dad?"

"No, my Dad was a good man. I can't believe someone did this to him."

Taylor nodded and decided he had what he needed. "Ladies, thank you again for coming in this morning. I'm going to do everything I can to find whoever did this. If you think of anything, call the number on my card. It goes straight to my phone, so you won't have to dial the switchboard. Again, I'm sorry for your loss." The two women left the interview room after thanking him for his efforts.

As they left, Taylor replayed the conversation again in his mind. He could say that by both accounts, Randal Morris was a good and reputable businessman, husband, and father. No enemies, and only the typical number of disagreements between family members and business relations. In short, everything was pointing toward a break-in gone wrong, but why shoot at Rebecca? Did she startle him by coming in at the wrong time? That would mean he just happened to enter through the incomplete sunroom and get surprised by Randal and then be surprised again by Rebecca. She just happened to walk in at the wrong time. Not impossible; just too coincidental.

He decided he would get Barnes to follow up with the two office workers as soon as possible. In the meantime, he would dig deeper into Morris's business dealings, starting with his competitors. Then he would investigate recent customers of Morris's remodeling business to see if there really weren't any problems. Now was the time for some good old-fashioned police work.

CHAPTER
SIX

Sunday was supposed to be Taylor's day off. Instead, he and Barnes were checking out the Morris family's neighborhood. It was a typical middle-class subdivision similar to the one he grew up in years ago. The houses were not overly large, but they had a comfortable feeling about them. This was not the neighborhood where one expected a murder investigation. In many of the windows and mailboxes of several homes were ribbons and signs of support for the Morris family.

It always bothered Taylor when bad things happened in a place like this. You felt safe and secure, and the next thing you knew, tragedy struck and took away all that comfort you had grown to expect. The neighborhood was pulling together, though, for the loss of one of their own. When he arrived, Taylor saw several people taking food and paying respects to the family.

Barnes showed up a few minutes after him. She did not protest when he had called her last night and asked her to join him to walk the scene. As Barnes got out of the car, she yawned and took a sip of her coffee. He guessed she had not been awake very long and almost felt bad for asking her to come in on her off day. The thought vanished when he reminded himself he was also here on his off day.

"Nice to see you're wide awake this morning," he said as she strode toward Taylor's car. She looked tired, and Taylor wondered what had kept her up, knowing she agreed to meet him today.

He did not want to ask her why she looked so tired, but curiosity got the better. "You look rough; what happened to you last night?" Instantly he regretted saying it like that. He reminded himself he needed to work on his interpersonal skills later. Still, by the look on Barnes's face, she did not seem to mind the question.

"Wouldn't you like to know?" she said with a sly smile. "That's why you called me out here on my day off? To find out what I do on the weekend? You could have just asked."

"Knock it off, Barnes. I wanted to talk over this whole scenario with you. I want to see it for myself and try to understand how our killer made his approach to the house."

At the scene, he learned the killer had made his way into the home through the sunporch window. He noted that the window was not locked, making it easy to gain access. Because the killer wore gloves, there was no way to know if he tried any of the other windows, but he suspected that's what he did. If that was the case, where did he stand the night of the murder before he broke into the house?

"So, the killer came in through the sunporch, right," said Barnes almost as if she had read his mind. "Where do you think he would have been? He would need a spot where he could watch the home and quickly access the back."

Taylor thought about where he would be if he wanted to enter the home. "I think maybe off to the side. Probably over there by those shrubs and trees. You could get a good view of the home and make a quick approach." The two walked over to that area just within sight of the house but easily concealed if you were trying not to be noticed. "See, you could walk unobserved this way toward the home and straight back to the sunporch."

They walked together down what they believed was the most likely path the killer took. As they walked, the pair scanned the ground for any clues. Nothing obvious stuck out to them. Soon they were by the sunporch examining the outside of the windows. Not even a fingerprint was found. Taylor studied the window closest to the house where they believed the killer let himself in that night.

"It's weird, you know," Taylor said as he looked over the window. "There really should be something here if he came through the window. There are a few scratches on the outside of the rear window, but it doesn't look like enough to get it open."

"Well, he did wear gloves," Barnes responded. "The guy was being careful. You know how these things go. Sometimes there's not a lot to go on. What about the door? Was it locked?"

"No, the door was not locked, and neither were any windows, which bothers me. Maybe he knew that before coming inside. No one is that careful if they think they don't have to be. Think about it. He thinks there's no one home. He's got time. He gets inside, and then what? Did Morris walk down before he could get inside? So he hid and waited for him to turn his back or become distracted and then killed him? Why wait around then. Most people who just committed murder would take off." He thought for a moment. "Then again if the door was open, we have to consider the possibility the killer came into ambush him."

Barnes asked, "You're thinking he may have been looking to kill Morris from the beginning?" She thought for a moment, "Maybe whoever did this wasn't here to kill anyone but decided they would make it worth it? Maybe they thought, 'Hey, I just killed someone, so I need to get something out of it.' Just seems like a big waste of effort to leave empty-handed."

"Okay, but why wait until the wife comes back? Why not just go to a bedroom, grab what you can, and run? Take what you can and get out, but the killer was here for at least twenty minutes. Not to mention that he took the possessions off Randall Morris's body. No, I think he was looking for something."

"According to the list of missing items Mrs. Morris gave us, there doesn't seem to be anything overly important missing. Except for the jewelry from the bedroom and the items taken from the body," Barnes said. "What could he have been looking for inside?"

"That's what we need to find out," Taylor said as he turned to walk back to the car. The two walked in silence as they returned to the vehicles. "Sorry to call you out here on your off day. Thought that something might jump out at us or something like that if we came down here again. You got plans for the rest of the day?" He asked her before he could stop himself.

"Yeah, I'm going to get together with some friends this afternoon and watch the game. You know you should join us. It's going to be fun."

Taylor took a deep breath and released it slowly. "I'd like to, but I think I will read over some of the case details again. We'll meet up tomorrow at Morris's office and question the staff."

"Okay, sure. Hey, listen, Taylor, don't turn this into a bar day, okay? I know you're dealing with stuff, but—"

"Look, Barnes, you're not my mother, alright. I'm fine. I'll be at my place. If you need me, call me." With that, he got in his car and drove home. Barnes watched him drive off and sighed before going back to her place.

It was not a go to the bar day, but it was not a stay at home day either. He did not lie to Barnes because he spent an hour or two looking at the case file. Nothing new jumped out at him. Taylor rubbed his eyes in frustration, knowing that sometimes there was not much to go on. So, after looking over what he had, he decided to get in his car and drive around.

Warrenton was quiet. He drove through town, passing places he knew. He tried not to think about the past as he went through the mostly empty streets, but the memories returned despite his best efforts to hold them back. Lucky for him, the memories that flooded back today were the good ones.

He pulled into a parking lot beside the city hall. The front of the building was designed in the classical style with Corinthian columns, red brick with white windows and doors. It was built in the early 1920s as a courthouse. It served that purpose until about 2009, when the new courthouse was built across from the police station. It became Warrenton's city hall a few months later. Taylor did not intend to end up here, but the memory that came to him strongest today seemed to summon him to this spot.

During his third year on the force, he first saw Shelia Lee. On the front steps of the then courthouse, he was a junior detective, full of idealism and enthusiasm for bringing justice to the world. There he stood during a press conference as the lead detective, Matthew Bennett, delivered the details of an arrest made in a murder case. Taylor stood in silence, giving off a look of confidence and self-assurance that only youth can produce, until he saw her in the group of reporters.

He tried his best not to stare but thought she might have been the most beautiful woman he had ever seen. Her black hair was just below her shoulders. Her face was soft with high cheekbones and captivating eyes. The way she used her hand to push her hair back from her face as she took notes during the conference first drew his attention. He was mesmerized. Then almost by chance, they locked eyes for the first time, and instantly, all the bravado melted away.

Roger looked away and thought that was the end of it. Bennett answered questions from the press while Taylor stood in the background. He could not resist the urge to look toward her, and again their eyes met. This time she smiled slightly but was fully aware that

Roger saw her. Taylor tried to remain stoic like the tough young cop, but he could not help reflexively smiling back. He regained his senses and tried to put forward a professional face as the press conference ended.

Taylor wanted to make his way to her to introduce himself. Detective Bennett had other ideas and called him over. Taylor half expected to be reprimanded for his behavior; instead, Bennett wanted him to go back to the station and follow up on a witness statement. When he looked back toward where she was standing, Shelia was gone. So much for that.

A couple of days later, he was sitting at his desk when a uniformed officer told him he had a guest. To his surprise, it was Shelia. She came by the station to follow up on the press conference with a few questions. He told her Detective Bennett was the lead investigator, but she was not interested in talking to him. That was fine with her she said. She asked Taylor about the case, but there was more to this visit than a case clarification. He realized she was trying to recruit him as a police source.

He waited for her at a local establishment called Tavern on the Corner. It made the perfect place to meet because of its late hours. When she arrived, they would exchange information on various cases, although it took little time for a friendship to grow. After the first few meetings, they discussed less and less police work. Over the next few months, the two began meeting off the clock. It was not long before the meeting turned into a date.

As luck would have it, they both shared a love of baseball. One of their favorite places to go on a date was to see the local minor league baseball team. As true fans, the couple had their specific spot in the stadium where they sat to watch the game. It was here they shared their first kiss, and Taylor never felt happier.

Over time the romance turned to talk of marriage. When Roger finally popped the question, his hands were shaking so badly he thought he would drop the ring. She said yes, and the two were never happier. Plans were made, and the couple began to plan a life together. It seemed as if the pair really had it all. However, as the saying goes, all good things must end.

A few months before the wedding, Shelia got her big break. A Sacramento television studio offered her the lead crime reporter job. Unfortunately, Sacramento was a five-hour drive from Warrenton. Shelia asked Roger to come with her. She knew that with his experience, he could easily land a job in Sacramento. There was only one problem. Bennett was retiring, and this was Taylor's chance for his dream job, lead detective. Life was beginning to pull them apart.

Shelia left for Sacramento, promising to keep in touch and see him soon. It was not that he did not believe her, but somehow he knew this was the beginning of the end. Weeks went by between the times they spent together. By the year's end, the engagement was over. She tried to return the ring, but he told her to keep it.

"Who knows, maybe one day we'll need it again," he told her, trying to sound like he believed it. Almost three years passed before he saw her again.

Taylor had been sitting alone at the stadium, enjoying his favorite pastime. The evening air was thick. As always, he was keeping score when a familiar voice asked if anyone was seated next to him. Roger knew it was Shelia before ever looking up. Suddenly, Taylor began to feel the same way he had when they met years ago. Without missing a beat, Shelia told him she had left the station in Sacramento and taken a job at the local studio in Warrenton. So began the next phase of their relationship: Roger Taylor, the informant, and Shelia Lee, the reporter. Only this time, they worked less close than before.

That all changed when Lawson Pierson died. They began to reconnect as they investigated a case together for the first time in years. Taylor hoped their romance was blooming all over again. He loved being near her, and even though he knew it was dangerous, he could not resist being in her presence. In the end, that's what got her killed. He should have pushed her away or kept a closer watch on her. Now she was gone, and he knew somehow it was his fault.

Glancing at his phone, he saw it was now past six o'clock. The sun was beginning to settle in at the end of the day. Taylor roused himself from the trance. He started the car and drove back home. When he got home, Roger grabbed the nearly full beer bottle from off of the coffee table from last night. After pouring it out and throwing away the bottle, he took another one from the refrigerator.

Returning to the living room, he placed the bottle on the coffee table across from his couch. He sat and then took two sips from the bottle. Satisfied, he leaned back on the sofa. It was hard to say what time sleep took him, but he woke up around 11:30, still on the couch, before finally making it to bed.

The following day, he awoke to the sound of his alarm clock on his cell phone. He couldn't remember any of the dreams from last night so that probably meant there were no nightmares. Before heading to the shower, he stood and made his bed. After a quick breakfast, he was on his way to the station.

CHAPTER
SEVEN

Randall Morris's office was nothing special. It was located at the far end of a strip mall in Warrenton. Walking through the front door, Taylor spotted a small display area showcasing some kitchen cabinets. The office space was situated right behind the display. Morris and his secretary Jennifer Douglas shared their office space in the slightly larger office to the right side of a small hallway. Brenda Eaton, the designer, had an office by herself. Farther back was a small work area with a few power tools and building supplies.

Jennifer Douglas sat at her desk, visibly shaken as Taylor sat across from her. She received the news of Randall's murder Sunday morning. When she arrived at the office Monday morning, Jennifer began to organize files and paperwork from previous weeks. She'd started calling clients, letting them know the situation and giving them the option to be refunded any payments. She also assured customers that the contractors who worked for Morris could still finish the jobs as planned. To say the least, it had been a stressful morning.

"I really don't know how we're going to do this," she said as Taylor took the seat across from her desk. "Randall was such a well-organized boss. He seemed to know what to do all the time. He just had a way of dealing with people that just...I'm sorry, Detective, I'm struggling with this."

"Take your time Ms. Douglas," he said trying his best to prompt her in the right direction. "What can you tell me about any of your former employees? Did anyone ever leave on bad terms? Maybe fired for something they did on the job?"

She thought for a moment. "Well, there was Phil Borden. He worked for Randall for a couple of years. Randall caught him using some of the company's equipment on side jobs a couple of months ago. Phil was warned several times, but he was fired when Randall caught him again. It got pretty heated, and Randall threatened to call the police."

"Did he make any threats against Mr. Morris?"

"Yeah, maybe; I don't remember what was said exactly. I wasn't here when the argument took place. Randall said he caught Phil loading some tools onto his truck one evening. I don't think Phil would go as far as to kill Randall. I mean, that was months ago."

"You know where I can find Phil?" Taylor asked her.

"He's like many people who work for us, an independent contractor. So, he's self-employed, at least last time I heard. I have his phone number on file if you need it."

"Yes, that would be very helpful, thank you." She turned to her computer and located the number quickly. Taylor stored the contact information in his phone as she called out the numbers. Taylor then asked, "When you got to the office this morning, did you notice if anything was missing or out of place. Like maybe someone had been in the office over the weekend?"

"No, all the doors were still locked, and the office was like we left it on Friday evening. I went through the building first thing this morning. As far as I can see, nothing is missing or out of place."

He nodded as she spoke, writing down a few notes in the small notebook he kept with him. "Thank you for the information, Mrs. Douglas. Just have one more question. Where were you on Friday night?"

"Me?" she asked with a surprised inflection, "I was at home with my husband and kids. We went to dinner early Friday evening but were home before ten."

"Please," he said trying to sound as cheerful as possible, "don't take offense. It's just a standard question to ask in a situation like this. Again, thank you for your help." He stood up to leave and made his way to the door. Ms. Douglas walked with him to the door to lock it behind him.

"Detective," she asked him as he stepped on the sidewalk outside the office, "do I have to stay in town? You know, not go anywhere until you check my story?"

Taylor did his best not to laugh out loud at the question. "Well, if you go somewhere, be sure to let someone know where you're going. I'd hate to have a missing person's case to look into as well. Otherwise, no, thank you again for your help." He made his way to his car and drove away.

It didn't take long to track down Phil Borden. A call to the city Permits Department yielded Borden's work address in about thirty minutes. He was working on a remodeling job in a small house across town. As Taylor arrived, Borden was loading some tools into his truck. Taylor pulled into the driveway behind the man's truck. Borden looked up as Taylor stepped out of the car.

"Phil Borden?"

"Yeah, what can I do for you?"

"Detective Roger Taylor, Warrenton PD. I need to have a word with you," he said as he flashed his badge.

"Is this about my child support payment? Look, I told her lawyer I made the payment. I'm current, and I can't afford to pay more. Hell, I'm working extra jobs as it is."

"No, Mr. Borden, I'm here about Randall Morris."

"God, is he going to accuse me of something again? I thought we settled all that a month or so ago."

"Afraid not, Mr. Borden, he's dead. Murdered a few days ago. Surprised you haven't heard."

"Dead?" Borden asked sounding more than a little surprised. "Wow, yeah, that's...that's awful. Always hated how things went down between us. He was good to work for."

"I bet you did since you threatened to kill him," Taylor responded. "Why are you packing things up? You going somewhere?"

"Wait a minute, I'm finished here. I need to get to the bank before it closes to deposit this check, that's all."

"Really? Did you pay a little visit to the Morris house a couple of nights ago? You know, settle that argument once and for all?"

"Hey, look, I haven't seen or spoken to Randall since that night we argued."

"Is that right? Where were you Friday night, Phil?"

"I was with a lady Friday night. Her name is Vera Holmes. Got her phone number If you want it. And I was with her all night if you get my drift." He gave the number. "You happy now?"

"Not yet. I'll call her to make sure your story checks out. I'll be in touch, so stay where I can find you." Taylor turned to go as Borden returned to packing up his tools.

As it turned out, one phone call later, Borden's story checked out. Taylor could confirm that he and Vera were together when Morris was killed. In short, Borden was not the killer. Taylor thought it was a long shot anyway, but he needed to be sure. He was beginning to believe that Barnes was right about this being a robbery gone wrong.

CHAPTER
EIGHT

Across town, Barnes arrived at the office of Custom Builders and Remodeling, the biggest competitor of Randall Morris. Walking inside, she noticed that the reception area was neatly decorated with a set of sample kitchen cabinets to the left of the office. On the right were photographs of some of the remodeling jobs the company completed since its creation about nine years ago.

The secretary looked up when the door chime rang as Barnes opened the door. She was a young African American woman in her twenties. Her hair was long and straight, and the makeup she used was complementary to her skin tone. Her outfit complemented her slender body.

Barnes showed her badge and asked to speak with the owner Gregory Seals. He was about the same age as Randall Morris, but the similarities ended there. Seals had an athletic build and was well-dressed in a gray blazer and a neatly pressed shirt. He stood at an average height with a small, sculpted mustache and thin goatee. His dark, bald head reflected the light in his office as he came out to greet her in the reception area. "Detective Barnes, right? A pleasure to meet you. Please come back to my office. Katrina, hold all my calls, please. Detective, this way, please."

They went into the office, which seemed more appropriate for a banker or financial analyst. The walls were light blue and the floors were colored to match. The desk was stained dark brown with a high sheen. The pictures looked like they were hand-painted and not reproductions. He motioned for Barnes to sit in a leather chair.

"I have to say, Mr. Seals, I really love your office."

"Thank you. I want my customers to feel like they're at home here. If they feel at home in here, then they'll believe I can give them the same feeling in their home after I'm finished," Seals said in a lively voice. He sat across from her at his desk, leaning back in his chair, which seemed to almost swallow him whole. "It's also a place I can relax. Customers see that. It shows confidence, and confidence sells. Now, what can I do for you, Detective Barnes?"

"Did you know that Randall Morris died Friday night?"

"Yes, I heard that. So sad. You know we worked together for a while. Randall taught me a lot about the remodeling business. A good man hated to hear that. How'd he die?"

"He was murdered."

"Oh God. Who would do such a thing?"

"I was hoping you could help me with that," she said trying not to sound like she was accusing him. His reaction seemed one of surprise when he heard about the murder. Body language could always be faked, but he did seem genuinely shocked. "Any ideas on who might want to hurt Randall Morris?"

"I worked with Randall for five years before opening up my own business, and in that time, I never heard anyone have a bad thing to say about him. Personally about him anyway." He exhaled loudly, "Detective, I can't tell you we had happy customers after every job, but it wasn't because we didn't try."

"So, what made you decide to strike out on your own? You two have some falling out?"

"Not even close," he said defensively. "My mother raised me to be a man who wanted to do something with his life. I always planned on being a positive role model in my old neighborhood, even before I knew what that meant. I wanted to learn a trade, so I took classes after high school on construction work, electrical work, and skills I thought I would need. Randall Morris helped me along the way, teaching me how to run a business and run it right. So when I told him I wanted to own my business, he gave me his blessing."

"Looks like you've done well for yourself," Barnes said.

"It wasn't easy, but I got people to trust me. I even convinced some investors to back me on the Arbor Glenn subdivision project several years ago. That's where all of this started," he said as he gestured at the things adorning his office.

"I guess you don't work on job sites much anymore?"

"No, I have others who do that for me now. We stayed busy even when the housing market collapsed a few years back. Heck, I even sent a couple of smaller jobs to Randall. As I said, he taught me what I know, which was my way of trying to repay him."

"I have to ask, where were you Friday night around 9:00 pm?"

"At home with my wife and kids. Michelle cooked a roast that would melt in your mouth. Then we watched a kids' movie after dinner, and what did we do after the movie? Well, that's private between my lady and me if you get what I'm saying."

"I think I do, yes. Did you ever have employees who worked for Randall before they came to you?"

"In this business, it's not uncommon to have people who work for a while and then up and leave, so yes, I had a few. I've had guys quit because their raise didn't show up on the paycheck before it went into effect. He had some of my former guys too. You meet some strange people sometimes."

"Anyone strange enough to kill a man?"

"I believe in giving people a second chance in life, so I have employed guys with records. Randall did too, but most of those guys weren't the dangerous types."

"Did any employees have money troubles?"

"In this line of business, that's all we get sometimes. My guys know what's expected of them. You steal from the company; you're gone. That simple. Randall was the same way. Our work can be dangerous. The last thing I need is someone high or drunk operating power tools or falling on a ladder. They also know not to ask for advances on their paychecks. Now would any of these guys rob our houses? I doubt it, but anything is possible, I guess."

Barnes collected her thoughts for a moment. "Thank you for your help Mr. Seals; here's my card. If you think of anything that might help, please give me a call." She gathered her belongings and stood to leave. Seals also stood to his feet and offered his hand to her, which she took immediately.

"Detective, before you leave, I have a question for you."

"Alright, what can I do for you?" she asked him.

"I don't see a ring on your finger, so I assume you're not married. If you don't mind me asking," he said, trying not to sound strange. "Tell me, do you live in an apartment by any chance?"

"Ummm…yeah, I do," she said as she began to wonder where he was going with this.

"Listen, why live in an apartment when you can have your own home? Think about it, why pay rent on something you will never own? I'm building seven new garden homes on Lakeside Drive. Two bedrooms, living room, spacious kitchen, and a good-sized bathroom. If you want, I can send you the information. I plan to start moving people into these houses soon, so don't wait too long."

"Okay, sure, send me the information, and I'll give you a call," she said as she quickened her pace to leave. Seals promised her she couldn't go wrong with a new house as he walked her to the door. Finally making it to her car, she sat in the driver's seat and rubbed her eyes, feeling some tension release.

Fishing out the phone in her purse, she called Taylor. After he answered, she told him what she had found out. "I honestly don't think he had anything to do with it. He's got a lot of business and didn't seem to be in direct competition with Morris. He even wanted me to buy a garden home he's building."

"So, when do you move in?" Taylor asked her.

"Yeah, I don't think I'm ready for that yet. Tempting as it might be."

"Well, too bad I was hoping to plan a housewarming party," Taylor said sarcastically. "Follow up on the information with the wife and anyone else that may have seen him to be sure. Otherwise, come on back."

"Got it. Be there shortly," Barnes said, then ended the call.

CHAPTER
NINE

He made his way to the agreed upon meeting point. It was a bright afternoon, and he wondered why anyone would want to meet in broad daylight. *Something like this*, he thought, *should be done under cover of night.* That seemed to make more sense to him, but his contact insisted on meeting during the day. The whole idea of secrecy was flawed by meeting in the daytime. Doesn't this guy know that in all the spy movies, you meet at night in the shadows? *Usually, don't they wear a trench coat and fedora decked out with dark sunglasses? Yeah, okay, that would seem suspicious to anyone who saw us.*

Honestly, he did not really know why he was doing this. It was not like he had anything against the guy. In fact, he hardly knew him at all. He told himself it wasn't personal. *It's just a job like any other. Okay, the guy is dead now, but it was just a job.* From what he heard about him, the guy had it coming. What he did hurt many people, so it was not like this guy was a saint. Even if he was, it is too late to back out now. Not like you can make him undead even if you wanted.

He sat on a bench near the bus stop close to Red Oak Park in the upper part of Warrenton. He hoped his contact would show soon, so he stretched out, relaxed as best as he could, and waited. Usually, he didn't have to wait long. The man was almost always right on time. He checked his watch for the second time since arriving, only about five minutes before the scheduled meeting.

As he sat on the bench, people jogged by where he sat. To his right was a playground where soccer moms brought their kids and gossiped about whatever the latest story was around Warrenton. To his left, a group from one of the retirement homes was out for their daily walk routine. The park was bustling with people, so it was easy to understand why they always met there. Sure there were a lot of eyes to see what they were doing, but most people didn't care much about people they didn't know. Most mind their business and go about their routine. *It's incredible how you can be nearly invisible in a crowd*, he thought.

About four minutes passed before he spotted a man approaching. He had the look of a businessman on his lunch break. He carried a briefcase in his right hand. His suit was pressed so sharply he could probably cut meat with it. The man looked in his fifties with more gray hair than brown. He had a sharp nose with well-proportioned green eyes. He was not an overly tall man, nor was he particularly well built physically, though maybe he could have been athletic once in his life. It was hard to tell, and he was not about to share any of that information.

The man strode nonchalantly toward the bench giving no indication to anyone around that he was there for an arranged meeting. He sat on the bench, resting his briefcase on his lap.

"Mr. Smith, did you get the task taken care of?" he asked without any emotion in his voice. It was nothing new; the contact never said much and kept their meetings short. That was probably the nicest thing he could say about their encounters.

"Of course I did; you don't think I would show up here if I

didn't?" Mr. Smith answered, sounding a bit defensive. He tried to read the expression on his contact's face and look for any clue that might indicate what he was thinking. "Did the guy really need to die, though? I could have just gone in and got what I needed, and no one would have been the wiser."

"Tell me, Mr. Smith, do you play chess?" Smith shook his head to say no. "I thought not. Each piece has its own job and function. The knight does not ask why he takes a pawn; it only does its job. Do your job the way we tell you to; that's all you need to know." He reached into the case he was carrying and pulled out an envelope. "Did you bring the files?"

"Yeah, they're all here. Look for yourself if you don't believe me."

The man opened the file Smith handed him and took a quick look. As the contact looked through the file, Smith sat there with a happy face that bordered on arrogance. Satisfied, the man put the files in his case and handed the envelope to Smith.

It was now Smith's turn to open what was given to him. Just a quick look told him the money was all there. "Nice. Very nice. You know it's great doing business with you," Smith said. "By the way, I got to know; why is it you call me Smith anyway? Why not Jones or Miller? Something a little flashier?" His contact looked at him with a blank stare. Smith shrugged, "Okay, be that way. When do we meet again?"

The man regarded him with a look bordering somewhere between disgust and hatred. Smith should have been used to that by now, but it always angered him how his contact seemed to believe he was superior. True, he was dressed in a fancy suit, and it was evident that whatever he did for a living afforded him a more comfortable lifestyle. Still, Smith knew he was being looked down on, and it riled him more than a little.

"Soon," the man said. "Keep your phone on at all times. I will call you when my employer is ready to move forward. Until then, keep quiet."

"Hey, fine man, whatever you say." Smith stood up to go. "You know where to find me. Oh, and if you need me to make things look a little more professional next time, it will cost extra."

The contact did not respond. He did not need to respond. Smith wondered what the guy he killed had done as he walked away. The job was simple: break-in, find a couple of files in the home office, and then take as many valuables as possible to cover up his theft of the files.

Part two of the job was to take out the man and his wife. The first part was easy enough. He got in without trouble, but part two did not go as planned. He was supposed to get them both, but the wife had managed to escape. When he told his contact about her inconvenient survival, he surprised Smith by saying it was not that important. As long as the husband was dead, that was all that mattered. Sure it would have been nice to get her too, but if his boss was not upset, then neither was he going to be. After all, it was just another job.

The arrogant bastard didn't know that after he took the files, Smith had made copies of them for himself. It was always good to have an insurance policy, just in case. He knew the contact supposedly worked for some organization or influential person. Smith wanted to know who he worked for, so the copied files might give a clue to their real identity. It might even be something he could use against them later.

Smith didn't intend to be used by these people forever. He was working on a way out. All he needed was the proper leverage against whoever they were, and he could make a clean break. It all sounded easy, but nothing in this line of work was easy. Still, Smith had no intention of doing their dirty work for the rest of his life.

CHAPTER
TEN

Taylor and Barnes arrived at the funeral home to attend the service for Randall Morris. It was well attended, and the family graciously received mourners. Taylor's mind drifted as he surveyed the people. The Morris office was professionally cleaned and nothing was out of place. Nobody he and Barnes interviewed could imagine who would kill Randall Morris.

Trying to blend in as best they could, the two detectives smiled and nodded politely to everyone who walked past them. He also saw several familiar faces from around town as they paid their respects to the family. Going to the funeral was as much strategy as respect; it was a tried and true strategy to rub elbows with the killer. In the back of his mind, Taylor knew anyone in attendance could have played a role in the killing.

As he surveyed the crowd, he noticed several people from city hall and the local school in attendance. It was not surprising. Randall Morris was a chamber of commerce member and was known to attend city council meetings. Mayor Clemmons was there to pay her respects along with about half of the council. The high school principal and a couple of Lauren Morris's teachers also attended.

Spotting an old friend in the entourage of people from city hall, Taylor excused himself from Barnes and made his way toward the group. He greeted the mayor and the members of the city council. Next, he turned his attention to Seth Willard, the city's building inspector. Seth was someone Taylor had met early in his career with the department. The two often found themselves at the same locations during their lunchtimes, so the friendship developed from there. It had been several months since they last met for lunch. Taylor was glad to see him.

Seth waved "Well, Detective Taylor, it's been a while. Where've you been hiding?" he asked as he extended his hand. Roger took his hand and told him how busy he had been over the last several months. It was not a complete lie, but the truth, he just was not in a social mood. "It's good to see you. Did you know Randall?"

"Hey, Seth, I'm the one that usually asks the questions, " Taylor responded light-heartedly. "Actually, no, I'm investigating the case. Not surprised that you knew him, though. How did you two meet?" He felt strange asking, but he needed to know. Seth could add some essential details about the case or might have some insight as to who might have the motive to kill Morris.

"Well, he came by my office several times for permits, and I often met him at his work sites to check for code compliance. He was good at what he did. Can't say he ever had a major code violation. He took a lot of pride in his work. You know, tried to make people happy."

"Did he ever have a problem with a client?"

"Not that I know of, no. He really went out of the way to do a quality job. Honestly, I can't think of a single reason anyone would want to complain about his work, much less kill him."

Taylor nodded. "Yeah, that's what I'm hearing about him. Sounds like he was a good guy. What about his competitors? Would any of them have a reason to go after him? A rival that maybe took things too seriously?"

"None he ever told me, and you know I can't play favorites with contractors. I understood he often referred people to his competitors if he couldn't help them. That's just the kind of guy he was." Seth glanced at his watch, "Oh man, I need to go speak to the family. Hey, we need to catch up. Want to do lunch sometime?"

"Sure, call me. Good seeing you," Taylor said as Willard tried to catch up with the mayor's group. Taylor made his way back to Barnes, contemplating the irony of having a building full of people who were suspects – or not. Maybe it was a waste of time, but at least a lot was confirmed about Morris's business dealings and personal relationships.

After following the long line of cars to a short graveside service, the crowd began to disperse. The service was well attended, and the minister delivered a stirring eulogy in which many nice things were said about the deceased. Taylor left the gravesite with Barnes. He tried to think of a motive someone at the funeral would have to kill Morris. When he thought about it, he knew he had nothing. He decided to pursue this as a robbery gone wrong. He reasoned that sometimes things are not what they seem, but sometimes they are. Occam's Razor came to mind, which says that the most straightforward answer is usually the correct one or something like that.

CHAPTER
ELEVEN

Officer McClendon sat along the roadside just outside of town late that morning. He'd gotten home late the night before and was grateful he did not have to stay on the scene of an 11:00 pm traffic accident with the other officers. Even so, he was still out later than he would have liked, especially since he promised Officer Boykin he would cover her shift today so she and her husband could go to a football game. Sitting on the side of the road only made the desire to sleep greater. McClendon decided to drive around for a while, but before starting his engine, a car passed him at high speed.

Instinctively he hit his lights and sped off after the car. He chased it for about half a mile before the driver pulled to the side of the road.

McClendon called in the plates to find out what he could about the car and its owner. It was not stolen, so he got out of the cruise and cautiously approached the vehicle. McClendon placed his hand on the car's trunk as he made his approach. Nothing out of the ordinary yet, but he knew to remain vigilant.

Inside, a single black man sat behind the wheel, nervously fidgeting as McClendon approached. "Driver's license and registration, please, sir," McClendon said as he came to the window. The driver huffed and muttered something McClendon could not and probably did not want to hear. He could tell the man was nervous about something, and from his smell, he was sure he knew why.

McClendon went back to his car and called in the driver's license number and the name Darrell Dortch. There were no active warrants on Dortch, but there were several prior arrests for everything from petty theft to drug possession and distribution. McClendon got out again and walked back to the car. "Sir, do you know why I stopped you?"

"'Cause y'all ain't got nothing better to do. I ain't got nothin', and I been clean for months. Why you messin' with me?"

"Well, that's what I'm trying to tell you. I clocked you doing 58 miles per hour in a 35-mile zone," responded McClendon as calmly as he could. He had done this song and dance many times, and it sounded the same every time. He tried to hide his frustration with the whole ordeal, and if Dortch was mad now, he was really about to lose his cool. "I also need to know if you've been drinking today or have you smoked anything today?"

"I told you I been clean for months," Dortch shouted, clearly getting angrier with each passing second.

"Not to doubt your word, sir, but the smell from your car says otherwise. Now tell the truth, have you smoked anything today?"

"No, I was at a friend's house, and they did, but I'm clean."

"Okay, so where does this friend live? He got a name?"

"Yeah, Kentrell over on Overland Street."

"Overland Street? You were heading back into town toward the direction of Overland. So you left Kentrell's to go where and drive back? Is that it?"

"Naw, I left an hour ago to get something to eat."

"From where?" asked McClendon.

"The gas station 'bout a mile up the road that way," he pointed back the way he came.

"So, you passed how many places to get food so you could go to that particular gas station? And it took you an hour? Come on, man, what were you really doing?"

"I told you, man. I know the guy there. He gives me free stuff when I go there."

"Alright, man, I need you to step out of the car for a minute." Dortch cursed aloud but complied, slamming the door behind him. "Look, what you're saying is not making any sense. Not to mention I can smell weed in there. If all you did was go get a little weed, I don't have an issue with that. I have an issue because I think you may be too impaired to drive."

Again, Dortch proclaimed that he was sober and did not have any weed. McClendon had only heard the same story about a hundred times over the last month.

McClendon performed several field sobriety tests on him; no surprise, Dortch failed almost all of them. As he was placing Dortch under arrest, Officer Miller arrived. Braden Miller was in his third year on the force. He had an easygoing demeanor that did not tell the whole story. Miller was sharp and had a way of putting people at ease, but he knew his job and performed it well.

"Darrell, I thought you said you went clean a while back," Miller said as he walked up to the scene.

"You know this guy, Miller?" asked McClendon as he double locked the cuffs on Dortch.

"Oh yeah, arrested him a couple of times. Nothing big. Let me guess, driving high?"

"Man, I should have known you'd be around," complained Dortch. "Somehow, you always find me." Miller ignored him. He walked to the window of the car and peeked inside. He spotted a bag half open in the floorboard of the passenger seat.

"Hey McClendon, put him in the car and come here," said Miller.

McClendon took Dortch by the arm and led him to the car. He opened the door, placed him inside, and fastened the seat belt. He told him to sit tight as he shut the door and walked back to Miller. "Hey, did you see that bag there?"

"Yeah, I haven't asked him about it yet. What do you think? We got grounds to search?"

"I think so. He's definitely under the influence, and his behavior is erratic. Could be drugs in there, and he has obviously just smoked. So yeah, we should be good."

Miller opened the door and reached in, and pulled out the bag. When they opened the bag, they found some weed, but the jewelry inside interested them the most. "Well, look at that," McClendon said, "There was a break-in a few nights back, and some jewelry was taken."

"You sure about that?" asked Miller.

"Yeah, I took Taylor there and hung around the scene for a while. Heard the detectives talking about some of the missing items before I left."

The two men walked to the back of McClendon's car and opened the door. "You want to tell us about the jewelry in that bag?"

"I ain't got nothin' to say about it. I don't know nothin' about it."

McClendon shut the door hard. "Yeah, that's what I thought. I'm going to call Detective Taylor; he will want to talk to this guy."

"Probably so. Had to play cabbie with Taylor the other night?"

"Yeah, it wasn't a big deal. I don't think Taylor had even drunk anything yet, and if he did, I think he was being cautious and did not drive. I can respect that, I guess," replied McClendon. In the back of his mind, it did bother him that he had to play chauffeur to a detective. He did not have a grudge against Taylor, but he knew many of the other officers did. Especially those officers were close to the recently fired ones.

"Yeah, I guess he's alright," replied Miller. "Detectives, you know, they're a different breed."

"I guess," McClendon said. "I plan on finding out someday. Don't really plan on working traffic stops the rest of my life, you know?"

"Sure, I get that. Go ahead and call this into Taylor. I'm going to get back out there."

Miller returned to his car and soon drove off with a wave. McClendon watched him drive off, and he regretted saying what he did about giving up patrol. It was true he wanted to be a detective, but he still needed more time on the force to be considered. He was not trying to sound like he hated patrol duty to Miller, who by all accounts loved working patrol and driving the marked police car. He might offer to buy him a drink later to apologize, even if Miller did not take offense. In the meantime, he needed to call Detective Taylor.

CHAPTER
TWELVE

The call from McClendon lifted Taylor's spirits in ways that were difficult to explain. After a week of few clues and no witnesses, he was beginning to lose hope of finding Randall Morris's killer. A chance encounter changed everything and gave him a much needed piece of good news.

As he drove into the station, he told himself to settle down, relax, and not get his hopes up too much. Often, these things work out differently than hoped. Just because someone was found with some of the stolen property did not make them the killer. On the other hand, it was possible that he received the property from the killer. It was now a matter of getting to the truth and seeing what this guy knew.

Taylor arrived at the station and went to his small office. He gathered a few items to take to the interview room with him. Next, he found Officer McClendon, who was talking with a couple of officers.

"McClendon," he began as he strode toward the group, "nice work out there today. I appreciate it."

"Of course, detective. My pleasure" responded McClendon.

Taylor turned to leave but then felt a small wave of guilt wash over him. "Hey McClendon," he said, "about the other night. Look, I've been going through some things, and I thought you should know. Well, it's just that..." he trailed off, not really knowing what to say. *What would I tell him?* he thought. Taylor was off duty, and even if he had too much to drink, which he didn't, he had a way home and did not plan to drive.

"Detective, it's okay. I was just glad I could help," McClendon said. He gave Taylor a nod and walked toward the parking lot to resume his patrol. As McClendon pulled out of the lot and into the street, he could not help but feel a sense of pride.

As Taylor returned to the interrogation room, he thought about his first collar. A man ran a stop sign and hit a couple of teenagers riding a dune buggy. The driver of the dune buggy, a star football player at the local high school, lost his leg in the crash. The other kid, a sixteen-year-old girl, spent several weeks in the hospital. The man who hit them had a long record of drunk driving and had a suspended license at the time of the crash. He fled in his pickup truck, leaving the two injured teens alone on the street.

It did not take long for Taylor to find the suspect. A woman who'd been watering her flowers had seen accident. She described the truck with startling accuracy – even had a partial plate number. When Taylor and several officers found the truck, the driver was passed out behind the wheel. When asked why he ran, all he could say was that he did not want to have another DUI on his record.

The teens were lucky, all things considered. Both could have been killed. Eventually, they both recovered from their injuries. The boy grew up and started an insurance business in Warrenton. The girl had moved away for college. He hoped life had treated her well since the accident.

Watching McClendon celebrate his first big arrest today brought back the memory. It was not the same, of course, but there was something satisfying in knowing what he had done to bring some closure to someone's life. It reminded him of a time when he really believed he could make a difference in the world. Still, after all of the years since his first case, he knew there was still some idealism left inside him.

He opened the door to the interrogation room where Darrell Dortch waited for him.

"Mr. Dortch, I'm Detective Roger Taylor. It's been a rough day for you, hasn't it?"

Dortch looked up from his seat next to a small table facing the door to the interrogation room. Whatever he had drunk or taken or smoked seemed to be wearing off. He sat resting his elbow on the table, cupping his left hand over his eyes. It looked to Taylor like Dortch was a man who had not slept in a couple of days.

"Yeah, man, you can say that," Dortch weakly replied. "Look, you got anything to drink?"

Taylor smiled. "Sure, no problem. Hang on a second." He opened the room door and got an officer's attention. "Hey, Everett, will you get me bottled water from the break room. Thanks." He shut the door and turned his attention back to Dortch. "He'll get it here in just a minute or two. You look like you need a nap. Were you up too late last night?" Taylor asked as he sat. He moved his chair toward the wall behind him, trying to relax.

"Yeah, man, it was a real late night. Played spades with my friends all night and drank some," Dortch said with a chuckle. "Got pretty serious for a couple of hands, you know." His voice was betraying just how exhausted he was feeling. His movements were slow, and when he leaned back, Taylor thought he might fall over.

"From the looks of you, seems like you guys did a little bit more than drink, right?" Taylor said, keeping the conversation light. To his surprise, Dortch laughed. "Yeah, you guys did more than drink and gamble, right. Come on, tell the truth; I won't charge you with anything like that. It's just us, right? What did you do last night?"

"Aww man, no, we just smoked a little weed, that's all. Just weed," Dortch said.

"Just weed? Are you sure? You look awful tired for just some weed," Taylor said in a light and almost playful tone. "Come on, man, just weed?"

"I swear, man, just a little weed and liquor. You know, can't lose it too much. I had money on the table."

Taylor laughed a little. "I can understand, man, okay." Officer Everett knocked on the door. "Looks like our water is here. Let me get that." Taylor thanked Everette for the water and handed one of the bottles to Dortch. "Hey, sorry about this, but I guess we don't have any cold ones. Here take mine. I think it's a little cooler." He handed the bottle to Dortch, who thanked him for the water and then wasted no time breaking it open and taking a drink. Taylor let him sit there for a moment as he took another sip from the water bottle.

Deciding it was time, Taylor began the questioning. "So, do you know why you're here?" he started subtly enough. His demeanor began to change slightly, taking on a more serious tone. The interrogation was like fishing to Taylor. Jerk the bait too soon or harshly, and you may lose the fish. Better to be slow and deliberate. Lure him in, and he may tell you what you want to know.

"Look, I didn't feel like I was too drunk to drive, man. I just wanted something to eat."

"I understand that. I probably would want something, too, especially if I had been drinking and toking up all night. Sure, that makes a lot of sense." Taylor leaned forward to rest his elbows on his knees. He still kept several feet away from the suspect. "But that's not why I want to talk to you. Why don't you tell me about that bag we found? It's your bag, right?"

"Yeah, that's my bag, but I didn't put any of that stuff in it."

"Darrell, come on, man. Are you trying to tell me you got jewelry in a bag and didn't put it there?" Taylor responded without raising his voice too much. "Look, let me tell you the truth, alright? Those pieces of jewelry came from a burglary several days ago. Now I want to believe you, but you got to help me out here. How would that jewelry get in your bag if you didn't put it there?" Dortch leaned forward in his seat and swore under his breath. "Darrell, this is your chance to tell your side of the story because right now, the evidence tells me you are the one who was in that house."

"Come on, man, I ain't never broke in nobody's house. That ain't me."

"Really, Darrell? So how does jewelry from a robbery wind up in your bag if you didn't put it there?"

"Man, I don't know. Someone must have put it there," Dortch said defensively.

Taylor opened the file he had brought in with him. He produced a picture of Randall Morris and slid it over to Dortch. "You recognize this guy?" Dortch shook his head and said no. "His name is Randall Morris. You sure you don't recognize him." Again, Dortch denied he had ever seen Morris before. "Take a good look at him, Darrell. He's dead. Died the night someone broke into his home. You see where I'm going with this?" Taylor's voice got serious. "What do you think happened to him?"

Dortch sat back in his chair and put his hands in his lap. "I guess somebody killed him."

"That's right, Darrell, they did. How do you think they did it?"

"With a gun, I guess," Dortch responded weakly.

"A gun. Why would you say that?"

"Cause ain't that the way most people kill someone?" Dortch responded defensively.

"Not always, but it's funny that's your first guess. You own any guns?"

"I can't own no guns, man I'm a convicted felon. I don't...."

"Darrell, when has that ever stopped someone who wanted to commit a crime. Lots of ex-cons have guns. So did you use a gun to kill Randall Morris?"

"No, I didn't kill nobody, and I didn't break into no house either."

"Hey, look. I want to help you out here, but you've got to do better. That jewelry didn't just jump into your car. So tell me how they got there because from where I'm sitting, you look pretty guilty right now. Think about it. You broke into a man's home, killed him, and made off with some valuables. That's felony murder. It means you go down for this and never walk away from it. You might even end up on death row. That man had a wife and kid. It will not play well in front of a jury, and a judge will not take it easy on you." Dortch began to squirm and fidget. Suddenly he forgot all about his lack of sleep over the last couple of days. "I can help you, Darrell. We can get through this together, but you've got to start telling me the truth."

"I told you, man, it wasn't me. I didn't break in no house or kill nobody," Dortch said as he turned fully to face Taylor, slamming his elbows on the table. "Look, I got those from Tony. He gave them to me."

"Tony, who?"

"Tony Pritchard, one of the guys at the game last night."

"Are you lying to me again, Darrell?"

"No, I swear. That's where I got the jewels. I won them last night in the game. He didn't have any cash, so he used the jewelry. He nearly lost his mind when I beat him. Accused me of cheating, so we threw hands. The other guys broke it up and kicked him out."

"So Tony was the one who broke into the house?"

"I don't know, he didn't say that, but that's who I got them from. I swear."

"Where do I find this Tony guy? You got an address, picture, anything?"

"I can tell you where he stays. Even got a picture of him we took last night. Group picture on my phone." Dortch gave Taylor all the information and showed him the picture. He looked defeated and downtrodden. Taylor thought it was as much from lack of sleep and exhaustion as the interrogation.

Taylor took the picture that Dortch sent to him and got a good look at Tony Pritchard. He then looked back over at Dortch. "Darrell, I'm going to find Tony, and I hope his story matches your story. The good news for you is that I've got a place you can get some sleep for a few hours."

"What? I told you everything, man; what's this about?" Dortch growled.

"First off, the DUI that you were brought in for this afternoon. Second, you have the stolen property, so we'll hold you on that. Not to mention that you're also still a suspect in a murder investigation. Like I said, if what you told me is true, I'll help you out. Until then, get some sleep." With that, Taylor walked out of the room and shut the door.

CHAPTER
THIRTEEN

The sun was setting when Barnes arrived at her apartment. She had stopped on the way home and picked up a medium pepperoni pizza from a local shop. As she walked to the door, she spotted the white cat with a large brown spot on his left side. The cat didn't belong to her, but as cats often do, the cat adopted her. Not surprisingly, the cat was there waiting for her most nights. The first time it showed up, Barnes gave it part of a burger she had with her. Since then, she bought a small bag of cat food to feed her when she showed up.

She opened the door and set down her things. The cat food bag was by the door, so she gave the cat a scoop of the food and shut the door. Barnes thought she should name the cat. There was no collar, so she began to think of a few names.

The phone began to vibrate in her pocket, interrupting her train of thought. Looking at the screen, she saw it was her mother calling. "Hey, Mom," she said, putting the phone between her cheek and shoulder while taking off her shoes.

A laughing voice on the other end told her, "Sorry to disappoint kiddo, it's Dad."

"Dad, why are you using Mom's phone?"

"She's outside watering her flowers and wanted me to call you."

"Watering flowers at this time of night? Why is she doing that?"

"You know your mother, she forgot to do it when she got home and just had to go water them. Anyway, are you coming to the house this weekend?"

"What? Was I supposed to? I didn't miss an important birthday or something, did I?"

"No, we hoped you'd come by and see us."

"Sorry, Dad, I promised some friends I'd watch the Rams game this weekend."

"Oh, is someone important going to be there? Someone you're looking forward to seeing?"

In the background, she could hear her mother saying, "Howard, give me that phone. Hi, honey. Don't pay any attention to your father. It's fine that you're not coming this weekend, but please, can you come to see us soon?"

Barnes smiled, "Yes, you know I will. How're things going?"

"We're good. Your father has his eyes on a new boat, but I told him he better be working some overtime if he wants it. He's got a fishing tournament this weekend. That's why he wanted to know if you would come home." Barnes could hear her father say something.

"Oh, so the truth comes out. Sorry, but as I said, I've got plans. Tell Dad if he's really, really good, I might be his partner for the next one. Just let me know ahead of time."

"Well, he knows you were always better at catching fish." Again she heard her father say something loud in the background. "Yes, she is Howard. She was the reason you won the tournament last year."

"Anyway, we both miss you. How are things in Warrenton?"

"Same as always. Just trying to get used to the whole detective role. It's so much different than patrol."

"I'm sure you're doing fine. Are you still short staffed?"

"Yes, but we're managing. The department has replaced most of the patrol officers we lost, so some of them are doing double duty with some detective work."

"Well, you be careful anyway."

"Not to worry, Mom. Listen, I've got my food ready, so let me go, okay."

"Alright, love you."

"Love you too. Tell Dad I love him. Even if he tried to trick me into coming to see him this weekend."

"Alright, bye."

Barnes hung up the phone and sat it on a small table. The pizza had cooled to just the right temperature, so she wasted no time digging into it. She thought about getting a plate from the kitchen but opted to eat right out of the box.

Turning on the television, she flipped a few channels before finding a football game between two small colleges from a conference she didn't recognize. She didn't recognize either of the teams but watched the game anyway. As she watched the game, she pulled her hair from the ponytail holder, letting it fall to her shoulders. She closed her eyes briefly, rubbing them with her finger and thumb.

Barnes returned to the television and sat down to watch the rest of the game. During a commercial break, she took the leftovers to the refrigerator. She grabbed a bottle of water from the counter and walked to her bedroom to change into her night clothes.

Try as she might, Barnes couldn't brush the memory of the funeral service out of her mind. It was not the first funeral she had ever attended. When she was twelve, her grandfather on her mother's side died of a sudden heart attack. While she was not to him, it came as a shock. At the funeral, the realization hit her that she would never see him again, and things seemed to close in on her from there. She did not remember crying, but the feeling of loss and remorse stuck with her.

She regretted she did not get to know her grandfather better while he was alive. They lived two hours away and usually only saw each other a few times a year, mostly on holidays.

To compensate for her lack of knowledge of her grandfather, she tried to learn everything she could about him in the weeks and months after the funeral. Looking back, she knew it was because of her grandfather that she decided to become a cop. He was a police officer for nearly twenty years, working everything from patrol to investigation. He retired from the department and worked as a private investigator for another twelve years.

The Morris funeral was different. It was the first one where she was not there to mourn. She was there to investigate. Taylor told her on the way over that the killer was often someone at the funeral. While they would not necessarily turn the funeral into an open interrogation, they could observe and make a note of those in attendance. She was not exactly sure what she was looking for, but Taylor said to stay close, and he would guide her through the process. Admittedly all she seemed to do was stand before everything started and then sit quietly in the back of the chapel during the service.

On the way back to the station, she told Taylor she felt she was not very helpful. He assured her she had done fine. Their presence might have made the killer nervous. He assured her that she observed a lot more than she gave herself credit for. "Sometimes things won't make sense until later when you look back on the facts of the case, and a realization hits you," he said.

Taylor said investigations were like puzzles – and sometimes there were pieces missing. You only goy part of the picture, even in the most apparent open and shut cases. Some facts, details, and circumstances were always missing, whether large or small. Even closed cases sometimes left an investigator asking why. Consequently, every detail an investigator could find mattered because the victim mattered.

The last part stuck with her the most. Randall Morris was more than a body and case number. She took notice of the family. How Lauren Morris sat in almost complete silence, not looking at anyone for long. How Rebecca thanked everyone for coming and sharing some of Randall's life stories. She seemed to be holding up well while greeting the guests before the service. During the service, she wiped away tears often. Barnes watched as Rebecca reluctantly walked away from the graveside, her composure falling apart.

A sudden rush of excitement from the television snapped her out of her thoughts. One of the teams had just scored a touchdown with 1:28 left on the clock in the fourth quarter. She realized she must have been deeply thinking, taking her attention away for most of the final period. The game ended about fifteen minutes later. Barnes decided she was ready to call it a day and turned off the television and lights in her apartment.

As Laura lay in her bed a few minutes later, her mind wandered again. She remembered her first days working patrol. The car she was assigned smelled like an old ashtray sprinkled over spilled coffee. They told her they cleaned the vehicles regularly, but she was sure this was the car given to rookies. Her patrol sergeant told her she was lucky. It took almost six months for her to get a regular rotation on daytime patrol. In larger departments, she could have been on the night shift for well over a year, maybe two, before working daylight hours.

She met Roger Taylor in her third month of patrol. He did not strike her as remarkable at first. In fact, he made her mad as he cut his way through the crime scene tape she carefully placed around the scene. She had spent ten dollars of her own money to buy the tape since the department rarely used it. She thought her initiative would impress the detectives on her first crime scene, but she heard them ask who put all the damn tape up. After a while, his bursting through her tape became an inside joke between the two of them.

Still, he took notice of her. He saw she had a way of being in the right places when needed. Taylor noticed her listening to what he and the other detectives were saying. He didn't take it as eavesdropping or snooping. In fact, he often invited her to assist in the investigations over other, more senior officers. She became known as an officer who could be trusted. Shortly after the fall of the Pierson crime family, Taylor approached her about becoming a detective. One of the proudest moments of her career was the day she passed the detective test and became an investigator.

Now, months later, she was assisting on a murder case. She knew she had come a long way in a short time. Though she never was overly sarcastic, some of Taylor's caustic sense of humor had rubbed off on her. Barnes liked that to a point, but often she tried to remain more forceful with suspects. The bad cop persona of the duo in a lot of ways.

Finally managing to close her eyes, she began to drift off to sleep. As she fell asleep, she thought only one thing was missing in her life. About eight months ago, she had broken up with a guy she dated for seventeen months, two weeks, and four days. She hated walking away, but he would not commit to her regarding engagements, marriage, and especially children. It felt silly that she knew the exact information.

She didn't need a man in her life, but she wanted one. Barnes, at heart, wanted a family, kids, and a home. Steven would not talk about those things, and eventually, he told her he didn't want kids at all. End of story. The next day she broke it off with him. They had tried to talk a few times, but the last conversation was six months ago when she told him she was twenty-seven and should be married with one kid and another on the way.

Maybe it's for the best, she thought. She drifted deeper into sleep. *No sense in staying with someone who does not share at least some of your life's goals..* A minute or two later, sleep put an end to her thoughts.

CHAPTER
FOURTEEN

Lauren arrived home from school to an empty house. She placed her school bags on the kitchen table and walked to the refrigerator. Spotting a bottle of salsa, she took it and put it on the kitchen table. A new bag of tortilla chips was in the cabinet next to the refrigerator. Taking the bag, she opened it and ate one of the chips before sitting the rest down next to the salsa bottle. She took a small bowl from the dishwasher, making a mental note to unload it before Rebecca came home.

She poured the bowl about half full of salsa before returning the remainder to the refrigerator. While she opened the door, she decided to take out the hamburger meat and brown it to make spaghetti for dinner. She took out the jar of sauce from the cabinet and the noodles. The pots and pans she found inside a cabinet on the island. A few minutes later, the noodles were boiling, and the hamburger was browning on the stovetop.

While the food was cooking, she sat down and dipped a chip into the salsa. She took out her math book and began working on the problems, occasionally stopping to stir the cooking meat and noodles. By the time she finished her homework, the meat was ready.

She drained the beef and then added it to the sauce. She retrieved the strainer and drained the noodles, then poured the sauce into a serving bowl.

Checking the clock on the wall, she saw that it was nearly 5:00 pm, and Rebecca would soon get off from the hospital if she didn't have to stay late. Lauren decided to put the frozen garlic bread in the oven anyway. Ten minutes later, the bread was ready, so she took it out of the oven and sat the sheet on top of the stove. She peeked outside to see that Rebecca's car was not in the driveway. Shrugging her shoulders, she prepared her plate and had dinner alone.

Once she finished her spaghetti, she washed the dish and placed it back in the cabinet. Lauren put away her homework and school books into her backpack. After hanging the bag by the door, she walked back to her room to begin planning for the next day.

She peered inside her father and stepmother's bedroom as she walked by on her way to her room. The last time she saw her father inside the house, he was standing by the bed saying something to Rebecca. She could not hear what they were saying, but it sounded friendly. He had turned to her and asked if she was ready to go to school.

After a few minutes, she tore herself from the bedroom, walked into her own bedroom, and sat down on her bed. Wrapping her arms around herself, she refused to let herself cry. Over and over, she kept telling herself to hold it together. Forcing herself to get up after several minutes, she picked out her clothes for the next day and took them to the ironing board in the laundry room. Finishing that task, she placed her clothes in her room.

Walking to the center of the house, Lauren almost opened the door to the sunporch. She had not yet brought herself to open the door in the days since her father's death. Much less walk down there to take a look. Standing by the door, she tried to muster up the courage to open the door and look inside. Breathing deeply, she placed her hand on the doorknob. Summoning all of her courage, Lauren turned the knob, pulling the door toward her, stopping herself before she opened it fully. She closed her eyes, took one last deep breath, and fully flung the door open.

Lauren strolled down the stairs. There were only a half dozen steps, but each took a great effort to complete. Each step was a task in and of itself. Finally, she reached the bottom of the steps where her father's body had been. She wasn't sure what she would feel at this moment. Somehow it was not what she thought it would be when she finally made it down to the sunporch. Looking around, she saw the familiar sight of a room in the middle of a renovation.

Crossing her arms, she stood in silence as the moments seemed to pass more like hours. She wanted to be strong, to keep her emotions under control, but as she stood, she could almost feel her heart in her throat. It wasn't sadness she felt. It was anger. Anger against whoever did this. She wanted to lash out, to find them, and kill them in the same way they killed her father. She knew she didn't want justice. She wanted revenge.

A warm tear streaked down her face, but she wiped it away as quickly as it fell. Her chest felt heavy as she stood there trembling at the site where her father lay. She let the anger settle on her. She wanted to burn the entire house to the ground, to leave Warrenton, and never return. Standing a while longer did not help the anger to pass, but she could at least get herself under control. Lauren turned to walk back upstairs, climbing the steps faster than she did on her way down. She shut the door and decided never to walk down there again.

Checking her cellphone, she saw that it was nearly 7:00 pm. Rebecca still had yet to arrive home from the hospital. Lauren walked across the room and into the living room. Lauren took the remote from the small table underneath the television and turned it on. Sitting near the back of the room on the recliner, she settled on an old sitcom she'd watched a few times before. When the show ended, the next episode began even as the credits started to roll on the screen.

Rebecca pulled into the driveway, parked her car, and fished her keys out of her purse. She opened the door with the key and hung her purse on one of the hooks on the wall next to Lauren's school bag. Rebecca saw the spaghetti sitting on the stove. She walked to the cabinet, took out a plate, and served herself the food Lauren had left for her. She placed the plate in the microwave and warmed it for a couple of minutes before taking it out and beginning to eat.

She walked into the living room and spotted Lauren. "Did you finish your homework?" she asked trying to make conversation. "Lauren," she said, "did you finish your homework." She took a seat on the couch without waiting for an answer.

"I finished it this afternoon," Lauren responded hoping her response didn't sound too angry. Rebecca didn't seem to take notice of the short reply. "Did you have to work overtime again?"

"What?" Rebecca asked her.

"Did you have to work overtime again?"

"Oh, yeah. It's been busy at the hospital. We're so understaffed everyone is having to pitch in and cover shifts."

Lauren nodded her head in acknowledgment. "So what are we going to do about the house?"

"What do you mean?"

"You said a few days ago you wanted to sell it. Said you didn't want to live here after Dad died. You still want that?"

"Lauren, if you're worried I'm going to kick you out and send you to live with your cousins, I'm not. Your father made me promise that I would take care of you if anything ever happened to him. Nothing has changed."

"But you do want to sell the house?"

"Maybe. I don't know. Randall's death has me shaken. It's just so empty feeling without him."

"So, what do you plan to do?"

"I don't know yet, okay?" Rebecca said, feeling anger building inside her. "You graduate in a few months. Once you do, we'll figure it out from there." She calmed herself before speaking again. "These last few days have been hard on both of us. Let's try to get through them best we can."

"Yeah. I'm sorry. I wasn't trying to make you mad. I just want this all to be over."

"Me too," Rebecca said. She stood up, took her empty plate into the kitchen, and washed it in the sink. After drying it, Rebecca placed it in the cabinet and walked to her bedroom. She shut the door behind her and started to undress out of her scrubs when her phone rang. "Hey, how are you?" she said as she wedged the phone between her shoulder and ear. "Yeah, no, I think I will stay in this weekend."

Lauren was going to her bedroom when she heard Rebecca on the phone. She quietly stood by the door, listening in on the conversation Rebecca was having. A wave of embarrassment overcame her.

"Look, I can't," she heard Rebecca say. "No. No, I can't. Not this weekend. Look, Lauren is going to be here, so no."

The mention of her name sent a slight chill down Lauren's spine. She couldn't say precisely why, but she didn't like what was being said. The relationship between her and Rebecca had not begun well, but it had improved over time. It wasn't that she didn't want her dad to be happy, but some of her wanted him at least to try to get back with her mother. Even knowing that her mother was the one to run off with another man and leave them alone, there was a fantasy that things could return to the way they were.

As Lauren got older, the relationship improved. Rebecca would probably never be overly friendly, but they learned to get along.

Lauren knew her father and stepmother often fought about money, his time away from home, and the sunporch project. Still, she knew her father wanted his marriage to work. It wasn't a perfect relationship, but Rebecca made Dad happy, even if they seemed to have had difficulties for the last couple of years.

In the days before his death, he talked with her about his relationship with Rebecca. He told Lauren that he loved Rebecca and wanted to stay with her. He told Lauren about his plan to surprise Rebecca with the date night, and she promised not to let on about his plans. Lauren told him she was happy for him and hoped things worked out the way he planned. When he dropped her off at school that Friday, she hugged him and told him to have fun. That was the last thing she ever said to him.

She couldn't hear everything that was being said. She could tell whoever she was on the phone with was someone Rebecca knew well. It wasn't easy to keep up with the conversation, but she was sure Rebecca was trying to be discrete. She sometimes lowered her voice to almost a whisper as if she knew someone might be listening. Lauren was about to leave when she heard Rebecca say she had to go. As she started to walk off, Lauren heard Rebecca say, "I love you too."

Lauren went to her room without a word, shutting the door behind her. The thought of Rebecca telling whoever she was on the phone that she loved them weighed heavy on her. Lauren told herself it was nothing. She had said that to her friends before, but something struck her as strange with how Rebecca said it.

Lying in her bed, Lauren replayed it over in her mind. It bothered her because it wasn't the first time, she had heard Rebecca say that to someone over the phone. *Was it the same person?* Lauren wondered? She reasoned it was probably nothing and tried to fall asleep. Still, the thought would not let her rest.

CHAPTER
FIFTEEN

Finding Pritchard turned out to be an exercise in frustration. Taylor wanted to keep the investigation as quiet as possible. Still, word must have gotten out because Pritchard was nowhere to be seen. Pritchard had an extensive rap sheet. Most recently, he served three years on a drug charge, but his arrests included everything from drugs and assault to auto theft. With such a lengthy criminal record, it was no surprise that he was an expert at how to stay hidden.

Trying to do something different, Taylor began clearing some of his other cases. He spent about three hours going through files, making phone calls, and handling other investigations. Looking at one of the files, he came across a familiar name. He sprang to his feet and made for the door.

He drove several minutes to the not so nice part of town. He turned down an all too familiar street. It did not take him long to find the target of his search outside a small house with a couple other men. He pulled to the curb and parked the car. Taylor strode toward his mark as he called to the man. "Russell Crane," he announced as he approached a well-built African American man in his late thirties, "I've got an arrest warrant for you."

Crane was none too happy to hear what Taylor had to say. He had a reputation as a tough guy in his neighborhood and on more than one occasion had put a man in the hospital. Taylor didn't recognize the other men with Crane. They appeared to be playing cards or shooting dice when he arrived. None of them seemed tiny muscle-wise.

"Man, what are you talking about? I ain't done nothing." The other men with Crane on the porch added their protests to Taylor's presence. "What's it for?" Crane asked in a combative voice.

"Assault. Seems you were in a fight a couple of weeks ago, and the guy you beat the crap out of filed charges," Taylor responded. He reached behind him and pulled out his cuffs. "Come on, man, let's do this the easy way. My friends behind me don't have to get involved," he said as a couple of marked police cars pulled up to the scene.

Crane cursed loudly. His friends lost their resolve to fight and sat down on the porch furniture. Crane looked back at them, cursing them for their loss of nerve. He put his hands in the air and walked toward Taylor, who, without further comments, slapped the cuffs on him. The two walked back to Taylor's car, and Crane took a seat in the back.

An hour later, Crane was sitting in the interrogation room at the station. He was beginning to get impatient with all the waiting when finally, Taylor walked into the room carrying a brown paper bag. He placed it directly on the table and locked eyes with Crane.

Taylor took the seat across the table, telling him, "I got some really bad news for you, my friend," he said in the sternest voice he could manage. "I forgot the ketchup."

"What are you kidding me? How can I eat fries without ketchup?"

"Hey, look, sorry, I was in a hurry. It's not like I'm the guy who likes to eat a little French fry with my ketchup," he said as he handed the bag to Crane. "Still, I think the double helping of Ulysses S. Grant will help those fries taste better."

"Two fifties and not a C-note?"

"Unbelievable, Russell. Are you really going to complain when a man gives you a burger and $100?"

"With no ketchup. It's not like you're giving it to me anyway. You want something and judging by the fact you gave me a hundred bucks, it must be important," Crane shot back.

"Guilty. I need some info, and this one is getting a little personal. You know a guy named Tony Pritchard?"

Crane took a big bite of his burger and answered, "Yeah, I know him. Not real well, but I know him."

"What's the word on the street about him? What's he been doing lately?"

Crane swallowed and took another bite of his burger. He said, "Heard he's been gambling a lot lately." "Been losing so bad that he's been dealing more than usual. Someone told me he's been robbing houses recently too. From what I hear, he can't hold a dollar long."

"Man, didn't anyone ever tell you not to talk with your mouth full?" Taylor said, disgusted by the sight of Crane talking while chewing. Crane rolled his eyes and continued eating his burger. "You know some of the places he's robbed in the last couple of weeks?"

"Naw, couldn't tell you that. I know he and a couple of his boys have recently hit a few houses. That's all I know."

Taylor exhaled loudly. "Do you know where I might find him?"

"Yeah, he likes to hang out and deal in Sally Davis Park."

"Alright, man, thanks for your help, as always. How long do you want to stay this time? A couple of hours?"

"Yeah, man, give me a couple hours and a shower. I got a big night planned with my lady, and I got to look good."

Taylor chuckled, "Sure, no problem. Have fun tonight."

As Taylor stood up, Crane yelled back at him, "Hey, Taylor. Next time you pick me up, do something different than that cheap got a warrant bit, huh. You've pulled that one three times now. Somebody's gonna get suspicious. I got a reputation to protect."

"Come on, Russell, it makes you look good in front of your homies. Makes you look like you are beating the man at his own game."

"Yeah, well, try some new material how about it," Crane replied as Taylor exited the room. Crane sat and finished his burger in peace.

CHAPTER
SIXTEEN

When people think of crime, they often conjure an image of shady people hiding in the dark. Truth is, there are plenty of crimes that happen in broad daylight. McClendon reflected on that fact as he sat on a park bench in plain clothes with fellow officer Rosalia Perez. The two had spent the last couple of days staking the area where Tony Pritchard was known to hang out, according to their source. The weather was nice, but the work was tedious. Sitting there all day pretending to be a loving couple seemed an exciting assignment, but the thrill wore off quickly.

Taylor sat at the opposite end of the park. He was beginning to think that Pritchard must have a sixth sense telling him when someone was looking for him. It probably was partially true. Pritchard had a lengthy criminal history that ranged from assault to dealing drugs. He served time a couple of years back. It was no surprise that Pritchard tried to stay under the radar, but his gambling habits always made him short on money, so he probably would take up his old habits sooner rather than later.

It was getting late in the day, and Taylor was getting ready to call off the search when McClendon spotted the target. "Taylor, I got eyes on him and two others walking up behind us." Taylor got an anxious feeling in the pit of his stomach. On the surface, he was calm and collected, but inside there was the same nervous energy he had felt since his early days on the force. It did not seem to matter that he worked this job for years; there was always the moment of truth when things could go wrong.

"Okay, everybody, this is it. I will make the approach; everyone else be ready in case they run," Taylor said as he got out of his car. He tried to be as calm as possible while walking at an angle to intercept the three men. If he walked too quickly, he might scare off his intended targets, but if he were too slow, he would miss them completely. It was a delicate game of cat and mouse. Taylor watched from the corner of his eye as he finally found himself in front of the suspect. He turned to face the three men. "Tony Pritchard, I'm Detective Taylor. I got a few questions for you."

Almost on cue, the three men bolted. His two friends ran off in the opposite direction as Pritchard ran back the way he came. It was the wrong move. Right as he neared the park bench, McClendon lunged at him in a near-perfect form tackle that folded Pritchard like a book. McClendon and Perez flipped him on his face and cuffed him.

Taylor calmly strode over to where Pritchard was finally catching his breath and being brought to his feet by the two undercover officers. "Tony, man, that looked like it hurt. McClendon, you play football or something?"

"All county two years in a row. Should have gotten a scholarship," McClendon responded. As he searched Pritchard, he felt something. Reaching into Pritchard's rear waistband, he found a revolver. "Hey, Taylor, look what I found."

"A revolver? Oh, Tony, a felon in possession of a firearm? I guess you know what that means don't you? Man, Tony, today is not your day, is it? Think I might make it a lot worse for you." He reached for his radio, "Barnes, did you guys get his buddies?"

Barnes radioed back, "We got them. Transporting them to the station even as we speak."

"Good deal Barnes, nice work." Looking back at his officers, Taylor said, "McClendon, Perez, give our friend here a lift to the station. We have a lot to talk about."

Three hours later, Tony Pritchard was sitting in the interrogation room at the Warrenton Police Department. He sat stewing over the events of the day but otherwise making no protest other than cursing to himself. He seemed calmer than one would expect for someone who had just been arrested for an illegal firearm. Pritchard mostly sat with his arms crossed, staring blankly at the back wall.

Taylor walked in and took a seat at the edge of the table. He leaned back, trying to look relaxed. "Tony, we need to talk. You're in a lot of trouble, my friend."

"I ain't saying nothing till my lawyer gets here," he said without looking up at Taylor.

"Hey, that's fine, Tony. You don't have to talk if you don't want to. I want to make sure you understand why you're here, that's all." Taylor steadied himself and leaned forward. "First off, that gun we found, but tell you what, we'll get to that later. You're also here because we think you may have something to do with several break-ins around town. Sure you don't want to talk about that?"

"I didn't break in nowhere. I don't know what you're talkin' about."

Taylor laid it out for him, "Yeah? Well, that's not what your boy Derrick is saying. He told us about you and him breaking into that house on West Fountain Street a couple of weeks ago. I think it was all his idea between the two of us, but he is blaming you, Tony."

"Man, he's lying. He wasn't even with us when me and Kylen robbed that house. The only one he helped with was...Aww, man,"

Pritchard said, putting his elbows on the table and hiding his face in his hands.

"See Tony, you told the truth just then. Feels good to get that off your chest, doesn't it?"

"I want my lawyer. I ain't saying nothing else until I get them here."

"That's fine, Tony, that's fine. Don't say another word, but I would listen real good."

Taylor took out a picture of Randall Morris. "You see this guy?" Taylor asked sliding the picture to Pritchard slowly. "He lives on West Fountain. At least, he used to. He's dead, Tony. Shot and killed by someone who broke into his house." Taylor's voice got serious, all traces of humor and sarcasm gone. "He was killed with a .38 caliber revolver Tony. One just like the one we took off you today."

Pritchard looked away from the photograph.

"You see, this is what I think happened. You broke in when you saw the wife leave, thinking no one would be home. But there was someone home. He saw you, and you panicked. So, you shot him. You know most people would have run off after that, but you're in deep with your bookies, aren't you? Maybe you lost some money on football games, so you needed a score. So, you finished the job. The problem was that you stayed too long, and the wife returned, so you shot at her." Pritchard was starting to get nervous. Taylor could tell he had rattled him.

"I want my lawyer," Pritchard angrily said.

Getting up to leave the room, Taylor gave him one final push. "Clock is ticking, Tony. You got a small window here to make things right. Better think about your next move. If we tie that gun to the murder. Tony, you're going away for life."

CHAPTER
SEVENTEEN

The evening he found himself again at the bar he had frequented over the years. In reality, it was more of a bar and grill, although he usually found himself in the bar area. The Tavern on the Corner was once a family-owned place that dated back to sometime in the 1920s. Under its original owner, Dalton Tanner, the tavern survived Prohibition and the Depression. The family fell on hard times in the 1960s when David Tanner, grandson, died in a helicopter crash over Chu Lai in Vietnam.

Eventually, the Tanners sold out to a new owner who nearly bankrupted the place. By the Eighties, the Warrenton landmark was all but lost.

However, things began to look up near the end of the decade when Garrett Palmer, who moved to Warrenton in the mid-Nineties, bought the place and made it what it was today. It was classy and welcoming. The Palmers were good people, and they hired good people. The food was excellent, and Garrett always walked among the customers making sure everything was perfect with their meals. It was the kind of place with that rare combination of being able to cater to the drink after work crowd and the family dining crowd.

A change came again just a few years ago. Garrett retired and sold the restaurant to its current owner. Many of their customers worried about the change; after all, it did not have the best track record of owners. Garrett chose his successor well, though. Eddie Sutter was a Marine Food Service Specialist. While in Iraq, Eddie was on his way to cater a function with several high-ranking officers sometime after the end of the troop surge in 2007. His convoy came under attack by insurgents. His Humvee hit an IED and killed the driver. Eddie lost his right leg after the Humvee flipped over, pinning him inside. After his discharge, he went to Warrenton and started work for Garrett. Now Eddie owned the place and continued the excellent reputation of Tavern on the Corner.

Taylor and Sutton hit it off almost immediately. They talked about their time in the service and their love of baseball. When Shelia returned to his life, Sutton quickly agreed to let his place be where they met to discuss cases. Sometimes they would be there well into the morning, but Eddie never complained. Anything they wanted, Eddie made sure they got it. After Shelia died, Eddie was one of the first to be there for Roger in his time of need. Many nights they just sat at the bar not saying a word.

As he sat at the bar in his usual place, Taylor nursed the only drink he had ordered all night. It was not so much about the drink; it was more about the time he spent remembering. Eddie seemed to know when to come over and when to leave him to his thoughts. It was getting late, and Eddie made his way over to him. "Roger, we're closing in a few minutes. You want to stay for a while?"

Taylor thought about it for a moment before answering. "I don't know, Eddie; think I might head home." It must have been the way he said it because even Taylor did not believe what he said. Maybe he wanted some company tonight, but he did not want to come out and say it.

Eddie, to his credit, would not take no for an answer. "Come on.

I got some onion rings back there saved up for us. What do you say? It's on the house. I'll even get you a fresh drink." Despite having a prosthetic right leg, Eddie was in great shape. Roger wondered how a guy who cooked as well as Eddie stayed in shape. Of course, once a Marine, always a Marine, which meant he took good care of himself. Roger would never say it out loud, but he was pretty sure Eddie could still take him in a fight.

"Okay, maybe for a bit. Got an early day tomorrow."

"Yeah, like that ever stopped you before," Eddie responded as he walked back to the kitchen. About fifteen minutes later, he returned with the promised onion rings and a cold beer. The onion rings smelled great and were still hot. It was clear these were not simply leftovers from the night's business. "How's life treating you these days, Roger?" he asked as he took the seat across from Taylor.

Taylor took one of the onion rings and dipped it into the sauce, stuffing it into his mouth. It was hotter than he was ready for, and his tongue was burned. He quickly swallowed and chased it with a deep sip of beer. "Wow, Eddie, I thought these were leftovers, but you made these fresh," he said, then took another drink of his beer. "Good, though."

"Yeah, what can I say? Always give people more than they expect or something," he said, sipping his drink. "You still haven't answered the question. How've you been?"

"Same as always, I guess. Been really wrapped up in a case recently. It's taken my mind off things, you know."

"Has it really, Roger?"

"At times. Other times it's brought back some good and bad memories, feelings, and dark thoughts. On the other hand, I've noticed that old sense of humor coming back. I feel better than I have in a long time in some ways, but in other ways, I want to crawl in a hole and hide from the world."

Eddie ate a couple of onion rings, "You know this is such a

simple food. Fried pieces of onion, whoever came up with this was an absolute genius." He laughed to himself. "Aldo Brambilla. He loved onion rings. Crazy, isn't it, that an Italian from Pennsylvania would love onion rings of all things. Couldn't get enough of them." Eddie took a few more and held them in his hand. "He didn't want to drive me that day. I had to leave early to cook for some colonel whose name I don't remember, but I bribed Aldo with onion rings if he would drive me. So, he agreed and took the other guy's place."

He sat for what seemed like an hour before continuing his story. "I didn't want to drive with someone I didn't know. It was Aldo's day off, but I talked him into driving just because I wanted someone to talk to on the ride." He put his head down and closed his eyes. "Then we got hit. I was trapped in that thing for I don't know how long. I remember seeing Aldo in that driver's seat, staring at me with cold blank eyes. I've carried that guilt for a long time. I think about him every time I eat these. It's my way to remember him."

The two sat there in silence for several minutes. Roger finally broke the silence. "You know, I always thought we had time. Shelia and me. We were beginning to have the same chemistry as we did before. When we worked the case against Pierson, I think we both felt it." Taylor took another drink. "Then time ran out, and she was gone. I've spent the last year and a half trying to forget about her, but I just can't."

"Then don't," Eddie said. "Don't forget about her. Remember her in the good times. Those times you shared you want to remember, not the fact that she's gone. I knew her well enough to know that's what she'd want you to do. I also know she wouldn't blame you for what happened."

"Is that what you do, Eddie? Remember Aldo with onion rings?"

"It's not that simple, Roger. Me and Aldo served together, but you and Shelia were more than that. It's different, I know, but she would want you to live your life and be happy." He picked up a large onion ring and held it toward Taylor. "I do this to honor his memory, not wallow in guilt and blame."

"What if I'm not ready yet?" Taylor asked.

"I think you will be. Probably sooner than you think. Until then, I won't run out of onion rings."

Roger stayed long enough to finish off the onion rings. He and Eddie had gone through the same conversation before. Deep down, Roger knew Eddie was right but moving on was difficult at best. Still, he had to admit that life was starting to return to a version of what it was before Shelia died. No, life would never be the same, but maybe Roger could get to where Eddie was. That may be enough.

CHAPTER EIGHTEEN

Taylor sat in his office pouring over case files. The attorney for Tony Pritchard had asked to speak with him in the afternoon. Until then, Taylor had a lot of work to catch up on. He looked up and saw Barnes walking in looking like someone had cut her off in traffic and given her the finger. Curiosity got the better, so he walked out of his office and over to her desk area. He asked her as dispassionately as possible, "Well, what's wrong with you?"

She glanced at him with a look that said go to hell, and here are the directions to get there. She answered him, saying, "My car radio died on me. Stupid thing hardly turns on, and when it does, it's nothing but static."

"Really, is it so bad that you can't listen to your Top 40 crap on the drive to work and home?" he responded.

"Top 40? Really is that what you think of me. I'm more of a hard-rock girl. It's my way of getting ready for the day and unwinding once it's over." She leaned back in her chair. "I'm thinking about getting one of those satellite radios. Do you know anyone who can install one of those?"

"Not me. I gave up on music years ago."

"Hey, I can install that for you," came a familiar voice behind them. Officer Michael Davis turned around from his pile of paperwork to face them. "It's not hard, really. I could have it done pretty quick," he said with a know-it-all smirk on his face.

"Davis, what do you know about car radios?" Barnes asked him sarcastically.

"Hey, my Dad used to have a shop here in town. My brother and I worked there on the weekends and over the summer when we were in school. Chris owns it now since Dad passed, and I help him from time to time."

"Okay, you two talk this out; I've got real work to do," Taylor said dismissively and turned back to his office. It was not that he felt a tinge of jealousy for being interrupted, or did he? *No, it's not jealousy. She's too young, and your partner. Better to not get too close.*

Still, it bothered him, but he could not explain why. Davis was a good guy and, by all accounts, would probably make detective soon. They certainly could use a couple more hands out in the field. Then again, Davis has never shown any interest in becoming a detective, and he seemed to prefer patrol duty. *To each their own,* Taylor thought as he sat back down at his desk, trying to clear away any distractions from the last few minutes.

Barnes was interested in Davis's offer. "So, how long does it take to install? I got big plans for the weekend," she said.

"Really? What? Are you going to drive up the coast or something?" Davis asked.

"No, I get together with friends and watch the Rams' game on Sunday. We've been watching the games together for years. If I'm not here on Sunday."

"You're a Rams fan too, huh? I went to the Denver game couple of weeks back?"

"No kidding? You go by yourself?"

"I went with Joe Miller and Ty Bennett, a couple of my old high school friends. They have a place just outside of LA. It was a great game, but it didn't look good when we got down 10-0 in the first quarter. Big comeback win 24-10."

"Don't you mean 34-10?" Barnes laughed.

"No, it was 24-10. I was there."

"Dude, I watched the game on TV. Remember they missed the extra point and were down 10-6? That's before they caught fire and scored four more TDs. You sure you were at that game?"

"Yeah, you're right, you're right. Guess I had too many beers."

"Sounds like it. You know you could join us this weekend if you'd like. Always have room for one more Rams fan. May want to lay off the drinks a little bit, though, so you can remember the game."

"No worries, I usually don't drink that much. Of course, I could have a designated driver take me home after the game," Davis said in a near whisper cutting his eyes toward Taylor's office.

Barnes lowered her voice to match. "That sounds like a great idea. It really shows how responsible you are. I like that in a man." She whispered, "So does my friend Mike. He doesn't drink and is usually responsible for getting people home. He'd love to drive you." Davis's face looked dejected. "So, can you install the radio Saturday?"

"Yeah, sure, I can do that. No problem."

"Good, then maybe we can talk about Sunday afternoon then," she replied with a satisfied smile and got busy on the stack of papers on her desk.

CHAPTER
NINETEEN

It was nearly three o'clock that afternoon before Pritchard's attorney arrived for the interview. Aimee Wright began serving the public defender's office about four years ago. Over that time, she gained a reputation as a tough negotiator. Wright made no secret of her desire to become one of the best defense attorneys in the state. Self-promotion seemed to come easily to her, and it appeared to Taylor that she never missed an opportunity to make herself look important.

Taylor and Barnes walked into the interrogation room and took the seats across from Pritchard and Wright. He did not wait long to break the silence. "Your client would like to talk, so let's talk," he said as he sat back in his chair.

"Right to the point as always, Detective Taylor?" Wright responded with more than a bit of scorn in her voice. "My client is willing to tell you about the robberies and his involvement in them in return for a lenient sentence."

"Well, that's great. I'm glad to hear that I really am, but what he really needs to talk about is the murder of Randall Morris. What's he got to say about that?"

She glanced over at Pritchard, who sat showing no emotion. "We have nothing to discuss about a murder. In fact, my client denies any involvement in the break-in that resulted in Mr. Morris's death. The other break-ins, yes, but not that one. That's our position."

Taylor glanced over at Barnes and shook his head. "So, you're telling me he admits breaking into a home just down the street from the Morris home, but he had nothing to do with the Morris robbery and murder? Come on, you can do better than that."

Barnes joined the conversation, "Mr. Pritchard and his accomplices broke into three houses in the Robinwood subdivision over the course of a couple of weeks. They then moved on to Harper Meadows. It seems like they found another home in Harper Meadows before they moved on."

"Mr. Pritchard claims he and his accomplices were going to hit another home, but they couldn't agree on which one. They never got around to picking another house before his arrest," Wright responded in an apparent attempt to talk down to Barnes. "You've got all you're going to get out of my client."

"If that's the case, how does he explain the stolen jewelry?" Barnes countered. She let a few uncomfortable moments drag on before she continued. "We have a witness willing to testify that he received jewelry from Mr. Pritchard for a gambling debt."

"That puts you inside the house at the time of the murder, Tony," Taylor interjected. "We have more than enough to charge you and put you away for life."

Tony Pritchard cursed but said nothing else in his defense.

"My client says he found those items in a car he broke into a while back," Wright said, clearly having trouble finding excuses for her client.

"You will have to do better than that, Tony. You're going to stake the rest of your life on a story that means you got lucky and found the jewelry? No way. I don't believe you for a second." Taylor believed he had his man. The ridiculous story he was hearing made little to no sense. "Do you even have a description of this car?"

"Man, I don't remember what it looked like. It was just one of a bunch of cars I broke into," Pritchard blurted out. Aimee Wright rubbed her forehead in frustration at her client's thoughtless answer. "Look, I'm a thief, but I ain't no killer. Alright, I broke into a lot of houses and cars, but I never killed nobody."

Sensing they had got him on the break-ins, Barnes decided to change the subject. "Let's talk about the gun then," Barnes countered. "A felon in possession of a firearm is a serious charge. Is he going to plead to that? If so, we need to know where it came from and who he got it from."

"Not to mention," Taylor interjected, "if we trace that gun to the murder, your client's guilty pleas to all the other crimes aren't going to mean much." He looked over at Pritchard, "This is your last opportunity to tell us the truth, or else the DA is going for murder one Tony. Think about it."

Wright looked over at her client, who shook his head. "According to Mr. Pritchard, he bought the gun from a guy he knows in his neighborhood. He's had it about a week or two, not long enough to commit the murder with it."

"This guy have a name, Tony?" Barnes asked.

Pritchard looked over at his attorney, who nodded. "His name is Marvo. Lives a few houses down from me. I don't know where he got it. That's all I know."

"I'm going to need a description of this Marvo. Has he got a last name?" Taylor asked.

"I don't know it; everyone just calls him Marvo."

Taylor motioned to Barnes. "We're done here. You better hope this Marvo turns up; otherwise, this is all on you. Might want to try and talk some sense into your client. Mrs. Wright." With that, he and Barnes left the room. "What do you think, Barnes?" he asked after they had walked away from the door.

"He's definitely hiding something, but he wouldn't be the first to try and cover up a murder. You think he's our guy?"

Taylor thought for a moment. "Sure seems to be. I got to admit I'm almost one hundred percent sure about him. He has no alibi for the time of the murder, a history of violence, and he admits to similar crimes. Once the ballistics are back, we'll know for sure."

"What about his two friends?" Barnes asked.

"Same for them. We can charge them as accessories to the burglaries, but tying them to the murder will be more difficult. Mrs. Morris only saw the one person, and he had his face covered, but if we pressure them more, I think one of them will eventually crack."

"I don't know. I think one of them, Derrick, claimed he was out drinking with some friends the night of the murder. I have not been able to confirm that, but the story sounds believable. The other one was at a party at the time, and I can confirm his story because he showed me a picture taken at the approximate time of the murder. I think Tony may have gone solo on this one," Barnes said.

"Kind of hard to believe he would try a burglary by himself in that neighborhood. Maybe if he was desperate enough to pay off his gambling debts. Well, let's try and find this Marvo guy. If that's who he got the gun from, he should be able to tell us when he sold it to him."

CHAPTER
TWENTY

As he was leaving the station, Taylor's phone rang. Looking at the screen, he saw that it was Seth Willard's number.

"Seth, how's it going?" It had been a while since the two last spoke on the phone. Until recently, the two regularly talked and shared meals together. Taylor didn't overthink it; he just assumed life somehow got in the way of their friendship. It happens sometimes, but maybe this was a chance to reconnect.

Seth's voice sounded cheerful. "Roger, how are you? You want to grab a bite to eat and a drink or two for old times?"

"Yeah, I was just leaving the station. Where do you want to meet up?"

Seth laughed, "Same old Roger, you leave the station at the same time every day. How about Garrett's Seafood? Could really use some grilled shrimp and lobster tails."

"Okay, first, no, I don't leave the station at the same time every day, just most days. Second, yes, shrimp and lobster sound great. Half an hour good?" Seth eagerly agreed to the meeting time. It occurred to Taylor that he hadn't been very social over the last several months. He could have easily called Seth or anyone else to meet up for a bite. Eddie was right; after all, he did need to get out more.

Being mid-week, Garrett's wasn't crowded. It was often overlooked because the décor was not the most eye catching, but it was a great place to get quality seafood. In recent years, the dine-in area wasn't used as much as customers began to use the takeout option. Still, a noticeable core of the restaurant's usual customers continued to dine in. Roger was one of those who preferred the dine-in option, as did the man he was here to see.

He quickly spotted Seth sitting in a corner booth near the back of the small dining area. Seth looked out the window while talking on the phone as Roger made his way to the booth. Seth spotted him and began to wrap up his conversation. He nodded his head in recognition and finished the conversation. He rose and offered his hand. "Roger, my apology; some builders don't seem to understand the concept of office hours."

Roger took his hand with a chuckle. "Yeah, I know a little about people who don't keep regular office hours."

"Yeah, I bet you do. Sit down. How've you been?"

Roger sat across from the man and made himself comfortable. A waitress who had worked at Garrett's since she graduated high school, took his drink order. "I can't say anything bad about life, I guess. Been a bit busy recently. What about you?"

"About the same, I guess. Work mostly. Been trying to get out a little more recently," Seth said, then took a long drink from his tea. "You know it's funny how funerals can bring people together again, isn't it?" He took another drink and then set the glass down, "You know that's happened before to me. I had a high school classmate die a few years ago of a heart attack. While there, several of my classmates talked it over, and the next week we had an impromptu class reunion. We got together at one of the guys' houses to hang out at his pool."

"Sounds like you have a thing with reconnecting with people at funerals," Roger poked at him.

"Yeah, I guess so. Man, that is a terrible thing that happened to Randall. I hope you find that guy." Seth stopped himself, "Sorry, you probably want to talk about anything other than work. Are you doing alright? You seeing anyone right now?"

"It's fine," Roger said, "I get asked about work all the time, and no, I'm not seeing anyone right now. Honestly, I haven't wanted to since Shelia died."

"I'm sorry, Roger, I didn't mean to...."

"Hey, Seth, it's fine," he said as Annette arrived with his drink.

"You guys ready to order, or do you still need a minute?" she asked in the enthusiastic waitress voice she had perfected over the years. Roger thought she would have opened her own place by now, but from all indications, Annette was happy where she was. She had been employed at Garrett's longer than anyone other than the owners. She had proven herself a valuable employee over the years, learning everything she could about the restaurant business from the business's waiting, cooking, and administration.

"I'll have the shrimp and lobster platter with a baked potato and ranch dressing on my salad," Roger said as he handed the menu back to her. Seth ordered the same thing. With that, she left the table to turn in their orders to the kitchen.

"I'm starting to move past her death. Not that I'll ever forget her, but I'm trying to get out there again. Trying to live with it? Is that the right thing to say? I don't know."

"I get what you're trying to say," Seth said reassuringly. "I really do. I remember when Heather ended our marriage. I thought it was the end of the world. It's different, I know, but divorce is almost like death in a way. The difference is you know your ex is out there some-where living life with some sleaze bag they left you for, and you're all alone." Seth stopped and laughed despite himself. "Listen to me.

You'd think it happened yesterday instead of three years ago. I guess things like that never fully go away."

Roger nodded in agreement as he took a drink of his tea. "Anyway, I've put myself out there recently. Been on a few dates here and there. You know, just trying to see if there is someone out there for me."

"Any luck?" Roger asked him.

"Well, nothing serious. I had someone I saw a while back, but nothing came of it. We dated a few times, but no magic spark. Anyway, I'm still looking for Mrs. Right. Wouldn't mind a Mrs. Rightnow in the meantime if you know what I mean."

"Okay, too much information," Roger said with a laugh in his voice.

"You know me. I like to have someone in my life. Never was one who liked to be alone. That's why the divorce was so tough. Not just the physical part but the companionship. That was the hardest part, the empty house."

"At least you got to keep it. The house, that is."

"Just barely, but yeah. I got to keep the house and every other weekend with the kids. Heather got a new life. I guess she figured she couldn't take the house with her to Riverside. Got to have some place for the kids to stay when they visit."

Roger lifted his glass of tea, "To ex-wives and new lives," he sarcastically toasted.

"I'll drink to that," Seth said as he lifted his glass.

The food was as delicious as usual. An hour passed as the two friends swapped stories and caught up on the months since the last time they shared a meal. Eventually, with the food eaten and fatigue from the workday, they called it a night. They shook hands and promised to stay in better touch in the future.

Thirty minutes later, Taylor arrived home. He walked back to his kitchen and grabbed a beer from the refrigerator. Twisting off the top, he took a quick drink from the bottle. He set the bottle on the small table in front of his couch while he sat across from it, not bothering to move the bottle from the night before. Taylor turned on the television and flipped through the channels for several minutes, not interested in anything as he surfed the channels. At some point, he must have drifted off to sleep.

He found himself on a beach somewhere he didn't exactly recognize. Looking around, he saw a small-framed Asian woman in a one-piece swimsuit. Her hair was shoulder length and moved with the wind from the ocean. She spread a beach towel and sat on it with her knees drawn to her body.

Roger began to walk toward her. As he drew closer, she turned and made eye contact with him. She smiled as she rested her head on her knees, looking toward him. The wind continued to blow its warm breeze through her hair. After what seemed like an eternity, he finally arrived close to where she was sitting. Her face was aglow as she took her hand and slowly moved her hair behind her ear. Suddenly Roger stopped. He didn't want to get any closer because he knew how this ended. He didn't want her to say anything, but he couldn't stop her. "Roger," she said in a familiar voice, and he awoke with a start.

Looking at the clock on his cellphone, he saw it was ten minutes past one in the morning. The lights in the duplex were still on as was the television. He leaned over, grabbed the beer bottle, realizing he had only taken a single sip from it, stood up and walked to the kitchen with both bottles. He poured out the beer as he tried to shake off the effects of the dream.

He went to the bedroom and lay on top of the covers. The next hour was spent trying to force himself to fall back asleep. He also remembered he hadn't plugged his phone into its charger. He walked back into his sitting area and picked up the phone from the sofa where he had left it. He plugged the phone into the outlet, set it on the nightstand beside his bed, and tried to scroll through his social media accounts. Finally, after about thirty more minutes, he thought he should close his eyes again. This time he felt himself drift off to sleep.

CHAPTER
TWENTY-ONE

Finding Marvo proved more difficult than finding Tony Pritchard. Several days passed, and it seemed unlikely that Marvo would ever be seen. Taylor was sitting in his office getting ready to start the search again when an officer appeared at his door.

"Hey, Taylor, the chief wants to see you." He hardly looked up from his desk but thanked the officer. The police chief's office was only a couple of doors down from his, but it felt like a longer walk than it was.

Chief Amanda Vanderbeck was a fourteen-year veteran of the Los Angeles Police Department. She was the first person of color to lead the Warrenton Police Department. The relationship between Taylor and Vanderbeck was professional but not overly friendly. Many believed that Taylor deserved the job after his work on the Pierson case. Instead, the city decided to go with someone from outside the department. He did not take it personally; he couldn't blame them for hiring someone outside the department.

The problem was that Vanderbeck knew he was in line for the job at least in her mind, Taylor was a rival. Taylor, for his part, did not see it that way, but he had to admit his relationship with the last chief did not extend to the new chief. Regardless, Taylor respected her position as chief, but they seemed to have little in common on a personal level. Maybe over time things would change, and he was willing to do his part to try.

As he arrived at her office, he saw a gray haired man sitting across from her in a suit and tie. The two, who seemed to be having a conversation before he arrived, turned to greet him as he arrived.

"Detective Taylor, this is Sergeant McNeil of the Julian Police Department. He's got a few questions for you on an old case you investigated."

"Sure, how can I help you?" Taylor asked, extending his hand.

McNeil handed him a picture of a young man. "Detective Taylor, do you recognize this man?" He asked the question like someone who already knew the answer.

"Yeah, that's Jordan Byrd. We've been looking for him for a while. He's the creep who set up hidden cameras in hotel rooms and any other place Lawson Pierson took the girls he met online. Did you arrest him or something?"

"Not exactly. He was found dead a few weeks ago. He'd been living in Julian with his wife. She came home and found him shot to death. Whoever did it took several things, files, and at least one laptop and a couple of hard drives. Got any idea who might have done it?"

Taylor thought for a moment, "That's hard to say. We took down the Pierson crime syndicate about a year ago. It's possible that it could be someone associated with them we missed."

"We don't think it's a direct Pierson connection. Our theory is that Jordan tried to act on some information he obtained from Lawson, which got him killed. It's probably not drug-related, but it may be some business information or a blackmail scheme. Either way, it's impossible to tell without any of the stolen files or computers he kept at home. That's why we hoped you could help us."

"My department will lend any help we can," Vanderbeck added to the conversation.

Taylor should not have been annoyed by the interjection, but for some reason, he was. So maybe he really did want the job of police chief after all. The better possibility was that it was the personality conflict neither of them seemed to be able to move past. Whatever it was, there was just something about her he did not like. He could not explain why. Still, she was the chief, and he would do his job despite his personal misgivings.

"Yes, of course, I'll look through my case files and see what I can dig up for you," Taylor said. He shook hands with the man and excused himself from the office.

Taylor spent several hours reviewing and arranging the relevant files he had on the Pierson case and Jordan Byrd in particular. It was a tedious but necessary job. He could not help but reminisce about all the frustrations throughout his investigation of Leonard Pierson. He often came close to catching him, but Pierson always seemed to be one step ahead. That changed when Sheila got involved.

After Shelia approached him about the case, she relentlessly poured herself into it. She had a tendency to go off on her own. That frightened him more than facing off with an armed shooter. He tried to keep her away from the most dangerous aspects of the investigation. Still, she had a way of finding herself there anyway. It was her resilience that he admired most about her. As much as it worried him, he loved how she was involved in the case and how much she put into it. The problem was he got lost in the case, which made him careless – and got her killed.

He pushed those thoughts aside. Resolutely, he refused to give in to those thoughts again. It was Leonard Pierson who ordered the hit on Shelia. Even if Roger never got her entangled, he was sure Shelia would have gotten involved anyway. That was Shelia. When she set her mind to something, there really was no stopping her.

When an officer came to his door, he was putting together the last files. "Detective, there's someone here to see you." *Again,* he thought. The officer motioned a teenaged girl to the office. Lauren Morris walked into the office with a worried look on her face. Taylor glanced at his watch. It was 1:45 on a Wednesday afternoon, and to the best of his knowledge, there was no school holiday scheduled, so he doubted anyone knew she was there.

"Detective Taylor, can I talk to you?" she asked in a voice so quiet he almost did not hear her. She was dressed in her school uniform; he guessed she was skipping class to come to the station. He wondered how she got here since he knew she did not drive. Still, if she was here, she had something on her mind.

"Of course, please come in. Have a seat," Taylor said as he motioned her to sit down. He got up and shut the door behind her. Sitting back down himself, he wondered what brought her to see him. When he last spoke to her and her stepmother, Taylor felt Lauren was holding something back. That was not unusual. Teens often did not open up about their life in front of their parents. It was usual for teens to keep things hidden from parents; he understood that, but there seemed to be more. He hadn't thought much of it because she was not present at the time of the murder. "So, how did you get here? Your stepmom bring you?"

Lauren blushed. "No, I checked myself out of school and walked here. It's not that far, and I don't have any important classes after lunch." She looked uncomfortable, like she was keeping a secret for too long, and wanted to get it off her chest. "Uhm...I'm not sure how to say this or if it even matters," she began. She was hesitant, almost as if she did not believe she would be taken seriously.

"Lauren, it's okay. You can tell me. What's bothering you?" he asked, trying to sound reassuring.

"Well, I think my stepmother was having an affair. Before my Dad died, I mean."

Taylor was taken aback by her comment. "Oh, okay, well, are you sure? How do you know that?"

"I didn't want to say anything while she was here when you interviewed us, but I heard her talking to someone on her cellphone one night."

"What were they saying?"

"I couldn't hear who she was talking to, but she was talking about meeting up with him. Without my Dad."

"Well, okay. Are you sure it was a man on the other end? Could she have been talking to a friend or a woman?"

"No, I'm certain it was a man. She said she loved him and couldn't wait to be with him. Like she was planning on leaving my Dad."

Taylor thought for a moment. Everything so far pointed to ideal home life and marriage, and now that was being called into question. "Lauren, are you sure she wasn't talking to your Dad? She could have been talking to him, or maybe it was a friend. You know, sometimes friends say that they love each other from time to time."

"No, it wasn't like that. Not like you talk to a friend. It's the way she said it. She said it softly like she didn't want anyone to hear her. Look, if you don't believe me…."

"Hey, now wait, I never said that. I just have to consider all the possibilities. How long ago was this?"

"I'm not sure," she said. "Couple of months ago, maybe. People think they had a perfect marriage, but my Dad worked a lot. He didn't get home sometimes until late at night, and Rebecca would be out late too. I know she was supposed to be at the hospital, but it's like she was out later than she should be. She'd always get home just before my Dad. I don't know, but I think she was seeing someone else."

Taylor took in all that she said and came up with an idea. "Okay, let's do this. I want you to write down everything you just told me. I'll look into it and see what I can find, but we have a suspect in custody we think may have pulled the trigger." He paused. "Look, even if your stepmother did have an affair, it doesn't make her a killer, but it's a terrible thing to deal with. I know this won't be easy for you, but if there is a connection, I'll do my best to find it. Let me get you some paper to write down your statement. I'll look into it, I promise. Then, I'll get you a ride home before your stepmom gets there."

CHAPTER
TWENTY-TWO

Sunday afternoon found Barnes in her usual friend group at the home of Bret Meyer. She first met Bret at Victory Grill and Sports Bar shortly after moving to Warrenton. Meyer noticed Barnes was decked out in Rams gear and started conversing with her. He invited her to join their fan group. They watched the game every Sunday at The Victory. Two years later, the place burned to the ground due to bad wiring, so the group began to meet at Meyer's home instead.

By that time, Bret married his fiancée Gwenn, a Raiders fan to everyone's chagrin. The group had many loyal members. Sundays then were traditional get togethers over the years, and Barnes rarely missed a game. This Sunday was no exception.

She brought her signature buffalo chicken dip with her to the party. Her buffalo chicken dip was one of the few dishes she felt confident enough to make for the party given her meager cooking skills. Greeting each person as she walked through Meyer's home, Barnes felt a wave of excitement as the early game reached the two-minute warning. The Rams were playing the Cowboys, so the game had a lot riding on it.

Barnes made her way to the table and began to fix herself a plate.

"Laura how are you?" came a familiar voice behind her. She turned to see her friend Skylar Oliver approaching. Skylar had her arms spread wide, wearing a Rams jersey.

Skylar was a slender woman with long black hair giving her an exotic look. Her father was a Caucasian man, and her mother was a light-skinned African American woman. She had a lively personality, and Sky was one of the first people Barnes met when she moved to town. Over time they became best friends.

The two embraced and exchanged greetings. "When did you get here, and why haven't you called me lately?"

"You know how it is, Sky. I stay busy these days. It's great to see you. Still dating Nate?"

"Sure am. How about you? Seeing anyone yet?"

"Nope, still looking though."

Skylar gave her a curious look. "Really? Gwenn said you were bringing someone. Where is he? I need to see if he passes inspection," she teased.

Barnes lowered her head and stared back at Sky. "Inspection? Really Sky?"

"Hey, I'm just trying to look out for you, Laura. It's been a while since you've been out. You know I can still fix you up with Dan."

"No, absolutely not," she said nearly dropping the plate of food she was holding.

"Okay fine, but where is the new guy?"

"He's not my new guy. I worked patrol with him for a couple of years. He installed my new car radio yesterday, so I invited him over as a thank you."

"Fine, but where is he, and what's his name?"

"His name is Michael Davis, and he's on his way. He texted me and said he had to go by his brother's car shop and pick up some stuff he had left there yesterday. Should be here in about twenty minutes or so."

"So, he's a cop too; how romantic," Sky teased. "You must have impressed him pretty good yesterday if he left all of his stuff behind."

"Sky, it was nothing like that. I hardly saw him at all yesterday."

"Well, is he at least cute?" Sky asked her to try to get all the information she could.

Barnes smiled and blushed. "Okay, yes, he is. Very cute, actually, but please don't tell him I said that. He's a co-worker, and I don't want things to get weird."

"You got it. Not a word. Just promise me I'll get the intro when he gets here."

"Promise," Barnes said as she tried to finish putting food on her plate.

By the time Davis arrived, the first quarter had ended in a scoreless tie. He sent Barnes a text asking her to meet him outside when he arrived. She excused herself as she walked through the guests to meet Davis. He arrived about five minutes later, carrying a case of bottled beer. "Sorry I'm late had to wait on my brother to show up. I hope you all like a light beer."

"It's fine, but let's go. The game's on." She turned to lead him inside as Sky rushed out to meet them. *Oh no*, Barnes thought. She hoped Sky hadn't seen her leave, but she should have known her best friend would be watching.

"Hello," she said, holding the "o" for a while. "You must be Michael,"

"Hi, I'm Michael, but everyone calls me Davis."

"Okay, Davis, then. Laura, aren't you going to introduce me?"

Laura looked like she could cause serious bodily harm to her best friend. She introduced Davis. "Now, can we please get back to the game?" Barnes asked, trying not to sound too annoyed.

"Oh, you haven't missed much. Dallas just scored on a long pass. It's just 7-0," Sky announced clearly more interested in what was going on outside than the game.

"What?" exclaimed Barnes. "Alright, both of you inside."

By halftime, Davis felt at home among the party guests as he watched the game. Everyone seemed friendly enough and encouraged him to make himself at home. Several asked how he knew Laura and how long they had been dating. For her part, she tried not to be too embarrassed by all of the questions.

"Are your friends always this attentive to the new guy?" he asked as the game went to commercial before the start of the fourth quarter. He felt a little overwhelmed by all the attention, although he seemed to get along well.

"It's because you're here with me. They all know I haven't dated anyone since my breakup a few months ago, so they're curious. Don't take it personally." She finished the beer she was holding and sat it on the small table in front of her. "Sky never liked Steven. She never would say so, but I could tell. I think she's relieved I didn't get back to him and decided to move on." Suddenly she felt like awkward. "Sorry, I didn't mean to say too much about my ex."

"It's fine, but I have to agree with her. The only time I met the guy, I thought he was a jerk."

"Really? Just now getting around to telling me that bit of info?"

"Hey, you know how it is. Never criticize someone's boyfriend or girlfriend. Never ends well."

"You're probably right. Probably would have just pissed me off."

Tension filled the room as the Cowboys moved the ball, with the score tied at 17 with time running down. Barnes intently watched the game while doing what she could to try and cheer on the defense. Then with fifteen seconds left, the Cowboys completed a pass and got out of bounds at the Rams' 28-yard line. As the Cowboys lined up for the field goal, Barnes grabbed Davis's hand, squeezing it tightly.

The kick sailed straight through the uprights giving the Cowboys the win. Barnes stood and slung down her hands, not seeming to realize that she still held Davis's hand. He winced in pain as she stood. Barnes turned suddenly, embarrassed at what she did. "I'm sorry, Davis. I forgot, are you okay?"

"Yeah," Davis said as he tried to laugh it off. "I didn't realize you were such a rabid fan."

Barnes gave an embarrassed laugh. "Sorry, I do get into the game. You should see me when I go in person."

"Tell me you're not the one in body paint and clown wigs."

"Not body paint or stupid, face paint," she said defensively. "

"Is there a difference?"

"Well, yeah. One is on your body, and one is on your face. And no, I don't wear a clown wig." She sat back down, unhappy with the result of the game. "Look, you can take off. I'm going to stay and help clean up. I'll see you tomorrow, alright?"

"Yeah, sure. Did you drive, or do you need a ride home?"

"I got it, Davis, thanks. I swear I've only had one beer, officer," she said joking around with him. "Seriously, go on, and I, ummm… had a great time hanging out with you. Thanks for coming."

"Yeah, I enjoyed it. Thanks for the invite. Alright, I'll see you tomorrow then." He left, thanking Meyers for inviting him. They thanked him, and he walked to his car.

Sky wasted no time running over to Barnes as she gathered beer bottles for the recycling. "Laura, he's perfect for you. You two make such a cute couple."

"Sky, we are not a couple. I've literally only seen him outside of work a couple of times. And don't read anything into that," she quickly added.

"Laura, it's okay. You don't have to fall in love just yet. Have some fun, go out and live it up a bit. Then if the mood strikes you both right, then you know."

"Skylar, stop it. Uh, seriously? Look, he's cute and all, but I will not rush into anything." She returned to rounding up beer bottles and then turned back to her friend. "You really think he's into me?"

"Are you kidding? Did you not see the way he looked at you? Trust me, I can tell when someone is into someone else. He's into you alright."

"Oh," Barnes said as she placed the bottles in the recycling bin. As she stood up, she smiled and quickly wiped it from her face before turning around.

CHAPTER
TWENTY-THREE

A couple of days later, Taylor and Barnes were going over the details of the Tony Pritchard cases in his office. He confessed to three home robberies but not the one involving Randall Morris. Still, if they could determine any patterns and similarities in the robberies, they felt sure a conviction for the Morris killing would follow. The problem was that all the other robberies occurred when no one was home. Morris was the only case where someone was encountered, much less killed.

Still, the story fit. Pritchard breaks in and finds Morris. In a panic, he shoots him dead. He decides to go through the house because he needs the cash. It all fit. There were still some loose ends and details to be worked out just in case he decided to pull out of the plea deal under consideration, a deal they were both confident would include the confession to murder.

Barnes decided to ask about the visitor he got from Julian. "He was here investigating the murder of Jordan Byrd," he told her. "Do you remember him?"

"Not exactly. Remind me," Barnes said, then listened as Taylor recounted the story of Jordan Byrd and his role in the Lewis case a few years back. "Byrd disappeared for a long time but resurfaced in Julian. He must have tried to use some of the information Lawson Pierson had, which got him killed. The sergeant couldn't tell me what that information was, but it doesn't matter."

"What do you mean it doesn't matter?" she asked, surprised Taylor would say that.

"It's not our case. It's another loose end in a closed case that has finally resolved itself."

"You've got to be kidding, Taylor. Really? A guy from the biggest case you have ever worked turns up dead, and you're not in the least interested?"

He set the file down he was looking through and gave Barnes a cold stare. "It's not that I'm uninterested, but it's not our case. It's way out of our jurisdiction, and we closed the Pierson case months ago. It's not really related to what I investigated. True, it involves some information from the Pierson case. Still, Jordan wasn't smart enough to be involved in anything other than Lawson's porn fetish."

Barnes leaned back in her chair, "Yeah, but what if it's not. What if there was more to it?"

"Like what?"

"I don't know, Taylor; maybe he knew something we don't. You really don't want to know?"

"Look, I went down that rabbit hole for years. We got Pierson, and now he's dead. Now that techno pervert is dead too. I'm just glad he can't hurt someone else. Case closed." He went back to the file he was reading moments before. Barnes was right about one thing; he was curious as to what Jordan did that got him killed. He told himself they would call him if the Julian PD needed help. Until then, he had more to do than chasing the ghost of Leonard Pierson.

Several minutes later, his phone rang. It was the crime lab with the results of the ballistics report on the .38 revolver.

"Are you sure?" he said forcefully into the phone. "Well, good, yeah, fine. Yes, please send over the results as soon as you can. Alright, thanks." He hung up the phone and looked at Barnes. Almost instinctively, she knew it was the result they were waiting for.

"Well, don't keep me waiting; what did they say?"

"Ballistics on Tony's gun are not a match. No way his gun was used to kill Randall Morris."

"That means we're back to square one then," she said feeling a knot form in her stomach.

"Not necessarily. Pritchard could still be our killer; he might have used a different gun."

"Really? Do you think he has a thing for .38s? I don't think so."

"I know, it's not likely, but possible. On the bright side, the gun can be linked to several other unsolved cases. When I get the report later today, I'll know a little more about it. It might help to close a few of them. Until then, let's keep looking for this Marvo guy."

They spent the remainder of the day canvasing the hangouts Pritchard said Marvo liked to visit. Hours passed, but no one saw or knew where to find him. They were beginning to become frustrated especially since Taylor had a terrible feeling it was a waste of time as far as the Morris case was concerned. Exhausted by the end of their shift, they reluctantly called it a day and headed back to the station.

After leaving the station, Taylor checked his watch. It was just past six that evening, so he had a thought. It was a long shot, but he decided to give it a try. He drove across town to a subdivision that had recently become all too familiar to him. Slowly, Taylor drove past the home of Randall Morris. As he passed by, he noted that the family car was still there, so he believed Rebecca was home.

Taylor turned the car around a few streets down and found a spot where he could see the house without anyone inside easily seeing him. In a way, he felt connected to the masked killer, thinking maybe the killer did the same thing on that fateful night. Roger waited for what he was unsure about, but he waited, nonetheless. An hour passed, and then another. Checking his watch, he realized it was almost 9:30. No one had left the house, and no one had arrived at the house. Nothing. He decided to call it a night and drove home.

Walking through the door, his nightly routine of placing his jacket on the chair next to it repeated. He walked into the kitchen and made a sandwich. Grabbing a beer from the sixpack in the fridge, Taylor walked back to the couch to start flipping channels. Taylor set his beer down without taking a single drink.

After flipping through the channels a few times, he turned off the television. He logged in on his laptop and pulled up some of his old files from the Pierson case.

Jordan Byrd was a guy who was always low on his list of priorities during the Pierson investigation. In high school, Byrd was the geeky kid that somehow managed to get into the popular crowd. Why Lawson chose to pal around with him, Taylor did not know. After high school, Jordan set up the video equipment for Lawson when he brought home one of his conquests. While Lawson was out looking for women, Jordan would hide cameras in the hotel room.

What Jordan got out of the arrangement was a mystery to Taylor for a long time, but he had his guesses. He later discovered that Lawson would send a young lady his way from time to time, and he paid Jordan very well. Jordan was never in need of the newest computer and latest video equipment. Lawson made sure of that. During the investigation, Taylor learned that Jordan kept Lawson's personal and financial records for him. Jordan was becoming a more valuable target as the investigation went on.

Jordan tended to stay out of sight. He rarely left wherever Lawson was keeping him, and if he traveled, it was usually with Lawson. Though he couldn't prove it, Taylor always thought Jordan was aboard the yacht the night Lawson was killed. Soon after, he disappeared altogether. Finding him again became a low priority in the wake of the collapse of the Pierson family crime syndicate. Until recently, Taylor had no idea he was in Julian.

What information he had that was important enough to get him killed was a definite curiosity to Taylor. He spent so much of his career investigating the Piersons that it was difficult to believe it was really over. Of all the loose ends and missing pieces from those years, what did Jordan know that got him killed?

Taylor remembered the first time he came in contact with the Piersons. An eighteen-wheeler owned by Pierson was pulled over on its way to Santa Fe, New Mexico. The truck was caught speeding outside of town, and a patrol officer pulled it over. The driver acted nervous, so the officer searched the cab and found a gram of marijuana. A gram of weed in a passenger car was not a big deal, but this was an eighteen-wheeler, so the driver was arrested. Searching the trailer revealed much more than pallets of auto parts. The cocaine they found was worth about $500,000 on the streets.

When he first met Leonard Pierson, Taylor found the man charming and sophisticated. He had the perfect family man persona with a prosperous business and living the American Dream. The more often they met, the charm turned into a gloating arrogance that began to grate on Taylor. His smile, so disarming to many, mocked him in his attempts to find evidence to convict Leonard Pierson. Taylor believed Pierson's company was a front for his drug-running operation, but proving that became a source of frustration for years to come.

Not long after the driver was released, he skipped bail. A couple of months later, he was found with three gunshot wounds. They were all administered to the chest while he stared his killer in the face. This would not be the last time they found witnesses, associates of the Piersons, and others who ran afoul of them killed in this manner. All the while, Leonard Pierson smiled and continued to make a fortune on the misery of others.

Pierson was dead now. Taylor found Pierson on the night he went to arrest him at his office. He was preparing to flee the country with enough cash to live for two lifetimes. Taylor got there first. As Roger rushed up the stairs, excitement built. Something inside him was setting off alarms, saying things were not right. He called for Pierson to open the door. Somehow Roger knew the man had one last card to play. The officers battered down the door to Pierson's office, but it was too late. A shot rang out, and as the door flew open, they saw Pierson slumped in his office chair. A single gunshot to the head with an old Colt Peacemaker. Somehow, he was still alive when the officers reached him, but he died just short of arriving at the hospital. What was worse, it appeared to Taylor that he had the same sick smile when they found him.

Snapping himself back to reality, Taylor continued for an hour to browse his files. Finally, he decided that it was enough at around 11 pm. He called it a night and lay in his bed. He tried to push away the memories of the Pierson case. They inevitably brought back memories of Shelia and the last time he saw her. At Shelia's funeral, he began to feel the weight of her death. Her mother, father, and brother were all there. Surprisingly, they never blamed him for what happened, even though he knew they were wrong.

Taylor saw the wounds on her body. The glazed eyes somehow accused him of not being there to protect her. Seeing her body lying in a wooded area of a walking track would haunt him for the rest of his life. As much as he wanted to remember the good times, the times when they were young and in love, the times they spent at the ballpark, the times they made love, he couldn't tear those last images from his mind.

Taylor rolled over on his side to keep the outside light away from his eyes. How long he lay there, he couldn't say. He must have drifted to sleep because his cell phone startled him. Sitting on the side of the bed, he turned off the alarm and went to the shower. From there, his morning routine started again. Before long, he was on his way back to the station.

CHAPTER
TWENTY-FOUR

Mr. Smith waited in his car for the man he was following to emerge from a local eatery. He paid a couple of kids twenty bucks a piece to keep watch on his contact and see where he went after he left the park. Sure, enough, the gamble paid off, and Smith got a description of the man's car and a partial plate number. Smith found the silver car not far away, so he parked across the street and waited.

About an hour passed before his contact returned to his vehicle. When he got into his car, Smith could see him dial a number on his cellphone. Whoever he was talking to must have been important because the conversation lasted almost forty-five minutes. When the conversation ended, the man backed out of his parking spot and pulled into the light traffic.

Smith followed him being careful to stay far enough back to not raise any suspicions. He thought it was lucky his car didn't stick out. It was a late model car, not remarkable; there were dozens of similar cars around town. The man drove through town without being in any hurry. When he made a left turn on Stetson Street, Smith drove past him, making sure not to make eye contact. He made the next left turn one street over, knowing he should be able to pick up his target back down the road.

He spotted the silver car again. It was farther up the road than he would have liked, but Smith could keep up. He followed it to a building with a large parking lot. Smith watched the man pull in and park in a spot near the back.

He slowly passed by then took the next right turn. Circling the block, he found a spot close enough to watch his contact but far enough back not to attract attention. The man waited in his car fifteen minutes before a champagne colored SUV turned into the lot and took the adjacent spot. A man got out of the SUV as did his contact. They talked for several minutes before the man who arrived in the SUV handed the contact an envelope. The two shook hands, and the man got in the SUV and drove off.

The contact continued to stand in the empty parking lot for several minutes. Smith watched as the man took out his cell phone again. To his shock, Smith's phone began to ring. Taking the phone out of his pocket, he answered it.

"Did you find what you were hoping to see, Mr. Smith?" the contact asked.

Looking up, Smith could see the man waving back at him. While he couldn't see the exact expression on the man's face, he was certain he had a self-satisfied grin. "Honestly, Mr. Smith, what were you hoping to see?"

"Yeah, nothing, I guess. Just curious."

"Really? Would you like to see what I have in the envelope here?"

Smith realized he was being played, but curiosity was getting the better of him. "Fine, I'll be right there."

"Do be careful crossing the street, Mr. Smith," the man said as he hung up the phone.

A couple of cars passed as he waited to cross. He went after the second car cleared.

"I have to say you did a fantastic job of following me here. Tell me. Did you pay someone in the park to follow me? A child, perhaps?" The contact laughed to himself. "Oh, Mr. Smith, that's such an old trick."

Smith made his way to him, feeling more embarrassment than fear. "So, what's in the envelope that you want me to see? Some new task from your boss?"

"No, Mr. Smith, something far more exquisite than that, I assure you. Something I've wanted for some time now." He opened the clasps on the envelope, pulling out a small frame. He turned it around, revealing the photograph of a man in a suit with writing on it. "Do you recognize him, Mr. Smith?"

He shook his head no without saying a word. "This man was a living legend. His name was Bobby Fischer. A true legend of the game of chess. A grandmaster of the highest order. He died years ago, I'm afraid, so I will have to content myself with this. I ordered it off an auction site, and the man was kind enough to bring it."

"So, you called me over here to show me a picture?"

"Of course not. I called you over here to tell you never follow me again. Your usefulness to me is conditional at best. The biggest condition is that you don't give me a reason to doubt your usefulness. Now, if you are done playing detective, I bid you good night."

The man got into his car and drove off into the growing darkness. Smith cursed loudly, regretting the day he became involved with this man. He returned to his car and quickly drove back to his place.

Arriving home, he went inside and retrieved the files he had hidden under some floorboards in his bedroom. He left the portable hard drive in its place, deciding not to work on his computer tonight. He flipped through the files, trying to find anything he could use. The next hour passed slowly as he studied several photographs in his file. He wasn't sure where Jordan got all of these photos, but if his contact found out about it, that probably explained why Jordan Byrd was now dead.

After several more minutes, he decided to call it quits for the night. He returned the files to their hiding place and began to get ready for bed. He reminded himself of his escape plan. Soon he would not have to worry about these people anymore. He believed his plans would work. Then he thought Byrd probably believed the same thing before he died. Putting the fearful thought out of his mind, he turned his light off and tried to sleep.

CHAPTER
TWENTY-FIVE

Barnes came into his office that afternoon with a triumphant smirk on her face. Taylor guessed she had good news.

"Look who I found," she said placing a picture of a man on his desk. "Say hello to Marvo, aka Marcus Vincent Owens, who just happens to live several streets down from our guest of honor, Tony Pritchard." She crossed her arms and flashed a satisfied smile.

"How'd you find him?"

"I went door to door around Pritchard's neighborhood, and as usual, no luck. I started back to my car when this lady called out to me. She asked me what I wanted with Marvo. So, I told her I had some questions for him. She asked me if he was in trouble 'cause if he was, she'd love to help me get that lowdown bastard who ran off with her cousin." Taylor could not help but laugh. "Yeah, I know a woman scorned, right? So she gave me his real name and this picture to go with it."

Taylor agreed. "So where do we find old Marvo?"

"Well, that's the best part. It turns out he's a stationary target. I looked up police reports on him, and guess what? Marvo was involved in a car crash two weeks ago that put him in the hospital. I called the hospital here in town, and he's scheduled to be released. Tomorrow. So I thought I'd pay him a little visit today. Want to tag along?"

Taylor looked at his desk. "Looks like I'm snowed under with paperwork. I guess he's all yours." Instantly her eyes lit up with excitement. He sometimes forgot she had only been a detective for a short time. Her enthusiasm reminded him of the first time his supervisor turned him loose on a case. It was hard to imagine himself now as a bright-eyed detective out to make the world a better place. Seeing the excitement in her eyes brought the feeling back to him for a moment.

"If you insist, boss man. Let you know what he says." She got up to leave but suddenly stopped. "So, what paperwork do you have there?"

"This?" he answered. "Just routine stuff. Reports, statements, the usual stuff."

"The usual stuff?" she asked with more than a hint of disbelief. "Let me see that report then."

"Barnes, it's not your job to second guess me."

"Oh my god, you're looking at the Byrd file, aren't you?"

"Barnes, don't you need to go talk to Marvo?"

"What've you found? Anything in the files you didn't know before?"

"No, not yet. I've just started going through them, okay? If I find anything important, I will let you know. Would you please see Marvo before someone lets him know we're looking for him?"

"Fine, but I knew you wouldn't be able to resist looking into Byrd's death."

She strutted out of his office with a knowing smile on her face. It was true, though. From the moment the Julian police brought over the information they had, he was bound to look into Jordan's death. He poured over the file intently after she left. Mostly, he saw information he already knew, along with numerous names of Pierson associates.

What struck him was there seemed to be information missing from the files. Some of it he could fill in with what he already knew from his investigation, but there were still holes in the records. Maybe it was because most of the information was what Lawson thought was important. In many ways, it seemed to Taylor that he was looking at Pierson's business through Lawson's eyes. Still, it struck him as odd. There should be more in the files. Maybe Jordan didn't have a complete record, and was making do with what he had on hand. Nothing Taylor had read so far seemed important enough to get Jordan killed. Whatever it was may have been important only to the killer.

He worked on the Jordan Byrd file for about another hour before finally putting it away. There were too many other cases requiring his attention. For now, he decided to set aside Byrd's case and try to clear some of his regular caseload while Barnes talked with Marvo.

CHAPTER
TWENTY-SIX

After leaving the station, Barnes drove the short distance to the hospital. She stopped by the nurse's desk and was directed to Marvo's hospital room. It was a double room, but his roommate was discharged about two hours earlier, so Marvo was alone. Barnes walked in, "You, Marvo?" she asked, knowing full well who he was.

"Maybe. Who wants to know?" he said, annoyed at Barnes's presence.

She flashed her badge. "Detective Laura Barnes, I got some questions for you."

He briefly regarded her, "You awful hot for a cop. Bet you here to have some work done on that nose."

"Yeah, like I've never heard that one before. Really expected better from you, Marvo; you're a hard man to find."

"So, I hear. How'd you find me?"

"Scorn, that's how."

"What?" Marvo clearly did not understand what she meant. "So what do you want anyway?"

"You recognize this man?" she asked as she showed him a picture of Tony Pritchard.

"Yeah, that's Tony. What about him?"

"Word is you sold him a gun a while back. That true?"

"What if it is?"

She smiled and pulled out another picture. "You know this man?" Marvo shook his head. "This is Randall Morris. We think Tony shot him in his home. Concerned yet, Marvo?"

"Hey, I didn't kill no one."

"Did Tony? How many guns did you sell him, Marvo? Think carefully because I could charge you as an accessory to murder for providing the gun. Not to mention selling it to someone you knew to be a convicted felon. So, think real hard on those facts before you answer."

Marvo looked nervous. "Okay, look, I sold him the gun. Just one. I got it from a buddy of mine in LA. He wanted to get rid of it. No questions asked. So I did, but that's the only time I ever sold Tony a gun. I swear."

"You think Tony got a gun from someone else?"

"Naw, Tony is a son of a bitch, but he's no killer. Likes to drink and gamble, so it gets him in trouble, but he ain't no killer."

"Then why the gun?" she asked.

"You ever dealt before, cop lady? Never know who might want to put a bullet in you. So yeah, self-defense, sure, but he ain't got it in him to shoot someone out of the blue. I'm telling you, he ain't the guy you want."

"You better not be lying to me, Marvo. If I have to come find you again, it will not be a good day for you. You got it, Marvo? Stay where I can find you in case I have more questions. Got it?"

"Yeah, whatever. I got you."

Barnes left the hospital and called Taylor from her car to recount her visit with Marvo. "Yeah, for what it's worth, I believe him. We should consider the possibility that Tony Pritchard is not our man." She could not help the feeling of disappointment that came over her.

Everything seemed to point at Pritchard, but the case seemed to fall apart in just a few minutes. "Well, we've got him and his buddies for the burglaries, so that's something," Taylor said.

"Any chance the other two had anything to do with Morris's death?"

"No, their alibies for that night all checked out. Come on back and do what you can here."

"What about you? You sound like you got somewhere to be."

"I do, actually, so you'll have to carry on without me."

"Sounds like a hot date. Anyone, I know?"

"Yeah, you could say that. Let you know how it turns out." With that, he hung up the phone. She couldn't help but wonder who he was going to see. Roger had not dated anyone she was aware of over the time she worked with him. After what he went through, she could hardly blame him. Still, a small wave of jealousy floated through her. He was her senior officer and at least ten years older than her, but still. She pushed the thought out of her mind and told herself to keep it professional as she started the drive back to the station.

By the time she arrived, Taylor had already left for the day. Looking across the station, she saw another professional problem headed to the locker room. She hesitated to follow him but somehow felt compelled to go back there. Davis was a nice-looking guy who was much closer to her own age. Technically there was no hard and fast rule about dating a fellow officer, but he was in patrol, and she did outrank him. That could be a problem even if only in her mind.

Nothing had happened the Saturday she took her car to him at his brother's repair shop. They made some small talk and that was all. True to his word, the work was done quickly. When he handed her the keys, she asked if he wanted to join her group on Sunday. Davis said he would love to, but he promised his brother he would help him at the shop on Sunday afternoon for a few hours. He asked her if it would be alright if he was a little late. Barnes told him it would not be a problem. That was the last time they spoke until the party. She was so wrapped up in her caseload that she had not seen him since. Barnes was not avoiding him per se, but well, maybe she was.

She decided to walk to the back as casually as possible. As she walked through the door, it occurred to her she was acting like a teenager with a secret crush. Was that what she was feeling? A crush? She took a deep breath, let it out all at once, and walked into the locker room area.

Spotting him by his locker, she called out. "Hey, Davis, you got a minute?"

He looked up, surprised to see her. "Hey, yeah, just about grab my stuff and head out for the day. What's up?"

She thought about how thankful she was for not playing the Prince Charming bit with her. Davis could be full of himself at times, but apparently, he was dropping the act for now.

"Yeah, I just wanted to say thanks for installing my radio. I bought the stupid thing and didn't consider what to do with all those wires," she said, trying not to sound silly.

"It's not a problem. Happens more than you think," Davis replied in a smooth but not condescending voice. "Really, I was glad to do it for you. So…"

"Yeah, so…" she said as she twirled a lock of her hair in her finger without realizing she was doing it. When she did, she suddenly stopped. *Ok, this is getting ridiculous*, she thought.

"So… I was just about to grab a bite. You…ah… you want to tag along?" Davis asked.

"Tag along? Do I look like I'm three?" she said with a coy smirk on her face.

"What? No, not at all. I was just…."

"Hey, just kidding, sure, why not? I'm paying for my own meal, though, got it?"

"Whatever you say, sure. Just let me… oh crap," Davis exclaimed as a leather folder fell out of his locker, scattering papers to the floor. "Man, I thought I zipped that thing closed."

"Here, let me help," she said, bending down to help round up the loose papers. "What've you got in this thing?"

"It's where I keep all my sales and gas receipts."

"You keep all of these receipts?" Barnes said with a mocking laugh. "What are you, some kind of packrat?"

"Hey, I got plans that don't include driving around in a squad car all my life. It helps me keep track of where my money is going. It's old fashioned, I know, but believe it or not, it keeps me from overspending."

"Yeah, okay," she said as she picked up the last piece of fallen paper. Looking at the paper, she noticed it was a receipt from a gas station in Julian. "So, what on earth were you in Julian for?"

"That's where Joe and Ty live. I filled up there before I got to their house to go to the game."

"Well, here," she said handing back the receipt to Davis, "better keep up with this one, or you might be off in your check register."

"Oh, real funny. You like Chinese?"

"Love it," she said.

"Well, I know just the place."

"Great, but I mean it; I'm buying my own. Got it?"

"Yes, ma'am," he said giving a mock salute.

"Ha, ha, cute," she shot back. "Lead the way."

The Jade Palace was about half full when they arrived. Davis opened the door for Barnes as she walked in. She hoped it didn't make her blush as the couple walked to the host. They were shown to seats at a table by a window. The server took their drink orders and then disappeared into the kitchen.

The restaurant was in its second year of operation, but it had quickly become a favorite spot for many of Warrenton's residents. Barnes was especially fond of their Szechuan chicken and hot and sour soup. She quickly decided that was what she wanted to order. Davis decided on the Kung Pao chicken.

"So, what are these big plans you've made for yourself?" she asked as they waited for their food to arrive.

"Well, it's nothing definite just yet," he said tensing a little. "I started saving a portion of my monthly paycheck to have something to fall back on if I need it. Then I decided that I wanted to retire in my fifties. Maybe travel the world or something like that."

"Sounds like you've got it all planned out," she teased.

"Not even close," he responded. "What about you? You want to do police work your whole life?"

"Sure, why not?" she replied as the waitress brought them eggrolls. "It's not a bad life, really. I get to help a lot of people, so I like it."

"Yeah, but don't you get tired of seeing the worst of society? Meeting people on the worst days of their lives? Doesn't that get to be a bit too much? Even a little?"

"That's just part of it," she said before taking a bite of her eggroll. Barnes lurched forward as the heat from the eggroll proved too much for her. "Man, that's hot," she said in embarrassment. She grabbed her glass of tea and took a quick sip.

"You should be more careful," Davis teased. "Did you burn your mouth?"

"No, I'm fine. Should have known better than to bite into a hot eggroll."

Their food arrived, and they continued to make small talk as they ate. As usual, the food was excellent. They sat there for another half hour before paying their bills and leaving. Davis tried to pay for

Barnes's food, but she refused to let him. He insisted on walking her to the car.

Arriving at her car Davis said, "I had a great time tonight, Barnes. We should do this again." He held his breath for a moment without a thought. The moments seemed to hang in the air endlessly. Almost as if she were purposefully prolonging the moment.

She finally broke the silence. ""Are you asking me out?" 'Cause if you are, then yes, we definitely should."

"Then yes, I am asking you out. Again."

"Okay, yes, that sounds good. Next weekend this time?" Barnes asked him in a playful voice.

"How's Saturday?"

"Perfect," she answered. Barnes was smiling despite her efforts to hide it. Both continued to stand there without knowing exactly how to part ways. Without warning, she leaned in and quickly kissed him on his lips. It ended just as soon as it began, but for tonight it was enough. "Good night, call me," she said as she opened her door and stepped into the vehicle. She drove away slowly enough to wave goodnight as he smiled and returned the wave.

CHAPTER
TWENTY-SEVEN

This was the fifth night that Taylor had staked out the Morris residence. He tried to park in a different location each time to avoid being seen or raising suspicion. Even so, he showed his badge to a passerby on more than a couple of occasions. Usually, someone from the newly formed community watch program that just started. One lady commented how sad it was that someone had to die before they got any police protection.

After each encounter, he moved on and drove around the neighborhood, constantly circling back by the Morris home. It was good that the community believed the police were conducting extra patrols. The fact he was in an unmarked car added a little more weight to the idea he was trying to catch the people who burglarized homes in the neighborhood.

There was something about what Lauren Morris told him driving him to see if the information was true. He had no doubt that she heard her stepmother talking to someone on the phone, but when you heard only half of the conversation, it was easy to misunderstand what was said. Even if she were right, it does not make Rebecca Morris a killer. She would be a cheater, and it would be a good motive. He hoped Lauren was wrong, even if it meant the case went cold.

It was getting dark, and he was just about ready to leave when a car turned into the driveway of the Morris home. Roger sat up straight, trying to get a good look at whoever got out of the car.

"Oh, no way," he said to himself when he saw the man get out and ring the doorbell. Rebecca opened the door, said something to him, and then kissed him. She took his hand and led him inside, shutting the door.

He waited ten minutes to see if the couple would come out of the house. Deciding they may be in for a while, he made his move. He parked near the curb by the house and made his way to the door. He rang the doorbell and waited. It did not take long for Rebecca to open the door. "Detective Taylor, what a surprise. What brings you here?"

"Good evening Mrs. Morris. May I come in? I have a few questions for you."

"Well, I have company now. Could you maybe come back tomorrow..."

"Oh, that's okay. I have some questions for him too. Hey, Seth, why don't you come out and answer a few questions."

Seth Willard walked around the corner slowly with a disgusted look on his face. "It's alright, sweetie; we have nothing to hide anymore." Rebecca looked over her shoulder at him, then closed her eyes in frustration, exhaling loudly.

She invited Taylor to come on into the living room. "Would you like to have a seat, Detective? Can I get you anything?"

"No, I'd rather stand. I won't be long. Just a few questions for you both, that's all."

Seth began, "Look, Roger, I know what you're thinking and...."

"I don't know, Seth; what am I thinking?"

"Roger, we weren't having an affair. At least not physically."

"What's that supposed to mean? You haven't what slept together, held hands, what? Please walk me through this. Make me believe it."

"Detective," Rebecca began, "we've known each other for a long time. We met years ago when I worked for Randall on my days off from the hospital. I used to take permit applications and paperwork to city hall. I met Seth there, and we became friends, that's all." She shuffled uncomfortably in her seat, clearly embarrassed by what she was about to say. "I don't know when I realized I had feelings for him, but Seth and I started seeing each other more often then I saw my late husband. He worked so much, and our marriage was starting to fall apart. I know people think we were the perfect family, but Randall came home, and we just...we just grew apart more every day."

"I told her to stick it out," Seth added, "I told her once he got past the workload, he'd come around." He took a deep breath, "I wanted her to make it work. Randall was a nice guy, but I started giving into temptation after Terra left me."

"So you what? Did you have him killed? Is that it? You two in it together?"

"No, Detective Taylor," Rebecca protested, "I would never hurt my husband, or have someone else hurt him. I loved Randall, and even with our problems, I would never want to hurt him." She ran her hands through her hair, "Seth was a shoulder for me to cry on, and maybe we shouldn't have gotten that close, but we didn't cheat."

"You have to admit the timing couldn't be worse," Taylor countered. "Your husband's been dead about a month, and you already got someone taking his place?"

"As I said, Roger, it's been a lonely couple of years. I admit I had feelings for her while she was married, but I didn't act on them, I swear."

Taylor was calming down. He wanted to believe them, but something was not ringing true. "Just for the record, where were you on the night of the murder, Seth?"

"You can't be serious, Roger. You know me, I'd never do something like that."

"I thought I knew you." Taylor responded, "now I'm not so sure. Where were you?"

"Oak Glen. I was in Oak Glen visiting my former neighbors, the Watsons. Kevin and Glenda Watson are their names." Seth reached into his pocket and pulled out his cell phone. "Here's their number. Call them, and they'll tell you I was there. Is that all?"

"For now. I hope you're both telling the truth here." Roger turned to leave, "Don't worry, I'll show myself out. I'll be in touch. Don't leave town anytime soon." With that, he walked outside and shut the door. Before he left, he snapped a shot of Seth's car, a white Volvo S60, and his license plate. He then returned to his car, got in, and drove off.

When he got home, he slammed the door behind him and threw his keys, missing the coffee table. He swore under his breath, picking up the keys and placing them on the coffee table as he sat down on his couch. He took out his phone and dialed the number for the Watsons. Four rings later, a man's voice answered.

"Mr. Watson? This is Detective Roger Taylor of the Warrenton Police Department. Sorry to bother you at this hour, but I have a couple of questions that can't wait."

"It's no bother. Detective Glenda and I are night owls. How can I help you?"

"Do you know a Seth Willard?"

"Sure, we used to be neighbors until we moved to Oak Glen. How is he? Is everything alright with him?"

"Yes, sir, everything is fine. Did he come to visit you about a month ago?"

"Yeah, we had a dinner party here at the house. He was here."

"Do you remember what time he left?"

"Not exactly, but maybe sometime around 8:00 or 8:30. Sorry, I'm not sure, so best guess."

"No, that's fine, Mr. Watson, that's fine. Look, thanks for talking to me. I'll call you back if I need anything else, okay?"

"You're welcome, have a good night."

"Thanks, you do the same. Good night." Roger hung up the phone, not sure what to believe. Seth's story checked out, but it did not completely put him in the clear. Oak Glen was about half an hour from Warrenton, and Morris was killed sometime between 9:15 and 9:30 that night. That meant there was an opening in which he could have made it, but it was a small window of opportunity. Maybe too small. Either way, he decided to check it out first thing tomorrow morning.

CHAPTER
TWENTY-EIGHT

When he arrived at the station the next morning, the desk sarge told him to report to Chief Vanderbeck. By the look on the chief's face, Taylor could tell she was not in a good mood. "Detective Taylor shut the door and have a seat," she said as he walked into her office. "I need an update on the Morris case. The DA is ready to make a move, and now I'm having to tell him to wait."

Taylor squirmed nervously in his seat. Her straight to the point and spare the niceties approach rubbed him the wrong way. She was forceful and blunt; in some ways, he could respect that because you never had to guess how she felt about an issue. In other ways, he did not appreciate being addressed that way. It was not so much what she said to him as how she said it. Then again, she is the police chief, and he respected her if for only that reason.

"Chief, with all due respect, Tony Pritchard is not our killer. Now he is plenty guilty of the burglaries and possession of a firearm, but he's not our killer."

She folded her hands on her desk and asked, "Do we have any leads on who did it then? People will want to know if we still have a killer on the loose breaking into houses."

"That's what I wanted to talk to you about today. I need a search warrant for a suspect's cell phone location and records," he told her, trying to sound confident he was on the right track despite his misgivings.

"For who,?"

"Seth Willard."

"The building inspector? You better have a damn good reason to want that kind of information about a member of city hall. What makes him a suspect?"

He recounted his conversation with Lauren Morris and her suspicions about her stepmother. Then he discussed last night's encounter with Seth Willard and Rebecca Morris at her home. He told her they denied the affair was physical, but he was confident they were lying about how long they saw each other. Vanderbeck listened intently to all he had to say before she finally spoke. "Are you saying that Rebecca Morris and Seth Willard are in this together?"

"Honestly, Chief, I hope I'm wrong. Do I think they were sleeping together? Yes, I do, but that's a far cry from planning a murder. He had time to drive back to Warrenton, and the affair gave him motive. If we get the cell phone records, we can either put him at the scene or clear him, and if Rebecca was in communication with him that night, we'd know that too."

"I don't like it. Blaming the wife for murdering her husband is one thing. Accusing a respected member of killing someone is another." She thought for an uncomfortably long amount of time. He almost thought she would not go for the idea. "I'll get started on the warrant and see if a judge will sign off. You better tread carefully on this."

"Chief, I hope I'm wrong. Seth was a friend until last night, but I got to follow this lead to the end. Whatever that end might be."

He left the chief's office feeling both worried and vindicated. On the one hand, he hated the thought of a friend being a killer. On the other, he felt he was blind to the possibility that the wife may have had something to do with the murder. Was an extramarital affair worth a man's life? If the killer or killers thought so, then they would not be the first or the last to kill over an affair. Then again, maybe there was something else.

Spotting Barnes at her desk, he asked her to join him in his office. When she got up to leave her desk, she smiled slightly at Davis who more obviously returned it. Taylor rolled his eyes and took his seat just before Barnes walked in. He updated her on the case and the information he learned last night.

"So what's our next move?" she asked not quite knowing what to believe.

"First, check up on Rebecca Morris's friends and coworkers. See if they know anything we don't know about their financial situation, spending habits, and other things that might motivate her to want Randall Morris dead. While you do that, I will head to the county jail to talk to Tony Pritchard again. Maybe I can jog his memory some more."

"Why? We already know he's not our killer."

"Yes, but he said he stole the jewelry out of a car, so maybe I can help him remember what the car looked like."

An hour and a half later, Tony Pritchard was led into a small meeting room at the county jail. From the look on his face, he was not too pleased to see Taylor there. "Man, what do you want now?" he said taking a seat across from Taylor.

"Tony, you're looking better these days. Can't say much about the outfit, though. I need some info from you, and I promise I'll leave you alone."

Pritchard was annoyed, but the possibility of being rid of Taylor seemed to intrigue him. "Whatever, man, just tell me what you want."

"Take a look at this car," Taylor said showing him a picture of the car Seth Willard drove last night. "Is that like the car you stole the jewelry from?"

Pritchard took a look and then shook his head. "Naw, that ain't it."

"You sure? Look again. Take a good look."

"I told you, man, that ain't the car. The car I took that stuff from was gray. No, wait, silver, yeah, it was silver. A silver..." he stopped to think. "I don't know some fancy car. Like a ummm...."

"A foreign car?"

"A what?"

"Was it an American car like a Ford or Chevy?"

"Naw, it was Japanese. Not Toyota, but that other one. Lexus, a silver Lexus, that's it."

"You sure? Because last time you said you didn't know."

"Yeah, I'm sure. I remember it was parked in the lot of some gym. Guess he left his gym bag or something, so I busted the back window out."

"Which side, driver or passenger?"

"Driver's side."

"Did you see the driver, and could you describe him?"

"Naw, I didn't get a look at him."

"Then how do you know it was a man's car then?"

"Cause the bag had dude's clothes in it. "

"What about a wallet or ID or something?"

"Naw, just clothes. Dude's clothes. That's all."

"What did you do with the clothes? You keep them?"

"Tossed them. I ain't got them."

Taylor got up to leave, "I think we're done here, Tony; believe it or not, you've been a big help."

"Hey, what you going to do to help me out?"

"Well, I'll put in a good word for you with the judge when you see him. Otherwise, I hope you enjoy prison because you'll probably be there for a while. Assuming you get out, you might want to watch that third strike. It's 25 years for a third felony in this state. See you, Tony."

As he left the county jail, he felt a pit of dread growing in his stomach. He knew the car Seth drove last night was not the one Pritchard stole the bag from, but he also knew Seth drove a silver Lexus at one time. What he could not remember was the model. Of course, the word of a now twice convicted felon was hardly creditable in court. Taylor decided to check the Department of Motor Vehicles to locate the VIN number of Seth's car. He could probably locate the car and find out if its window had broken out as Pritchard described.

It was well after lunch when he returned to the station. He did not even make it to his office before Chief Vanderbeck called him over. "Taylor, Judge Corley signed off on your warrant. I want to know as soon as you find something. Got it?"

"You got it, Chief," he said and got to work.

CHAPTER
TWENTY-NINE

It was raining when Smith sat on the usual bench and waited for his contact to arrive. The rain did not really amount to much, just enough to get his clothes wet and make them uncomfortable. His contact told him to be here at nine o'clock, but now it was well past ten. The fact that he was late was unusual. He was usually punctual enough to set a watch by, so Smith was worried by the delay.

Smith glanced at his watch again, and as if by magic, he spotted his contact's approach. The man sat next to him without speaking. "You know I will have to start charging you overtime for keeping me waiting like this."

The man opened his briefcase and handed Smith a large, sealed envelope. Opening it, he found a small stack of bills and a cell phone, as usual. Inside there was also a file folder with his next assignment. He glanced through the folder and froze when he saw the picture of his next target. "Oh, hell no. No way."

The man looked at him scornfully, "He's getting too close to the truth."

Smith hated that look from him; it summarized everything he

despised about this arrangement. "You needn't worry about your payment. You will be handsomely rewarded."

"It's not that, man, it's not that at all," Smith responded, feeling a sense of fear well up in him. "That's Roger Taylor. Next in line to the chief."

"I am quite aware of who he is, Mr. Smith. Detective Roger Taylor destroyed my life. Everything I worked for collapsed when he took down the Piersons. I want him dead. If you can't do it, then you are of no further use to me. I'm certain you know what that means." The man reached inside the case and pulled out a small pistol with a silencer concealed inside.

Smith instinctively backed away from the man. "Whoa, hey, let's not get crazy here. I'm only saying that if I do this, it's the end for me here. I will never be able to come back here, and I'll have to lay low in some nice and quiet place like somewhere in South America. I'm going to need a lot of cash to set me up. Probably for life."

His contact hardly blinked an eye as he coldly stared at him like a shark circling a helpless swimmer. Smith was starting to feel like maybe he had demanded too much from the mystery man.

It was a relief when the man finally broke the awkward silence and placed the gun back in the case. "Very well," he began, "my employer will provide enough money for you to escape and provide for yourself in exile." Smith felt relieved. "Next time we meet will be our last. Call me when you have completed the job. We will meet then to remit your payment."

"Not a chance, man," Smith shot back. "No, I will give you a bank account, and you will wire the money to me. I don't want to meet you again. I'll carry out this last job, then I'm done."

"Oh, Mr. Smith, is that how you think this works?" came the reply from the contact. "You do not get to tell us how this ends. You are one of many tools we have at our disposal. If you want your money, you will meet me again. Otherwise, you are of no use to my employer."

"Yeah, and what if I don't?" Smith said more out of fear than courage.

"I don't think you want to find out. Not when you are so close to getting what you want. We own you, Mr. Smith. Did you really think we would let you run away and not know how to find you?" The man flashed a quick smile at Smith. "Oh, I see that you did. My dear Mr. Smith, I'm afraid you are very wrong." Smith began feeling like he would hyperventilate, and the water on his head was not just from the rain any longer but from a cold sweat. "Finish your job. Then we will discuss what comes next." The contact got up and began to walk away. As he did, he turned back to Smith, who was feeling lucky to be alive, "Just remember, Mr. Smith, you will never be anywhere I can't find you."

Smith was alone at last. He could still feel his heart beating inside his throat. What had he gotten himself into? The relationship started simply enough, do a job and get paid. Now he felt he had sold his soul to the devil, and there seemed no way out of his situation. He knew better, but he did not act on his knowledge, and now it was too late to back out.

Something the man said stuck with him. He said that Taylor ruined his life. It was the first time he didn't mention an employer. It was also the first time he seemed to lose his cool as if the mask he wore slipped just a little. When he mentioned Taylor, Smith could sense a fit of anger that could not be hidden as if this job was personal.

It also cast doubt in Smith's mind if the man was all he said. Smith believed whoever his contact was, he wasn't simply a messenger. Smith did some digging on the man, and while he had yet to uncover who he was or worked for, he was sure there was more to him. At this point, Smith wasn't even sure he worked for anyone. In fact, he was becoming more convinced his contact was really the man in charge.

He couldn't prove anything yet, but Smith was collecting evidence. He'd followed the contact a couple of times. Snapped a few photographs and conducted some research. All he had come up with so far was that he had some connections to the Piersons. Precisely what that connection was, he didn't know, but he was confident the answer was somewhere on the Jordan Byrd files and hard drive.

Whether or not Smith ever found out the exact identity of his so-called contact, he decided there would not be the next job for him. One way or the other, Smith would flee after this job to some isolated place and never be seen again, whether his contact liked it or not. He did not care about the threats; he could handle them. Stay on the move, do not settle down for too long. He would cover his tracks and vanish. Even if they eventually found him, so what? Anything was better than living under submission to their will.

No, I'm done, he thought. *I can reinvent myself with a new name, new history, everything.* He knew people who could make that happen.

Smith decided to do what they wanted one last time. Kill Taylor; well, no big loss there. At least they didn't give a timeline to get it done. This one had to be done carefully.

Can't get sloppy like the last guy. If this job is done right, maybe they will let me be after all. If they don't, it won't matter.

Either way, Smith was done and planned to never be found again.

CHAPTER
THIRTY

Barnes arrived at the home of the Morris's neighbor, Mrs. Madalyn O'Rear, a retired art teacher. O'Rear still gave art lessons several days a week at the community center in the afternoon but she was regularly home. She spent most of her time in the small vegetable garden behind her house.

When Barnes rang the doorbell, a symphony of barking began. None of the dogs sounded exceptionally large, but to her, it sounded as if there were at least three of them. No one came to the door, so she tried again. Still, nothing. Barnes surveyed the home and saw nothing out of place. She walked around, peered through the garage door windows, and saw the car was still there.

Cautiously, she made her way toward the rear of the home. No signs of forced entry on the windows as she walked to the backyard fence. Arriving at the gate, she spotted Mrs. O'Rear in the back wearing an orange-yellowish housecoat. She appeared to be attending to her garden, but when Barnes called out, there was no response. She tried again, and still no response. From the angle where she stood, Barnes could not tell whether Mrs. O'Rear was moving.

Barnes opened the gate and moved toward the form of Madalyn O'Rear, seated or squatting in her garden. A thousand thoughts raced through Barnes's mind as she carefully approached the garden. A sense of dread began to take hold of her, and she started thinking the worst. Barnes had covered about three-quarters of the distance between the fence and Mrs. O'Rear. As she got closer, there was still no movement.

Mrs. O'Rear was partially seated with her back toward Barnes. Slowly, Barnes reached out and touched the woman's shoulder.

"Mrs. O'Rear," she timidly said.

Without warning, the retired teacher sprang to her feet with a shout that Barnes thought would pierce her eardrums.

Mrs. O'Rear flailed in panic, screaming. "Oh my god, I don't have any money. Take whatever you want; just don't hurt my dogs."

Holding out the badge around her neck, "Mrs. O'Rear, I'm a police officer. Detective Laura Barnes, please calm down." O'Rear finally calmed down enough to stop screaming. Both women tried to recover from their fright as Madalyn placed her hand on her chest and her breath started to return to normal.

O'Rear reached up to her ears and removed her earbuds, "I'm sorry, dear, I didn't hear you. I was listening to Jefferson Airplane. Oh, how I miss the 60s. Do you like the Jefferson Airplane? I bet you're a Stones fan, aren't you? Oh, who am I kidding? Those bands are too old for you. You are so young. I bet your parents weren't even born in the 60s. Oh, too bad, what a time. Then that awful Richard Nixon, don't get me started on that one. Promised to bring our boys home and then invaded Cambodia. Can you believe that? Of course, that was the 70s. I never cared for disco. I'm a McCartney fan."

Barnes was finally calming as O'Rear went down a list of reasons why the 60s were so much better than the 70s. She could hardly get a word in O'Rear was talking so fast. Finally, she took a breath, and that was Barnes's cue.

"Mrs. O'Rear, I'm sorry to have startled you. My name again is Detective Laura Barnes, and I need to ask you a few questions." She was almost relieved to get the information out.

"Is this about those tickets I owe? I've been parking in the spot for years during my yoga class. Then one day, I came out, and there was a ticket on my windshield. I thought it was a mistake, but they put another one there the next Thursday. I called the DMV, and they told me I'd have to call the police department about it. Then the department told me I had to call the courthouse. Everyone is telling me to call somebody else, so I don't know who to call. You're not here to arrest me, are you? I've tried to...."

"No, Mrs. O'Rear, no, I'm not with traffic. I promise I'm not here to arrest you. I wanted to talk about your neighbors, the Morris."

"Oh yes, that's terrible. Randall was such a nice man. He fixed my gutters once when a tree limb damaged them in a storm. He was such a sweet man. He didn't even charge me. I could tell his wife didn't like that, though."

"Wait, hold on. How'd you know that?

"Well, I couldn't exactly hear what she was saying, but she kept pointing over here angrily. He spent over half a day fixing my gutters and even put a screen over them so I wouldn't have to climb up a ladder to clean them. My son lives in Oregon, you see. Works for some brokerage or something and doesn't have time to visit his mother? Can you believe that? No time for his own mother?"

"Yes, that's terrible, but how well do you know Rebecca Morris?"

"Well enough. I see things, you know. You see that spot over there?" she said pointing to a flat area outside her house. "That's where I set up my easel. I can see the Morris's driveway from here. She always leaves and comes back with all kinds of bags. She goes to work, and the delivery trucks leave stuff at their door." She crossed her arms and shook her head in what looked like frustration. "Don't get me wrong, she's friendly enough most of the time, but she likes to spend money, and not on the rest of the family if you know what I mean."

"Have you ever noticed any," Barnes hesitated for a moment, "other people that come by regularly."

"You mean, do I think she's giving it out to other men?" she asked without hesitation. "I'm a 60s girl. I had my share of the free love, sweetie, but that all changed when I married Trevor. My Trevor was a good man; rest his soul. He could really be a tiger when…."

"Okay, I get the idea, sorry, but could you tell me about Mrs. Morris?"

"Oh, sure. I'm not one to judge, mind you, but she had her fun. You know they worked different schedules. She was off sometimes, seven days at a time. I know she worked for Randall's business while at home, but a car would show up every now and then and stay there an hour or two."

"Did you get a good look at him?"

"Him? Oh no, honey, more like them, at least two different men over the years. I don't think he ever caught her in the act, but he came close once. A guy in a red truck was pulling out of the driveway as Randall was driving down the street." She paused to catch her breath, "They tied into it real good that day. She saw me watching that time. She told me later that a contractor came to give an estimate on the sunporch, and that's what made him mad, but I know different. He was there for over two hours. Who stays that long to give an estimate? Not to mention her husband is a contractor too."

"Do you remember when that took place?"

"It's been six or seven months ago now. Never saw that one again. But the other guy, oh yes, he used to come by a lot. They were more careful this time, though. She'd leave and stay gone all day and get back just in time to meet Lauren when she came home from school or Randall when he got home."

"She didn't pick up her stepdaughter from school?"

"Not often," she said as she readjusted her housecoat. "Usually, Lauren would be there by herself for a few hours. She either rode the bus or had a friend bring her home." Sighing, she continued, "She's such a quiet girl, Lauren; you hardly know she's here sometimes. I think she tries to avoid her stepmom."

"Why do you say that?"

"Well, I don't see her much. She comes home and, I think, goes straight to her room. I speak to her occasionally, but she's not much for conversation. I think she's intimidated by her stepmother."

"Like physically abused?"

"No, not like that. Maybe Rebecca is mean to her, but not like she hits her. I've heard what she said to her husband, so imagine what she could say to a child. Just my opinion."

"This guy that came over, can you describe him?"

"Pretty tall, well dressed. Looks like his hair is graying. You know, a trim guy, not overly muscular, with a scruffy beard, one that's kept in a permanent five o'clock shadow. Kind of a long face."

"Did he drive a car that looks like this?" showing her the picture of Seth Willard's car from last night.

"He does now. He's been coming here for at least a year, and until a couple of weeks ago, he's been driving a silver car. He must have sold it because he's driving that white car now."

"How long did you say you've noticed this going on?"

"Oh honey, at least a year, maybe longer. I try not to be nosey, but it's hard not to notice. I go to yoga, and he's there. I come back, and he's still there. Tell me nothing's going on."

"Do you think any of the neighbors can confirm any of this information?"

"Probably not. The Millers, that was their name, they moved out years ago, and no one has bought the house. The lot next to them is vacant, and no one lives in the house across the street. What a shame, too; it's such a lovely house. We used to play…"

"Okay, sorry, Mrs. O'Rear, I understand. Anything else you think I should know?"

"I don't think so. Rebecca is not in any trouble, is she?"

Barnes smiled, "No, I'm just trying to learn all I can to find who killed Mr. Morris. Thank you for your time, Mrs. O'Rear."

Barnes turned to go with her mind mulling everything Mrs. O'Rear told her. She had undoubtedly painted a picture very different from the person they had met a month ago. Barnes heard Mrs. O'Rear shouting her name. Barnes turned.

"Oh, Detective Barnes. I hate to ask, but do you think you can do something to help me out with those parking tickets. I hate to ask, but they sent this letter the other day saying I need to pay them in the next thirty days."

Barnes smiled. "I'll see what I can do, Mrs. O'Rear." She turned away and walked back to her car as fast as she could without being too obvious that she was trying to make an escape.

Barnes left the station earlier than usual for her that evening. She wasted no time once she got home to step in the shower and get ready for her date. She did not usually go out on a weekday, but Davis had the day off tomorrow, so she made an exception. Their first date was about a week ago, and she enjoyed herself more than she thought she would. She was initially uncertain about Davis, but she had to admit he had a certain charm about him. A little rough around the edges, maybe, but charming. It helped that he was a handsome man with a mischievous look. His humor surprised her, and she laughed at his corny jokes even though they sounded more like something her dad would say.

As she was finishing her outfit for the night, the expected knock came on the door. She ran barefoot to the door, peering through the peephole to see Davis with flowers in his hands. She opened the door and greeted him, apologizing for running late and promising she would only be a few more minutes. Davis stood outside almost speechless, then clumsily handed her the bouquet of flowers. "You look amazing," he finally managed.

"Thanks. It's the hair. I wear it up so much that I sometimes forget how long it is. Takes forever to dry. Come in and have a seat. I'll only be a few more minutes." She directed him to sit on the couch while she finished getting ready in her bathroom. Twenty minutes later, she turned down the short hallway putting her slip-on shoe on her foot. "Okay, ready."

"Barnes, you look… amazing," he said again as he rose to his feet.

"Yeah, you said that," she teased. "I guess I clean up nice, don't I? I was raised as something of a tomboy, but I like to dress up like a lady occasionally."

"It's good to see this side of you," he responded and then regretted it in the back of his mind. "Did that sound weird?"

"Maybe a little, but it's okay," she said, smiling back at him. "Should we go now, or are we just going to talk about my outfit all night?"

"Sure, I got us a spot reserved at Village Steakhouse. Ever been there?"

"Are you kidding? I love a good steak. I can't wait."

"Well then, madam," he said, putting his hand flat above his naval and giving a slight bow, "allow me to escort the lady to dinner."

The Village Steakhouse was another Warrenton landmark the locals flocked to for good food. It had opened about ten years before and quickly became a local favorite. The owners, Jack and Cindy Varner, were lifetime residents of Warrenton. The couple risked their savings to open the restaurant after Jack lost his job at a paving company where he worked as an office manager. His friends always told him he had a knack for cooking, so he took the gamble and opened the restaurant. The move paid off in ways the Varners never imagined.

Barnes and Davis talked the night away over their meal and drinks. She was impressed with Davis's ability to converse about many different topics. She felt comfortable around him, like she could talk about almost anything. He put her at ease and made her feel like she could relax.

"So, I hear you like fishing," he said as they waited for the check.

"Yeah, my Dad and I used to go fishing all the time. It drove my brother crazy because I always caught more fish than him. What about you?"

"I've got a trout fishing trip planned in a few weeks. I'm planning on doing some fly fishing."

"Sounds fun. Believe it or not, that's a type of fishing I've never tried?"

"Really?" he said, surprised. "You should go with me. It's a tough skill to master, but I think you'll get the hang of it quickly."

"I might just do that. I'd have to get a flyrod, though."

"You can use one of mine. No need to buy anything."

"I'll have to check my schedule, but I'm interested."

"Great, I'm already looking forward to it."

They finished their meals and went to a small ice cream shop where they got desserts. Davis got a milkshake, while Barnes opted for the strawberry ice cream in a waffle cone. The couple slowly walked back to Davis's car. When they got to the car, Davis opened the door for her. "Thanks," she said as she took her seat.

He started the car and began the drive back to her apartment. "So, do you want to come over and watch the game this Sunday?" she asked him as they drove along.

"It sounds fun, but I'm working Sunday. Sorry."

"Oh well, guess I should have known that," she said trying to hide her disappointment. "Sky asked about you the other night when I talked to her."

"Really? She's high energy, isn't she?"

"You don't know the half of it, but she's a good friend. Sky keeps me on my toes."

"I liked her. She reminded me of someone I knew in high school. Her name was Brenda, and she was high energy too."

"Did you date her?" Barnes asked.

"No, Brenda and her boyfriend dated throughout high school and got married after graduation. I lost track of her after that."

"Yeah, Sky's not married yet, but she's had a steady boyfriend for a while now. He'll probably ask her soon."

Davis pulled the car into the lot next to her apartment building. Again he opened her door for her. As they made their way to her apartment, Davis did not know what to do next. He reached out and took her hand as they walked, and to his surprise, she did not let go. The walk was short, but at that moment, he wished it would last forever.

Arriving at the door, she turned to face him, taking his other hand into hers. "This was really nice, Davis."

He looked down and nodded his head in agreement. "Yeah, but one thing. Call me Mike. At least outside the office."

She smiled shyly. "Okay, but only if you call me Laura."

"I would like that. Laura," he said softly as he leaned in. Her lips met his, and this time they stayed together for more than a quick moment. She looked away from him, avoiding eye contact, smiling even though she tried not to smile.

"Call me?" she asked, looking back at him.

"I will. Are you working next Saturday?"

"No, do you want to hang out here? Maybe watch a game? I like college football too."

"Can't wait," he said. "Might even wear my Bruins jersey."

"Do that," she said as she opened her door. "Goodnight." She took her time going through the door. Temptation called on her to invite him in. Barnes resisted and settled for waving at him as she slowly closed the door. When the door closed, she rested her back against it as she softly laughed at herself. She held on to the moment as long as she could before slipping off her shoes and getting ready for bed.

CHAPTER
THIRTY-ONE

The couple lay in bed covered only by the sheet. Rebecca reveled in the afterglow of their lovemaking and seemed completely satisfied. Seth, on the other hand, seemed out of place for someone who had just experienced the pleasures of sex with a beautiful woman. He was anything but relaxed as he lay beside her, the woman of his dreams or not.

Rebecca rolled over and put her hand on his chest, draping her leg across him simultaneously. She felt frisky that night, not a care in the world. "That was wonderful. You think you got another one in you?" she said as her hand slowly moved toward his midsection.

Seth grabbed her hand, stopping it short of her intended target. "Taylor suspects us now, and this is all you can think about?" he said, annoyance rising inside him. "I know him. He'll keep looking." He sat up in the bed and looked toward her. She had hardly moved, but he could sense the tension between them starting to rise. "This doesn't look good for us."

She sat up, pulling the sheet over her breasts. "Taylor doesn't have anything on us. All he knows is that we had an affair before

Randall died. That's all, and while it may not be the most moral thing, it's hardly illegal." Taking his face into her hand, she turned his head to meet her gaze face to face. "We're fine. He can't prove anything. Your friends told you they backed up your story, so there's nothing to worry about."

"What if he doesn't buy it? How do we explain all of this?" he responded. Seth was feeling the pressure of the situation, and it annoyed him how casual Rebecca was being. "No matter what we did or didn't do, there's a lot of circumstantial evidence that will keep us on his radar. That's the last thing we need."

"Are you saying we made a mistake starting a relationship?" she angrily responded. "If you will recall, you made the first move on me."

"You didn't exactly play hard to get," he shot back. "Besides, that's not what I'm saying. I fell for you even before my wife left me. I knew you and Randall were not as happy as you tried to make people believe. After the divorce, I wanted to believe we would end up together, but you were married. I tried to respect that, but you could have done much better. I just…"

"Seth," she said in a calm voice, surprising to him, "I don't regret what we did. Okay, sure, the timing could have been better, and yes, I should have left Randall, but I didn't. What's done is done, Seth. We can't worry about what people think about us."

He understood what she was saying but still couldn't shake the uneasy feeling that Taylor would find something to implicate them in Randall's murder. "I don't think you're taking this seriously enough. Even if he never finds any link between Randall's murder and us, there will always be a pall of suspicion around us. People will always say that we had something to do with it."

"People will think what they will, Seth. We live our lives the way we want, and that's all we can do." She put her arm around him and leaned her head on his shoulder. "I fell in love with you because of the person you were. I've stayed in love with you because of the way you try and protect me. That's all we're guilty of. Protecting one another. I fell in love. I can't help that. Maybe it was wrong the way we went about it, but that's over now. Let Taylor say what he wants. Let anyone say what they want. They will never be able to put any blame on us." She gently kissed his neck, taking her other arm and wrapping it around him. The sheet fell into her lap as she straddled him, pressing her body against his. "It's just you and me now."

His troubles seemed to melt away with every move of her body against his. Still, in the back of his mind, he was worried. He knew Roger Taylor as well as anyone, and he knew he would not let this case go. He remembered how doggedly he pursued Leonard Pierson. He also knew that Taylor was now suspicious of his relationship with Rebecca.

Seth didn't regret his relationship with Rebecca. What he did regret was how it came about. He saw her often when she delivered Randall's paperwork to city hall. Almost on impulse, he began to put himself where he knew she would be when she arrived.

It probably should not have been a surprise that she started noticing his presence and stopping by his office to say hello. Then he started showing up where she liked to go on her lunch break and days off. He kept his distance, trying to make it look like a coincidence that they were in the same place. The idea of the two of them together began to take shape over several months.

It all seemed to happen innocently enough. Seth sat alone at the coffee shop where he often went for lunch. Rebecca walked in and ordered. She spotted him, walked over to his table, and asked if she could sit with him. Of course, he agreed, and the two chatted away. He felt their fingers touch as they talked, and a charge of energy seemed to pass between them. His hand slightly recoiled at her touch, and she seemed embarrassed as she laughed it off. Yet there was more to it than a mistaken touch. She wrapped her hair around her fingers and looked away with a smile as they made eye contact. Seth noticed that her hand stayed on the table they shared, and before he could stop himself, his hand was reaching for hers.

Over the next several weeks, they continued to meet. Most of the time, they talked about small, trivial things, just two adults enjoying each other's company. One day as they sat in a more secluded place in a small park, the conversation turned more serious. She told him she was unhappy with her marriage. Randall worked all the time and made little effort to spend time with her. She admitted that although she was married, she was lonely. She felt isolated and ignored, and when Randall did speak to her, it usually resulted in an argument.

He looked around as she sat there, almost as if she could cry at any moment. Realizing they were alone, he leaned in and gently kissed her on the cheek. She lowered her head, gazing at him with receptive eyes. Their lips met for the first time ever so briefly. She trembled as he pulled her closer and kissed her deeply. She started to embrace him when a sudden fright overcame her.

"I can't," she said. "If Randall finds out." She walked away, and he thought that was the last he would see of her.

A couple of days later, she sent him a text wanting to meet him again after work. He agreed, and the two met at his house in the evening. She apologized for running out on him. Rebecca could not deny she developed feelings for him, but she worried about what would happen if they gave in to them. The thought of cheating on her husband caused her to feel guilty, but she could not help her feelings for Seth.

Slowly, he drew her near him, gently slipping his arm around her and kissing her neck. This time she did not pull away. She kissed him back shyly but became more passionate with every breath. They made love for the first time that night, and although he knew it was wrong, Seth could not resist. The relationship grew from there, and the guilt disappeared quickly.

His thoughts quickly shifted to the passion of the present moment with Rebecca. She had a way of taking his mind off of his worries. He lay back and decided to enjoy his time with her.

CHAPTER
THIRTY-TWO

The following day Barnes found Taylor in his office. "Hey, I've got a lead on a suspect in the Morris murder," she said. "Mrs. O'Rear told me she saw a man at the Morris home driving a red truck. According to her, Randall Morris arrived home early as the truck drove off. She said he and Rebecca got into an argument after the man in the truck left."

"Right, so tell me more," replied Taylor.

"I called Morris's secretary, and she gave me the name of an employee who drove a red truck matching the description Mrs. O'Rear gave me." She took out a photograph of the man in the truck. "Meet James Burnette."

"The former minor leaguer?" Taylor asked in a surprised voice. "He worked for Randall Morris?"

"Sure did, and it gets better. Burnette has a couple of DUIs and a prior arrest for breaking and entering. An affair with the boss's wife, the B and E charge, plus according to the secretary, he's had money troubles. Sounds like motive to me."

"Alright, bring him in."

In a neighborhood south of town, Burnette was busying himself trimming a cabinet filler for a home remodeling job. Outside the home, he set up a small portable table saw and measured the piece to ensure it was the right length before making his cut. Barnes spotted him right away as she pulled up to the site. She parked the car and approached Burnett, who either did not notice or ignored her arrival.

"James Burnette," she announced when she was only a few feet from the man.

"Yeah," was all the man said in response.

"Detective Laura Barnes. I need you to come to the station to answer a few questions."

"Can it wait? I got work to do," he responded, dismissive of her request.

"No, it can't. I'll give you a minute or two to put your stuff up if you want."

"And what if I don't want?" he asked in a voice bordering on threatening.

"Well, I can have some of my uniformed friends to help you," she said motioning to the police car pulling up near her vehicle. She crossed her arms, never taking her eyes off Burnette. "So, what's it going to be?" He cursed aloud and started putting his things into his truck.

About forty-five minutes later, he sat impatiently in the interrogation room for someone to speak to him. When Barnes and Taylor entered the room, he looked almost relieved. The two detectives sat across from him and tried to look as relaxed as possible while keeping stern looks on their faces.

"Mr. Burnette, I'm Detective Taylor. I think you've already met Detective Barnes." Burnette nodded in acknowledgment. "You know I've seen you play several times before," Taylor said. "You were pretty good. What happened?"

"I crashed my motorcycle going around a curve too fast.

Wrecked my right shoulder and broke my arm in three places." The question clearly made him uncomfortable.

"Seems like I remember hearing that. I guess the team cut you, didn't it? You're not supposed to ride motorcycles and other potentially dangerous things that can ruin your playing ability. Right?"

"Yeah, that's right," Burnette said defensively.

"Times have been tough since then, haven't they?" Taylor asked.

"What do you mean by that?"

"Well, let's take a look. Couple of DUIs, and this breaking and entering charge."

"Hey, those charges were dismissed. It was just a misunderstanding, that's all."

"I understand what you're saying. Big mistake, right? But the money dried up, didn't it? No more sponsors, no more possibilities of making the big league. Times got tough. So, you realize you have to get a real job, but no one wants a washed-up ballplayer on their payroll. So, you eventually start working odd jobs. Finally, landing a job with Randall Morris. How long did you work for him?"

"A little over a year."

"When did you start having relations with Rebecca Morris?"

"I didn't have a relationship with her."

"Yes, you did, James," interjected Barnes. "I have a witness that put your truck at her house about six months ago. Right after that, you got fired. I verified that with the office. So why don't you drop the act and tell us the truth? That's all we want."

"Hey, I didn't kill Randall, alright. That's what you're getting at. Okay, yes, I slept with her a couple of times. I'm not proud of it, but she came on to me first."

"Oh, that's really noble," Barnes countered. "Messing around with your boss's wife, I bet that went over well when he found out. He confronted you, didn't he. Tell us what happened."

"What's there to tell? He came in the next day and fired me.

Told me if I ever showed my face anywhere near him, he'd kick my ass."

"So, what did you do? Did you show up at his house? Take out a little payback on him?" she asked.

"No, I told you I broke it off with Rebecca and never went back."

"Is that so? Where were you when Randall Morris died?"

"I was with a lady friend at the Mexican restaurant bar."

Taylor asked him, "This lady friend got a name, and which Mexican restaurant were you at?"

"Her name is Bethany Pettis. We were at El Encanto until about 10:30. Then we went back to my place."

"I'm going to need her contact information. You can sit tight until I can verify the information you gave us," Taylor said as he and Barnes exited the room. Burnette sat with his arms crossed. As soon as the door shut, he slammed his fists on the table.

A couple of hours later, Taylor found Barnes at her desk. "Well, I just got off the phone with Bethany, and she confirmed that she was with Romeo in there on the night Randall Morris died," Barnes told him.

"Which means he's not our guy. Alright, cut him loose."

Barnes nodded and walked away to release Burnette. Taylor had a terrible feeling come over him as he returned to his office. He felt like he knew the truth but found it hard to admit. He felt the same way the day George Sullivan was revealed as a mole in the department working for Pierson. Over the years, Sullivan sabotaged investigations, misdirected leads, and planted or removed evidence to cover for his boss. This had most of the same feelings.

He had really hoped Burnette was the guy. It even seemed likely, but there was no denying the proof Barnes uncovered. Somehow, Taylor knew Seth Willard was involved and most likely the trigger-man. He didn't know whether or not he acted alone or if Rebecca

Morris put him up to the murder. Taylor knew Seth's divorce was difficult. Sometimes desperation made a person do things they ordinarily would not do. Sometimes unspeakable things.

Still, what would Rebecca get out of it? Randall had no other relatives except his daughter. A lot of his possessions would go to Rebecca. Lauren would inherit a nice sum from her father's estate. Rebecca told them at the start of the investigation that they were not overly wealthy. Still, they had an impressive nest egg saved up over the years, but was it enough to convince someone to commit a murder? People had been killed for far less.

His office phone rang, snapping him out of his thoughts. The voice on the other end told him that Willard's phone records were being sent over. Taylor thanked the person on the phone and wasted no time pouring over the phone records. What he found on the night in question made him feel no better than before.

CHAPTER
THIRTY-THREE

People were moving all around as Seth surveyed the site. He stopped here and there to check the wiring, the building quality, the structure strength, and other factors to ensure everything was up to code. So far, so good on this one. Raymond and Jernigan Construction was a newer company in the Warrenton area, but they did quality work. He kept that in the back of his mind as he made notations on his clipboard, checking off all the items on the list.

The house they were working on was situated on a small hill overlooking an artificial lake in a new subdivision called Lakeview Estates. So far, only five houses existed in the location. Still, lots were selling fast even with the exceedingly high price demanded for the property alone, much less the cost of the home. As the old saying goes, real estate is about location, and prime real estate demands a high price tag. The houses here were large, spacious homes built for people who wanted to flaunt their money and seclude themselves from everyone else at the same time. The home he was inspecting now was no exception.

Satisfied with what he saw, he searched out the construction foreman and, to his surprise, spotted Phillip Raymond talking with the man. Seth Willard was relieved to see him since it would keep him from driving to Raymond's office at the day's end. Making his way toward them, he stuck out his hand, which Raymond readily took. "Phillip didn't expect to see you here today. How are you?"

"Well, everything I've seen tells me you're up to code."

"Hey, that's great. Man, I'm glad to hear we're all good to go here," came a voice behind the group of men. They turned almost in unison to see the smiling face of Roger Taylor. "Seth, I'm going to need to talk with you downtown," he said keeping the lighthearted inflection in his voice.

"Hey, Roger, look, I'm busy right now. Can we do this later today?"

"Tell you what, if you come with me now, I'll let you do it without these," he said as he held up a pair of handcuffs. "Hey, I'll even be willing to drive you myself. What do you say?"

"Phillip, I'll have those papers sent over as soon as possible, okay?" The look on his face said more than any words he could have mustered at that moment. "Okay, Detective, lead the way."

"This way, then," Taylor said gesturing toward the dirt lot outside the unfinished home. "Gentlemen, it was nice meeting you." Raymond and his foreman stared back at him in confusion.

The ride to the station was one of awkward silence. Taylor watched his passenger in the rear-view mirror from time to time. When they made eye contact, he knew he was not wrong about what happened the night Randall Morris died. When they arrived at the station, Taylor knew what he needed to know.

He wasted no time once they made it to the interrogation room. Taylor sat across from Willard and went after him from the start. "You lied to me, Seth. You've been lying to me from the start. You can come up with any excuse you want, but the fact is you're a liar. Now, I want to know the truth from you."

"I told you I was at the Watson's until late—"

"Yeah, I know I called them. The problem is based on the time of death; there is a gap of about thirty minutes or so where you can't account for your whereabouts, but I can. You see, cell phones use towers to get their signal across the country, and every time you drive from place to place, you use a different tower." Taylor placed several papers in front of him, then stood up and walked behind his erstwhile friend. "You see this one right here?" he asked as he pointed to a line on the cell phone record. "That puts you within ten minutes of the Morris residence approximately thirty minutes before Morris died, and you sat there for a long while. Why?"

"There was a train that night, and I couldn't get around it."

"You weren't going home, were you? You live across town from the Morris's home, Seth. You had no reason to be there. So why were you?"

"I just wanted to drive by and see—"

"See what? See if they were home? You knew they were, didn't you?"

"No, Roger, please."

"Don't 'please Roger' me. You knew they were home because you planned this, didn't you?"

"No."

"Yes, you did. You're lying again. You lied about the affair. You two have been physical for about a year, and you know it. So tell me, Seth is this just you, or did she put you up to it?" Roger let his question sink in for a moment and then came at him with the next piece of evidence. "You also own a .38, don't you? I bet if we matched the ballistics in your gun to the one that killed Morris, we would get a match, wouldn't we? Where's the gun, Seth?"

"I sold it years ago."

"Really? To who? What was their name? Where are they from?"

"I don't remember. It was a long time ago."

"Stop lying to me, Seth," Taylor said forcefully. "All you are doing is digging yourself deeper. How about the truth." Taylor slammed his hand on the table. "Let me tell you what I think." He walked back to the seat across from Willard. "I think you went to the Morris's home and waited. Then, you're in luck; Rebecca leaves. So you took the gun and went to the back of the house, slowly, quietly. Opened the backdoor while Randall had his back turned, and you shot him. Then, you went to the bedroom, grabbed the jewelry box, and emptied it into your gym bag. You had to make it look good, so you waited for Rebecca to get home and took a shot at her as she opened the door. You weren't trying to shoot her, but it had to look good. Isn't that right?" Taylor paused to let his words sink in. He could tell he was close to the truth.

"The only thing that doesn't make sense is how you knew to be there that night. Rebecca told us their dinner was a surprise. Did she tell you to wait for her to leave? Did she arrange for you to be there so you could wait for the right time to go inside?"

"It wasn't supposed to happen this way," Seth exclaimed. "Okay, I waited outside their home. I just wanted to see her. I watched them walk in. I hated seeing her with him, so I waited for them to go to sleep. A few minutes later, I saw her come out, get in her car, and drive off. I knew they kept the sunporch door open because it was under construction, and they locked the door going into the house." Seth started to break down. His breathing became heavy, his eyes became wet, and his nose began to run. "I hated him. I hated him because he had her all to himself." Seth looked up at Taylor and, in a loud voice, declared, "It was me. I did it all. I wanted her to myself and not have to share her with that fool of a man."

Taylor felt a lump form in his throat. He could not help but have mixed feelings on this one. Seth had been a friend, someone who was close at one time. The other part of him felt sick that this same man could do something so terrible. What he had to do next sickened him all the more. "You're under arrest, Seth, for Randall

Morris's murder. Stand up and turn around." He cuffed Seth without a moment of hesitation. "I hope she was worth it. Have a seat." He opened the door and, spotting Officer McClendon, motioned for him to come to the door. "McClendon, you get the honors, book Mr. Willard on a charge of first degree murder."

Taylor walked into his office and slammed the door. He sat down at his desk and put his head in his hands. These were the times Taylor hated this job. He looked up just in time to see McClendon leading Willard to booking. The man looked beaten and defeated, and Taylor knew he was. Leaning back in his seat, Taylor exhaled loudly. He banged his fist on his desk and then picked up the phone.

CHAPTER
THIRTY-FOUR

The hospital was unusually quiet. Rebecca's shift ended, and she gathered her things to go home. Rebecca never let on to her coworkers that she and Seth were interviewed by the police at her house. Even so, she kept playing the event through her mind. She told herself she knew better to get involved with Seth, but she let her libido get the better of her again. *Stupid*, she thought.

As Rebecca walked out of the hospital, she spotted a blonde-haired woman talking to a male nurse who pointed toward her. Anticipating she was about to be stopped, she waited for the young, blonde-haired woman to approach her.

"Mrs. Morris, do you remember me? I'm Detective Laura Barnes; I've been investigating your husband's murder."

Rebecca smiled weakly. "Yes, I remember you; how are you?"

"I'm good, thank you. I wanted to let you know that we are close to finding your husband's killer, so I would like you to come to the station with me to answer a few more questions."

"Well, I would like to, but I need to get home. My stepdaughter is there by herself."

"Please, it will only take a few minutes. I would ask you here, but we discovered some documents we need your help with. Promise, it won't take long. Have you home before dinner time."

Rebecca thought for a moment. "Okay, sure, I'll stop by. I'll drive right over."

"Great, I'm parked next to you so we can follow each other."

The two women got in their cars and drove away from the hospital. Barnes's phone rang.

"Hey, boss man," she said. "Yep, I got her. We're on our way now." Minutes later, the two women arrived at the station. Barnes waited for Rebecca as she parked her car and headed inside. Barnes smiled again and guided her to the interview room, telling her that she would be with her shortly.

A few minutes later, Detective Taylor walked into the room. "Sorry to keep you waiting; this won't take long," he said as he sat down. He chuckled. "You were expecting Barnes? She got a call, so I'll discuss this with you."

Rebecca smiled back at him uneasily. "Okay, sure. Have you found out something about my husband's murder?"

"We did. In fact, I just arrested Seth for Randall's murder."

"No. Detective, there must be some mistake."

"Afraid not. Seth admitted to the affair and that he was in your home often. By the way, why would you lie to cover that up, Mrs. Morris?"

"I...I didn't want to believe Seth would...that he would hurt anyone. This has to be a mistake."

"He said you told him the door to the sunporch was always open and that you locked the door going into the house."

"I don't...wait, yes, I remember that. Yes, I told Seth about the door. But I didn't think he would do something like kill Randall."

"Tell me, Mrs. Morris, is it possible maybe you mentioned the door was unlocked hoping he would try to kill your husband? You know, dangle a piece of information in front of him to entice him into action?'

"No, absolutely not. Detective, Randall and I had our share of problems, and yes, I cheated on him—"

"More than once, right? Got a witness to say you and your husband got into a screaming match when he caught another guy leaving your house? What, about six months ago?"

"Okay, yes, I had other men besides Seth, but that doesn't mean I didn't love Randall. It's just he worked so much, and I was lonely. That does strange things to people, but we were working it out. We were going to stay together."

"You like to shop, Mrs. Morris? Because I hear you were spending more than Randall was bringing in. You've got some pretty bad spending habits. Did he confront you about that?"

"No, it wasn't like that. Yes, I like to shop, it's true. What woman doesn't? But I stayed within a budget."

"With a little help from Seth Willard, right? A nice job at city hall added to what you brought in from the hospital and Randall's money. With all that, you were sitting pretty. What happened? Did Randall get tired of it? Threaten to cut you off?"

"No, that's not how it was," she began with tears starting to streak her face. "We had a fight a couple of nights before Randall died. It was a bad one. We said things. He said he would leave me, but we calmed down the next day. I broke down with him and swore I would never cheat on him again. He said he was sorry, too, for not being there and that he would be home more and be more attentive as a husband. The night he died was his way of renewing our marriage."

With that, she lost control and sobbed. Taylor offered her the tissue box, and she took several. He told her he would give her some time to collect herself. Taylor left the room and stepped outside. Taking a deep breath, he opened the door to the adjoining room. Inside, Barnes and Seth Willard stood by the two-way mirror. "Did you get all of that?" Taylor asked.

Seth stood in disbelief in front of the window, tears streaming down his eyes. "I can't believe she did this to me," he said repeatedly. He turned to Taylor, "I'm ready, to tell the truth. All of it."

Rebecca Morris was getting nervous. She paced back and forth angrily, wanting to leave, to be anywhere but where she was. It was almost a relief to her when Taylor returned to the room. "Detective, I'm sorry, but I really need to get home. It's late, and I—"

"It's okay, Mrs. Morris, we are just about done. I have a couple more questions first. Did your husband have a life insurance policy by any chance?"

"We both do," she said defensively.

"Yeah, but his is worth what, say, $250,000?" Her face went pale. "That's what it's worth right?"

"I...ummm...yes, that's right. If one of us died, we needed it to pay off the house."

"Sure, many people have life insurance policies, but why did you tell Seth?"

She did not answer. "You planned this, didn't you? You planned it from the beginning." Taylor turned up the heat, "Seth told us everything. The plan was for a home invasion. Kill Randall, beat you up a bit, and tie you down in a separate room. Make it look like Randall resisted. The thing is, Randall, surprised you with dinner that night. So, you had to change the plan. Seth was going to confront you two in the driveway and make it look like a robbery gone wrong, but he got stuck by the train. So, you had to change the plan again. Seth waited, and you left. Then he made his move."

"That's a lie. I never—"

"Hold on, this is the best part. You got back, and Seth was finishing up, so he fired two shots into the wall by the door to make it look like you walked in on the thief. Then you screamed and rolled around in the flower bed outside. I got to admit you played your part well."

"You can't prove any of this. I don't know what he told you, but he's lying. I would never hurt Randall. We worked through our marital problems and were going to stay together."

"I thought you would say that, and you're right. I wouldn't just take Seth's word for it. So how about this?" he said as he began to read from a paper. "'Change of plan, we're going to dinner tonight. Meet us in the driveway.'" How about this one? 'Where are you?' Oh, this one is my favorite. 'I'm pulling out right now, be back in half an hour. Make it look good.' Remember those text messages you sent?" She said nothing. She crossed her arms, sat back in her chair, and said nothing. "See, most people think that if you delete a text, it's gone forever. But they're not. Takes a court order, but you can retrieve them. It also helps when the recipient puts context to those messages."

"You also should have gotten rid of the jewelry, but again you got greedy, and Seth got sloppy. He left it in his gym bag inside his car, and a random lowlife busted his window to get them. So, he panicked, traded the car in, and got a new one. It didn't work because we found the car and verified it had a broken window." He paused and continued. "He told us about the gun. Told us he buried it in his flower garden. My guys are over there digging it up right now. It's over, Rebecca."

"I want a lawyer," she said.

"You're going to need one." Minutes later, Barnes led a cuffed Rebecca Morris out of the interrogation room and down to the booking area. Several minutes later, she was led past a row of cells. In one of them sat Seth Willard. He rose to his feet as Rebecca walked by. The two locked eyes. It only lasted a moment, but it was all they needed. She continued down the cellblock stopping in front of an open cell door, and stepped inside. The door slid closed behind her, and she stood alone.

CHAPTER
THIRTY-FIVE

Several weeks later, a familiar face wandered into the Warrenton Police Department. Seeing Lauren Morris from across the room, Taylor walked over to greet her. "Lauren, how have you been? Everything alright?" he asked as she shook his outstretched hand.

"Yes, thank you. I just wanted to say thank you again for catching my Dad's killers. What's going to happen to Rebecca?"

"I talked to the DA, and they are both going to take a plea deal in exchange for no death penalty. Life in prison with no chance of parole. It's too good of a fate for them after what they did, but you'll never have to worry about Rebecca again." Lauren smiled at the thought. "So what about you? What are your plans now?"

"I'm living with my cousin Samantha and her family. They have a place here in town, so I can finish school here. After that, I plan to move away to college. Probably somewhere far away."

"Can't say I blame you, kid."

"Again, thanks for all you did, Detective. I really appreciate it."

"You got it. Take care now."

The rest of the day went the same as all the others. Crime never stops, and Warrenton was no exception to the rule. People came and went just as any other day. Taylor could not help but feel a little deflated after the events of the past several weeks. He reasoned it was only natural after such a high-profile case.

As he glanced out of his office window, he spotted Banes and Davis conversing. It seemed obvious what was going on after hours. It made sense; an attractive woman and a handsome man, both younger than himself, seemed like a good match. He sighed to himself anyway. He didn't think he was so much older. His own grandparents were nine years apart in age. It was not jealousy, he felt; it was something else. Something he could not quite understand, but he tried to put it out of his mind.

Why should it matter anyway? Was it a sense of betrayal that he felt? Deep down, Shelia was gone, and he knew she was gone a long time, even before she died. While she was alive, he always hoped she would come back to him. When they worked the Pierson case, he could feel them growing closer together, bonding over the shared danger. He hated that part, but it allowed him to be close to her. That is what got her killed. At least he told himself so. The truth was that no matter what he did, she would go after the truth of the Sidney Lewis case, with or without him. In many ways, he agreed to help her as his way to protect her, but she made it clear it was her choice, not his, to pursue the truth.

When Barnes and Davis parted, he sprang from his desk and asked Barnes to join him in his office. "Hey, I just wanted to go over a few things on our last big case," he began as Barnes listened. "You did a great job on that interview with the Morris's neighbor, Mrs.… ummm, what was her name?"

"Mrs. O'Rear. Too bad you didn't get to meet her. She's full of fun facts," Barnes said as Taylor fumbled through the case file.

"Yeah, I bet. I thought you also handled bringing in Rebecca Morris well too. It's not easy looking at someone you either know or at least greatly suspect committed a crime and keeping your cool. Seriously you did great."

"Thanks. You didn't do so bad yourself, you know."

"Are you kidding? I let my guard down. Got personally involved and let myself be led astray when I should have seen past that whole grieving widow bit."

"You can't blame yourself for that. We all thought Rebecca was the victim, but we discovered the truth, and now she and her lover boy are where they belong."

"Yeah, true enough." An uncomfortable pause took place between the two. Neither seemed to know what to say next. She was his partner and a junior detective. Still, something bothered him about her and Davis.

"You really want to ask, don't you?" Barnes said, finally breaking the uncomfortable silence. "It's okay, just ask."

"Ask?" he said, trying his best to not sound like a disappointed teenager. "Ask what?"

"Come on, Taylor, are we really going to play this game?" Her voice held just the slightest hint of a tease. "You want to know about Davis and me. Just ask."

"Look, it's none of my business."

"Of course not, but you still want to know."

"Who you date is not my concern. You're a big girl. You can make your own choices."

"I'm a big girl? Really?"

"You know what I mean, Barnes. You're a grown woman and don't need my permission to date a fellow officer. There's nothing in the rule book that expressly forbids it."

She could tell he was getting uncomfortable. Honestly, she was feeling a little uneasy as well. She had to admit that when she first joined the department, she was attracted to Taylor. Barnes still felt the pull, even if it was not the same sentiment she had for Davis. It was hard to explain, much less work out in her mind about what she felt for Taylor and Davis. It was similar but different. There was no love triangle because she was not in love with either of them, at least not yet. Besides, she was certain Taylor was still in love with someone else.

"Taylor, are you trying to tell me something here? If so, I'm all ears."

Now it was his turn to be defensive. He ran the facts through his mind as he formed his response. Barnes was several years younger, she was his partner, and more importantly, he was not sure he was over Shelia. In fact, he was sure he was not. Then again, this could be how he could begin to get over her. The problem was the game of cat and mouse was frustrating him. Somehow, he could not say what was really on his mind, mostly because he could not even say it to himself. He liked her, they had a strong partnership, and he did not want to screw that up. She seemed happy with Davis too, and he did not want to foul up her happiness. Now might not be the time.

"Barnes, I want you to be happy, that's all. If Davis makes you happy, then, by all means, go ahead. Just be careful, okay?"

"Sure, boss. No problem." She got up to leave and turned back around before walking out of the office. "Hey, I'm thinking about going for a drink if you want to join me. You know, to relax a bit. Might be fun."

He thought for a moment. "No better go on without me. I think I'm going home and going to bed."

"Suit yourself."

As she turned to go, he called back to her, "Hey, Barnes, can you give these to the chief before you go? I'm going to sneak out," he said, handing her a small stack of papers.

She laughed, "Sure, no problem. See you tomorrow? No, wait, it's Saturday, and you're off tomorrow. Lucky you."

"Yeah, thought I might go fishing or something tomorrow. Probably just stay home, though."

"Well, don't have too much fun," she said as she exited the office.

Taylor grabbed his things and headed to the exit. The night air was cool, and there was a gentle breeze. Taylor stood outside the police station for a few minutes and thought seriously about going to see Eddie again. He would probably fuss at him for not having that drink with Barnes. He laughed at the thought to himself as he made his way to his Charger. About halfway to his car, he heard Barnes calling for him. He pulled out his keys and pushed his automatic start button.

"Hey, Taylor," she yelled at him, causing him to turn around, "You forgot to sign this one," she said, holding one of the documents he just gave her. "Chief wanted me to catch you before you left." He could see the sarcastic grin on her face. Taylor let out a frustrated breath. He thought he signed all the papers, but he knew Chief Vanderbeck would not let him hear the end of it if he didn't sign them now. She started walking toward him to try and meet him halfway. "You still got time to reconsider that drink offer."

Taylor began walking back toward her and the station smiling and shaking his head simultaneously. "You know I just...." Suddenly a bright flash and an earsplitting explosion broke the otherwise quiet night. Taylor was blown toward the building while Barnes was knocked backward by the force of the blast. His ears were ringing as his vision blurred. His mind tried to make sense of what had just happened.

Barnes was sitting up. Her mouth was moving, saying something, but he could not make out what she was saying. She pointed at something behind him. It took a moment to register, but he realized she was pointing at his car. Looking behind him, he saw the vehicle engulfed in flames. It started to register with him that someone had just tried to kill him. Another few minutes, and he would have been sitting in that car somewhere down the road.

Barnes was finally on her feet and moving toward him. He still could not hear what she was saying, but she was clearly asking if he was okay. He tried to stand but soon found he could not stand. He was moving but felt clumsy and somehow out of place. Still, he felt his strength returning and, with it, pain. He could hear her voice as she called out to him. "Taylor are you all right. Are you injured? Talk to me. Are you okay?"

"What just happened?" he asked, partially knowing the answer. Officers were starting to run out of the building toward the two detectives. He started to hear sirens in the distance.

"Barnes," he said, looking to see if she was still there. He was dazed, his head swimming, and his vision was blurred. He was having difficulty focusing.

"Taylor, talk to me. Are you okay?"

The world was finally coming back into focus. Taylor took several deep breaths trying to focus his attention. "Barnes," he began, "my car?"

"It's gone. Fire Department will be here any minute now. Are you injured?"

"I don't think so," he responded, "At least not too bad. The last thing I remember was starting my car with my remote when you came out."

"A bomb? Tied into your car's remote? Who has access to this lot?" she asked him as the smoke smell began filling her senses.

"Only cops," he said, fighting the smoke and the ringing in his ears.

"Who would plant a bomb in your car? Who...," she stopped in midsentence. "Oh no. Oh god, no."

A block from the station, Smith waited for the explosion he knew would come. When it happened, it was not nearly as loud as he thought it would be. Smith waited several minutes longer and saw the ambulance and fire trucks dispatched to the police station. He smiled as he picked up the phone he had received from his contact. He dialed the only number stored in the phone. His contact picked up, "It's done," he told the man on the other end of the phone.

"Meet me tomorrow at nine o'clock, and you'll get your payment." Hanging up the phone, Smith opened the door and flung the phone down on the sidewalk. He got out of the car and smashed the phone more with his foot. Satisfied the device was destroyed, he returned to the car and drove away.

CHAPTER THIRTY-SIX

Davis woke up early in the morning to begin packing his bags. He had planned this trip months ago and was anxious to get on his way. He planned to drive north up the coast and get as far away as possible, picking up anything he needed along the way. Packing light, he only took what he thought necessary.

Grabbing the two bags, he made his way through the front door, locking it behind him. As he turned toward the street, he saw a familiar face leaning against his car. She smiled and waved at him, greeting him as he made his way down the few steps of his rental house.

"Hey there," Barnes greeted him with a warm smile. "Where are you off to?"

Surprised, he answered, "I have a couple of weeks' vacation, so I'm going to travel up the coast. No place special, really. Just plan to drive and see what I can get into. Do you want to join me? I got plenty of room. I travel light."

"Wow, yeah, I would love to, but I can't. I've got a big case I just started last night. Someone tried to kill Detective Taylor."

"Taylor? Is he alright?"

"He's in the hospital under observation. Will probably be there a couple of days," Barnes told him.

"Well, at least it sounds like he'll be okay. Hate to hear that."

"Yeah, me too," she said as she continued to stand between Davis and his car. "So, where were you last night? I tried to call, but it went to voicemail."

"I was here. I let my phone drain all the way down and forgot to turn it back on. Sorry."

"You know I want to believe you. I really do," she said, trying to fight back her emotions. "It was a car bomb. He hit his remote start, and it exploded just a short delay later. I got to thinking about who could do that. Then I remembered you told me you used to work at your Dad's place. If anyone could tune a bomb to a keyless remote frequency, you could."

"Hey, Barnes, you're not accusing me, are you?"

She started to move toward him slowly, deliberately. "You didn't know the score, did you?"

"What?"

"The score to the game. You said you were there with friends but couldn't remember the score. Seems to me you would, being it was just a week or two before. You didn't remember because you were never there."

"Barnes, that's crazy. My friends will—"

"They did. I called them. They told me you canceled on them. Then there's the gas receipt that fell out of your binder. It said you were in Julian but weren't there to pick up your friends. On the same day you were there, a man was murdered."

"Whoa, wait a minute. That's a big leap. I don't know what you're trying to prove, Barnes, but it's not working. Now I need to hit the road."

Barnes stood her ground between Davis and his car. She stared intently at him, watching for any dangerous move. "You're right; it would be except for who it was. Jordan Byrd, a loose end from the Pierson case?" She laughed. "You know Taylor always believed there were other cops on the take for Pierson, but we couldn't prove it. Not you, though. You were one of the good ones. At least, that's what we thought."

She pulled out a stack of papers from a file folder she was holding. "Took some doing, but I got a judge to sign off on a warrant for your bank records. Nothing too specific until I found this entry for an airline ticket to Miami. Not really up the coast, is it?"

Davis began to sway nervously. "Look, Barnes, I don't know what—"

"When did he get to you, Davis? Had to be while we were working patrol. Why now?"

Realizing that the deception was over, Davis sarcastically laughed. "Doesn't matter," he began, "Byrd was a loose end. Tried to use the information he had no business having. And Taylor? Well, let's just say he's also a loose end. He ruined a good thing for a lot of people." He took a deep breath, "So, what happens now?"

"I've got to take you in, Davis. That's why I'm here. I wanted to give you a chance to surrender without the embarrassment of being hauled in by someone else."

"You know it's not too late, Barnes. You could forget you saw me. Meet me in Miami, and we can go off together."

Barnes stood her ground. "I can't do that, Davis. You're going down for this."

Seeing he could not convince her, he began to move his right hand toward his back. There, he found the handle of the 9 mm pistol he carried in his waistband. "I'm sorry that you feel that way. I really am." He took hold of the weapon and slowly freed it from his waistband. "You know they tell you at the Academy' never confront a dangerous suspect without backup. Too bad you forgot that."

"She didn't," came a voice from behind him. Without turning

his body, Davis looked behind him to see Roger Taylor walking from behind the corner of the rental house. Davis felt the urge to pull his weapon even stronger. "Go ahead, Davis, do it. I want you to. Please pull that weapon. I'm begging you."

Davis thought about his situation. He tightened the grip on his gun for a moment but then decided the odds against him were too great. "Go ahead and shoot me, Taylor. I'm dead either way," he said as he slowly put his hands in the air. Taylor advanced on him quickly, grabbing Davis's weapon and tossing it to the ground. Before Davis could blink, he was cuffed.

"You're not taking the easy way out, Davis," Taylor said pushing him toward Barnes's car. "Besides, do you know how hard it is to find a car like the one you blew up?" Taylor slammed the car door shut. He looked at a visibly shaken Barnes. "Laura, are you alright?"

She looked at him and smiled weakly. "I will be. Let's get him booked before I change my mind and shoot him myself."

After Davis was processed, he sat alone in the interrogation room waiting, his wrists cuffed to the table. It was as uncomfortable as he imagined. Taylor and Barnes entered the room with determined looks on their faces. They sat across from him, silent for what seemed like an eternity before Davis broke the silence. "Well, aren't you two the cute couple. You know you really do deserve one another. The older man, the younger woman, it just seems to fit you. Will I be allowed to come to the wedding?"

"Shut up, Davis," Taylor commanded. "You tried to kill me. Why?"

"Wow, is that the best you got, Taylor? I really expected better."

"How long were you on the Pierson payroll? When did he get to you?"

"You know it was so long ago."

"Cut the crap, Davis. You killed Jordan Byrd, and you tried to kill me. Are you some holdout from the Piersons, or is someone else pulling your strings? Now answer."

"I want my lawyer."

Taylor got up and stormed out of the room, leaving Barnes with Davis. After the door slammed, she looked at Davis sitting across from her. "So, I guess you're the good cop now?" Her expression did not change. She stared at him stoically. Inside her mind, she wished she was anywhere but here.

"You know it's funny in a way," she began. "We've spent a lot of time together recently, but it's like I hardly knew you at all. Did you know I was near his car when it exploded? Did you even think about who else may have been hurt? Honestly, I don't care why. I don't. I want to know if everything between us was a lie."

"Laura…"

"Don't call me that," she yelled. "Don't you dare call me that! You look me in the eyes and tell me it wasn't all a lie! You do that. Hell, I might even believe you." Davis looked away, shifting his body away from her as much as he could. "You can't, can you?"

"Barnes," he began, "I meant what I said about you coming with me."

"Why, so I could be your hostage?"

"No, dammit, no. I wasn't trying to hurt you. I swear it was never about you."

"Then tell me why. Why?" Barnes demanded.

"Because I was trapped. Yes, I took money from Pierson. I turned a blind eye to what I saw and was paid well. Then weeks after Pierson died, I got a call from a guy telling me to meet him at Sally Davis Park, saying if I didn't show up, he'd release evidence I was on the take for Pierson."

"Then what?"

"I showed up, and he had the bank records showing money I'd

been paid. He told me my record would disappear if I did a few jobs for him."

"This guy got a name?"

"Yeah, I'm sure he does, but I don't know it. He always called me Mr. Smith. Said it was better if we didn't use our names. He paid me in cash to fix a few problems for his employer, nothing serious, but a few months ago, he upped the game. Told me to kill Byrd. He said if I did, I would only owe him one more favor, and after that, I would have a clean slate."

"Let me guess, he lied to you."

"Yeah, said he owned me. That his employer had plans for me or something. I wanted out."

"Which is why you were going to fly to Miami."

"I was going to lay low for a while and then charter a flight to Bogota or somewhere in South America and disappear. After a year or so, I planned to go to Switzerland or Thailand. Someplace far away from here. Start over with a lot of money."

"Guess me and Taylor were worth a lot more."

"It wasn't like that. Okay, yeah, sure, Taylor, but not you. I wouldn't purposely hurt you. I swear."

"Yeah, my family could have put that in my obituary. What a fitting tribute, 'I didn't do it on purpose,' what a tearjerker that would have been."

"Barnes, I need protection. When they find out I've been—"

"I don't care, Davis. I only need to know from you now if there are other names on their hit list."

"I don't know. They would let me escape to South America, but they would keep tabs on me. Told me they would bring me back at some point. That's why I was going to disappear to Europe or Asia. Hell, I don't know. I didn't want to plan too far ahead so they couldn't find out too soon."

"Well, don't count on going to South America. At best, you get protective custody in a concrete cell." She got up and walked out of the room leaving Davis to sit and ponder what fate might have for him. It was nothing good, he was certain.

Taylor waited for her at her desk. "Well, any luck?"

"Yeah, we need to guard him 'round the clock. I'll explain every-thing in your office." The detectives sat down, and Barnes recounted everything Davis told her.

Several hours passed as Davis sat and waited. Finally, a uniformed officer came in. "It's about time. I've had to piss for an hour."

The officer said nothing. He strolled behind Davis, reaching for a small silver reel concealed in his sleeve. "I told you there was nowhere you could hide from me, Mr. Smith," he said as he whipped the garrote around Davis's neck. The steel cord nearly decapitated the helpless man. Davis struggled in vain as the wire began to dig deeper into his neck. Finally, Davis gave up as his body began to relax, and death took him. His work now finished, the false officer exited the room and made his escape.

CHAPTER
THIRTY-SEVEN

"Just how the hell do you let a man dressed as one of us walk into a guarded room and kill a suspect? Do you know the hell I'm going to catch for this? Do you?" Chief Vanderbeck demanded of both Taylor and Barnes. They had listened to the chief for about an hour. She went on and on about how the media would scrutinize the department and its lax security. How sloppy the procedure was handling a suspect in custody.

"Chief, we followed every procedure correctly. I had Garner watching the door. He needed to take a piss, so he got someone to watch for him, just like he was supposed to. There were over a dozen cops in that station. Our killer stayed close by and took his spot when he left for the restroom. He slipped in and killed Davis, and when Garner returned, the killer walked away."

"And Garner didn't think to check to see if he knew the guy that took his watch?" Vanderbeck asked.

"Do you recognize every officer here? There have been a lot of new faces recently. We may not be the biggest department, but we still have over a hundred officers." Taylor's temper was beginning to get the better of him. He knew he had done everything right. "Fact is, Chief, the guy knew our routine and procedures. He also knew the fastest ways in and out of the department. He knew how to best avoid the cameras and keep most of his face obscured. In short, this wasn't the first time he's been here."

"That doesn't help us much," Vanderbeck responded harshly. "There are hundreds of people in and out of here on any given day."

"No, it doesn't help at all. In fact, it hardly narrows the suspect list," Taylor conceded.

"Not to mention this is the second security breach in a week," she added. Vanderbeck tried to calm herself. She switched her gaze between the two detectives. "What about you, Barnes? You got any brilliant insight to add here? Davis was your boyfriend, wasn't he?"

Barnes cut her eyes at Taylor and then quickly refocused. "I wouldn't say that, Chief. Yes, we were dating, but we weren't officially exclusive. We hadn't been physical yet, so…"

"Well, while that is certainly fascinating. I'm more interested in why Davis would try to kill Taylor here and then we find his throat cut open. You got any thoughts on that?"

"He told me he worked for the Piersons for around a year and wanted out. He admitted to killing Byrd and that he was afraid for his life. He told me he wanted to hide in South America and move around to various places."

Vanderbeck glared at them intensely, almost like she could stare completely through them. "So, what is your plan now, Taylor? Got any ideas?"

Taylor glanced over at Barnes and took in a deep breath. "I've got Davis's home locked down. No one in or out until Barnes and I get there. I have McClendon running a report on known Pierson associates to see if he can turn up any possible leads. If all of that fails, I'll go to the surviving members of the Pierson family myself to see if I can find any information."

"Steer clear of the Piersons themselves for now. Find out what you can from the house and keep me informed," Vanderbeck said putting on her glasses and looking down at a stack of papers. "That's all. Why are you still here?"

The two detectives were back at Davis's rental home several minutes later. It was late afternoon when they arrived. The two detectives entered the home and began looking around for anything useful. Taylor thought how small the house was and how few possessions Davis had.

"Hey Taylor come here," he heard Barnes call from the bedroom.

Taylor felt a warning run through his mind. He walked in a found her standing near his closet. "I may have got something here. I wanted to look at the top of his closet, and a couple of boards moved. She bent down to try to remove them from their place. "He had a couple of pairs of shoes on top of them, but the boards gave way too easy."

"Careful, Barnes, they might be rigged, a trap," he said as she moved the first one out of its place. She shined the flashlight from her phone into the hole in the floor.

"No worries. Nothing is holding it, and there are no wires. It looks clean," Barnes said as the second one was removed from its place. "Well, well. Look at this." She reached into the hole and removed a black file holder with a Velcro strap.

"Wonder what Davis was hiding," Taylor said as he moved to Barnes's side.

"I wouldn't know. Told you and the chief earlier I never got this far with him."

"Nice to hear you're keeping your sense of humor about this," he responded as he began to look through a notebook he found in the folder.

"It's the only thing keeping me from going crazy right now." She took out a file and flipped through it. "Taylor, look at this. Seems Davis was doing some investigative work on his own. There's a list of names here, and several have been crossed off. Do you recognize any of them?"

It didn't take long to realize a connection. "Yeah, they are all old Pierson associates, business partners, friends of friends and all. At least two or three of the names on this list are crossed off because they're dead. Others he's crossed off are still alive. I bet he was trying to find out who was blackmailing him. By the looks of it, he's narrowed it to about a dozen possibilities, but nothing solid. Does he have a computer by any chance?"

"Who doesn't these days? Should be around somewhere." After searching for several minutes, they finally found Davis's laptop. Neither was surprised when they discovered the laptop was password protected. "Guess the guys in the lab can try and crack it."

"Actually," Taylor said, "let me handle the laptop. I know just the guy who can do it. Keep searching here and see if you can turn up anything more." With that, he left with the laptop in hand.

CHAPTER
THIRTY-EIGHT

Monday morning Taylor arrived at a small, rented office in town. He walked right past the counter and into an office down the short hallway. The man Taylor was looking for was in his late twenties with long dreadlocks. One might mistake him as an athlete or bodybuilder but in fact, Tavon Garrett was one of the most talented computer guys Taylor knew. Tavon was staring on whatever was on the screen in front of him. Taylor noticed the earbuds and shouted.

"Tavon!"

Tavon nearly fell out of his chair. Ripping the devices from his ears, he angrily shouted, "Man, what the hell are you trying to do? You want to give me a heart attack?" Taylor laughed. "Oh, you think this is funny, Taylor? Why did I ever give you that key?"

"You didn't; the door was open. You ought to be more careful; there are a lot of bad people around here, you know?" Taylor responded as he set the laptop down on the desk.

"Look, Taylor, it's not that I don't like all the work the department gives me, but calling ahead would be nice."

Taylor pulled his phone from his pocket, "I did. Three times. How do you stay in business if that's your customer service?"

"Yeah, real funny. What did you do? Let me guess, bill the department for the laptop? Did you spill coffee on it?"

"No, this one is off the record. Mostly anyway. I was hoping you could get into it and extract files on the hard drive. Belongs to a guy named Davis. As usual, faster is better."

"This pro bono?"

"Not completely pro bono, no. But needs to be hush-hush for a while. You know, usual damaging stuff about people and whatnot. You know how it is."

Tavon snickered. "Yeah, when you're around, I do. I guess you want this now, don't you?" He didn't wait for a response. He opened the laptop. "Give me a couple of hours to work my magic, and I'll have access to everything you want."

"Tavon, you are a genius."

"Yeah, and I'm humble, too, don't forget that part. Just how much info do you want off this thing?"

"I want to know what this guy had for lunch yesterday and everything else you can get. I want pictures if he has a secret family in Idaho."

"Yeah, that's what I thought. I'll have it for you in an hour or so."

"An hour? You just said two hours."

"Yeah, but now you got me curious, and I want to know about the family in Idaho."

While Taylor busied himself with some of the files he kept from Davis's folder, Tavon got into the computer. His magic took forty-two minutes.

"Hey, Taylor come here," he said. "Your boy Davis was a real Boy Scout. Once you get past the porn, there's some interesting stuff. Take a look at this."

Taylor stared at the screen. "What am I supposed to see?"

"Nothing, and that's the point. You aren't supposed to see a thing, but when I do this," Tavon said as he continued his work, "it gives me a whole different perspective." Clearly confused, Taylor asked for clarification. "Look, do you see this line right here? It's part of a tracking program. Whoever set this up is pretty good. He could see and record everything Davis did on this computer. He probably knew what Davis was up to at all times, and I mean everything."

A wave of concern washed over Taylor. "Can he be watching us now?"

Tavon laughed. "No man, I said he was pretty good, but he ain't me. One of the first things I did was check for anything that could come back on me. As far as this cat knows, the computer is still sitting wherever it is you found it." He turned toward Taylor. "Now we get to the good stuff. Davis kept track of his money pretty well. Seems he has close to $700,000 hidden in accounts all over the place. The man must have been making some major bank. He was also really interested in this guy."

He called up a picture of a man with graying hair and a sharply defined nose. Taylor studied the picture for a moment. He didn't say anything, but he was confident he'd seen the man. "You recognize him, Taylor?"

"No, I may have seen him before, but I don't know him. Did Davis leave any clues as to who he was?"

"He didn't record a name, but there are several pictures of him." Tavon began to flip through the pictures. Most were of the guy alone, but one stuck out to Taylor. He asked Tavon to stop and enlarge the photo. In the picture were two men, the first was the sharp-nosed man; the other was one more familiar to him.

"That's George Sullivan. He used to be one of my detectives. Can you make me a copy of this picture?"

"Man, I just busted all into this computer, and you're going to ask me if I can copy a picture?"

"Yeah, I know. What was I thinking?"

"There's more, though. There are some encrypted files I found too. Way too sophisticated for the likes of Davis. These files had to come from someone other than him. He tried to get into the files but had no luck. My guess is he found something he thought he could use. If you ask me, he was a dead man walking even before you guys got to him."

"What, you're the detective now, Tavon?"

"No, but think about it. If you're the criminal type, will you let some fool expose you? Personally, I'd take him out before he could get to me."

"You've thought about that too long, Tavon, but it makes sense. Can you crack the files?"

"There's nothing I can't get into, but this level of encryption will take time. I'll call you when I've got something. Until then, you might as well go do cop things or whatever it is you do when you're not here bothering me."

"Tavon, you're the best," Taylor said as he turned to go.

"And humble," Tavon said as he turned his attention back to the screen. "Now, let's see what you're trying to hide."

While driving the ninety minutes to Chino Men's Prison, Taylor arranged a meeting with his old friend George Sullivan. Despite being told it was against protocol, the officials granted the request. Taylor waited over an hour in a small meeting room before Sullivan arrived.

When the door opened, Sullivan entered the room looking like he had seen better days. He looked haggard and beaten down by life and possibly a few inmates.

"Oh, what the hell is this?" Sullivan asked and tried to turn around and walk out. The guard told him to sit down and slammed the door behind him. The two men stared at each other. The last time they had seen one another was when Sullivan was on the witness stand fulfilling his part of a plea deal and testifying against several Pierson operatives.

"You look good, George. What's it been two years? Something like that?"

"Piss off, Taylor," the other shot back.

"George, is that any way to talk to a man who brought you a gift?" Taylor responded as he produced a brown sack with a burger inside it. "Probably a bit cold now, but I remembered these were your favorite. How've you been?"

"How the hell do you think I've been? Looks like I lost a little bit more than my pension, and let me tell you just how much ex-cops are loved in here. It makes you really popular in all the wrong ways. So, what the hell do you want so I get back to my next ten years?"

"Yeah, about that, I need some help from you. You recognize this guy?" he asked as he showed the picture to Sullivan.

"Maybe. What if I do?"

"Now, George, remember the little deal you made with the state. You come clean to everything you know about the Piersons, their operation, or the deals off. You remember that, right?"

"Yeah, I remember that, but you're barking up the wrong tree on this one."

"What do you mean?"

"I mean, that guy didn't work for Leonard Pierson. He worked for Lawson. His name is Edgar Reece. He was something of a go-between for the cartels and Lawson. Basically did a lot of dirty work for Lawson. The problem was Leonard didn't like the guy; he said he wasn't trustworthy. Lawson still used him for a side hustle without Daddy Pierson knowing."

"What kind of side hustle?"

"Guns mostly. Reece is ex-special forces, or at least he claimed. Said he ran missions in Central America during the Reagan and

Bush years. I thought he was full of crap, but Lawson liked him well enough."

"Daddy Pierson didn't know about Lawson's gun running?"

"After Lawson died, Reece disappeared. I just figured he melted into the jungle or something. Maybe a jaguar got him, or he blew himself up."

"How well did you know him? Did you ever interact with him?"

"Look, I didn't know him well. We met a few times here and there. He doesn't have much personality, and he's full of himself. Likes to think he's more important than he is. Obsessed with chess too. He likes to make comments using chess metaphors."

"Do you think he could still be doing go-between work?"

"Anything is possible, but I doubt it. Lawson always said the guy was about two steps away from being on the wrong side of a cartel bullet. I thought he was just a low-life masquerading as a big shot. That was the vibe I got from him."

Believing he had all he needed, Taylor stood up to go. "Hey, George, this was fun. We should do this more often. Next time I have a Pierson question, I'll let you know. We should get together and reminisce about the old days when you get out in a few years. Or maybe not." He knocked on the door to tell the guard he was ready to leave. As the door opened, he looked back at his one-time friend, "Hey George, you know what? Forget it."

George Sullivan sat there for a few minutes, sulking. Behind him, the door opened, and the guard returned and led him back to his area.

CHAPTER
THIRTY-NINE

The day was not particularly hot, but you could not tell it by the expression on the man's face as he contemplated his next move. He studied the board and carefully considered every possible move. Nothing seemed to satisfy him. The strain on the man's face was amusing to watch. He was sweating as his hand grasped the bishop and then his last knight.

Reece observed his opponent and reveled in the satisfaction of knowing that no matter what his next move was, it would be the wrong one. Usually, he did not play for money, but when his opponent insisted on making things interesting, the challenge was accepted. Now the trap was set, and the man seemed to realize there were moves left.

It wasn't about the mere $500 gamble. It was the satisfaction of a trap well laid. The planning, the moves, and the counter moves. The setup led to the anticipation of the coming trap. He was almost let down when the man seemed lulled into his trap so easily. Now, the game was about to come to a close. He was almost disappointed that it was all but over. At last, the man made his move and stopped his clock.

He chose the knight, Reece thought. He figured the move might prolong this for several more moves, but victory was inevitable. Unfortunately, there were more important things on his itinerary than wasting time with someone who obviously needed help understanding the man he challenged. Reece moved his rook.

"Check," he said as blankly as possible, concealing his satisfaction.

The man squirmed, not seeming to realize that it no longer mattered. He made his next move. He would not like the result. Reece moved his bishop, and the opponent's last knight quickly disappeared.

"Check." This time, a self-satisfied smile gently creased his lips. He regarded the opponent's hopeless situation with near delight. "Are you sure you wish to continue?"

To his credit, the opponent did not flinch. He countered the move the best he could with his remaining bishop, but as soon as he hit the button on top of the clock, he realized his mistake. Reece moved his queen.

"Checkmate," he said as he leaned back in his chair. "I believe this now belongs to me." He took the five one hundred dollar bills out from under the stone.

His opponent said something under his breath as he got up to leave. The Reece watched him leave with a sense of satisfaction. As he reveled in his self-congratulations, he spotted a familiar face from a distance. At first, he was not sure it was actually her. She was in the company of a young man and a child who looked to have just learned to walk. Perhaps he was mistaken, but he had to be sure.

Leaving his seat, he began to walk across the park. Closing on her, he noted she looked different from the last time he had seen her. The hair was a little lighter and shorter. She appeared to have put on some baby weight. She was still quite slender by the look of her, but she was different, nonetheless.

Sidney squatted down, stretching her arms out, calling her son Todd. She looked back for a quick glance at Jason as he stood in line at the small shaved-ice truck. She watched as Todd took several clumsy steps toward her. The child carried a sippy cup half full of apple juice in his left hand while his right hand flailed away. She waved him toward her; he finally reached her after nearly falling to the ground. "Good job," she said taking Todd by his free hand.

Reece began to quicken his pace as he walked toward Sidney. He had only seen her a couple of times when she was with Lawson, and he doubted she remembered him. Still, Reece couldn't forget her. He recalled one particular time she visited Lawson at his office shortly after their engagement. She came in and brought him a lunch she had prepared. They seemed happy, and Lawson wished her a good day with a kiss right before she left. He waited several minutes to ensure she was gone before promptly throwing the lunch in the garbage.

He knew what Lawson was doing with her, and he also knew that Lawson had other women. It was always something he hated about Lawson. The often off-color comments he made about her sickened him and did much to cement his opinion that Lawson was an unworthy successor to Leonard Pierson. Not long after the incident, Lawson was dead.

At first, Reece did not believe the reports that this mousey-looking woman had dared to kill the heir to the Pierson name. After Lawson's death, Reece lost his connections to the Piersons altogether. He spent some time in Mexico, convinced that Sidney Lewis would not survive Lawson for long. One day years later, he was surprised to find out that Leonard Pierson was dead and Sidney Lewis was still alive.

Reece had not thought much about her until now. A chance encounter placed them together; he had his opportunity. He was close now. Any doubt that it was her was removed as he closed the distance between them. He slowly reached into his jacket to find the shoulder holster. He grasped the pistol's handle as he fixed his eyes on his target.

Only a few steps were between them as the weapon started sliding from its holster. That's when the child broke from her and stumbled toward him. The sippy cup fell from his hand and rolled to a stop at Reece's feet. Looking down, Reece made eye contact with the child. The child looked back at him with a curious expression. Reece bent down and picked up the fallen cup without a word.

Embarrassed, Sidney rushed up to her son. "I am so sorry, sir," she said with an apologetic smile. "He got away from me, I guess."

Reece squatted down, returned the cup to the boy, and patted him on his head. "That is quite alright, young lady. A boy full of energy is a good thing. What is his name?"

"Todd," she said, "He's definitely got his dad's sense of adventure."

"Well, Mr. Todd," Reece said as he slowly rose, "I hope you enjoy what's left of your day. And you, madam as well." With that, he smiled and walked on his way, secretly securing the hidden gun back in its place.

Sidney thanked him as he left them. A few minutes later, Jason joined her with their shaved ice. Though she couldn't swear to it, Sidney felt she had seen the stranger before but could not remember where. Shrugging her shoulders, the happy family made their way back to their car and headed for home.

Reece watched as they drove away. He could have easily disposed of her today, he mused as he watched them drive off. Instead, Reece decided that Sidney Lewis, or whatever her name was now, probably did the world a favor by ridding it of Lawson Pierson. He knew he could have sought his revenge against Roger Taylor by either killing or kidnapping the girl. However, if Leonard Pierson had seen it fit to spare her, who was he to go against the man's wishes? Besides, he knew of a better way to draw out Roger Taylor.

CHAPTER
FORTY

It was nearly 7:00 pm before Taylor arrived home from his short meeting with George Sullivan. He stopped and got a burger from a fast-food restaurant before returning to his place. He sat the bag down, walked to his kitchen, and grabbed a beer from the refrigerator. He settled down in his usual spot and turned on the television. Baseball season had yet to start, so he flipped through the channels. After cycling through the choices of reruns, talk shows, news, reality television, and general stuff, he didn't want to watch, he turned off the set and focused on his meal.

It had just started to turn cold, and he half considered sticking it in the microwave. Instead, he finished his meal, leaving the beer on his coffee table. He thought about going to bed early. He heard a knock on the door. Instinctively he reached for his service pistol and made his way across the room trying not to make a sound.

"Who is it?" he asked. He usually wasn't so cautious about answering the door but considering that someone recently tried to kill him, he wanted to be sure.

"Roger," came a familiar if unexpected voice, "it's Dylan Lee. Shelia's brother. Can I come in?"

He put away the pistol and opened the door as fast as his fingers allowed. Flinging it open, he saw the familiar face of Dylan Lee. "Oh my god, man, how are you? Yes, come in. Can I get you something? Got an extra beer or two if you'd like."

Dylan smiled and told him no thanks for the beer.

"So, what brings you around here? You still living in San Francisco?" Roger asked.

"Yes, my two boys are growing up, man. One graduates next year from high school, and the other is just starting. Lyla is still working for the same firm she did last time we talked and me, well, still crunching numbers at the accounting firm. How about you?"

"Same old, same old, fighting crime, risking life with daring do. What brings you out here?"

"Well, I don't know if you heard, but Dad died a couple of weeks ago. He had a massive heart attack in his sleep. So, I've been down here trying to take care of his stuff and make arrangements to take care of Mom."

"Oh, wow, no, I didn't hear about that. Man, I've been so wrapped up in a case I'm working on that I must have missed it. Dylan, I am so sorry. He was a good man."

Dylan laughed, "Yep, same old Roger. Never takes a day off. It's okay, really. Dad always spoke well of you back when you and Shelia were engaged. I think he always hoped you two would get back together. That was before..." he trailed off.

Roger felt a lump begin to form in his throat. "Yeah." He fell silent, looking away from his guest in embarrassment. "Dylan, I tried to keep her safe. I warned her so many times..."

"Roger, it's okay. She was my sister, and I knew how she could be once she got hooked on a story. She was relentless, and nothing anyone said could change that. Believe me, Dad tried."

Dylan put his hand on Roger's shoulder. "It was not your fault. None of us blamed you. Dad was more concerned about you than he was any of us, I think. No one in the family thinks any less of you. In fact, we are grateful to you."

"Grateful?" he said in a surprised voice. "Grateful for what?"

Dylan sat back in the chair. "She always regretted leaving you. Her eyes lit up anytime your name came up. She never said so, but there was just something there. We're grateful to you for giving her that, at least."

Roger tried to say something. He was not often at a loss for words, but this was one of those times he did not know what to say. He finally managed to find his voice. "She really was special, wasn't she? I miss her every day, and I'm sure I always will."

"So do I," Dylan said as he fought back a tear. Suddenly he remembered. "Oh man, before I forget why I came, I have something for you." Dylan had a blue canvas shopping bag with him. "While we were cleaning some of Dad's things, we found some of Shelia's stuff we wanted you to have," he said while handing the bag to Roger.

Inside were old photographs of Roger and Shelia as a young couple. He found the picture they took after he proposed. She was showing off the ring. The happy images took him back to a time when life seemed so much easier, somehow simpler.

He remembered that night so well, how he planned for weeks for just the right moment and said just the right words. There they were by a small fountain in a small park after a beautiful dinner at their favorite place to eat. They held hands as they walked, smiling, laughing, and even stealing a quick kiss. They stopped by the park's fountain; he reached into his pocket just as her phone began to ring. She turned around and flashed a finger as a sign to hold on a second.

She chatted on the phone with her back to him, but she must have realized he was waiting, so she gave him a backward glance. That was when she saw him down on one knee, ring in hand, offering it to her. Shelia nearly dropped her phone and told whoever

235

it was on the other end she would call them back. With his knee killing him, he still managed to slip the ring on her finger. They embraced in a way that he hoped would last forever. Half an hour later, her mother took the photo he held in his hand.

"You know, I almost don't recognize these kids. Seems like forever and yesterday all in the same breath," he said.

Reaching down into the bag, he found a small box. Opening it revealed the engagement ring.

"Dylan, I can't accept this. It belongs with your family." He never thought he would see the ring again, assuming the Lee family would keep it. Roger felt it was proper for them to have it since he gave it to Shelia and refused to take it back when she offered.

"No, I think Shelia would want you to have it," Dylan said with a sad smile. "I saw her put it on several times when she visited Mom and Dad. She'd put it on and then take it off after she admired it. I think she regretted leaving for Sacramento. Funny, or maybe it's sad, how life works sometimes." He shook himself out of the blue glaze that had washed over him and smiled. "No, Roger, it's yours and belongs to you."

The two men continued to talk over old times and other things for about another hour before Dylan had to leave. He told Roger he would be in town a few more days before heading back to San Francisco and said they should meet again. Roger agreed. The two shook hands, which gave way to a warm embrace.

"Take care, Dylan," Roger said as the other man turned to go.

"You too, and I mean it. Call me, and let's get together again before I go home."

Roger agreed and shut the door when Dylan was halfway to his car. He sat back on the couch and realized the ring was still in his hand. He stared at it, the light every now and again giving color to the diamond mounted on its setting. He tried to think of how many times she'd worn that ring and the connection it made between the two of them.

Walking at last into his bedroom, he placed the picture of their engagement and the ring on his dresser cabinet. As he readied for bed, images of Shelia rushed by in a flurry of emotion. Sitting down on his bed, he felt a wave of sadness, followed by a peace he couldn't explain. When he was finally ready, he lay down and covered himself. The temperature in the bedroom was not hot, but something caused his eyes to sweat.

At least, that's the way he chose to remember it.

CHAPTER
FORTY-ONE

It was well after lunch before Tavon called him with news that he had cracked the encryption on Davis's laptop. Taylor finished the small task he'd started at his desk before peeking into the squad room to find Barnes. She was not at her desk, so walked outside and called her. When she answered, he told her to drop what she was doing and meet him at Tavon's.

She beat him to Tavon's office since she was only a few blocks away finishing up an incident report.

Tavon sat at his desk and gave Barnes his full attention. As Taylor walked in, Tavon told her how one of his customers kept deleting files he needed for his computer to work correctly. The man deleted the file three or four times, and Tavon had to reload it every time. Barnes, for her part, played the interested guest, but she was relieved when Taylor finally arrived.

Taylor wanted to get straight to the point. "What've you got for me, Tavon?" he said as he took his place next to Barnes. He could tell the lack of sleep the night before was starting to get to him since he was a little short with his speech. Tavon didn't seem to notice or mind.

"Hey, Taylor, I told you I work magic, but this took some extra abracadabra from yours truly." He turned back to his screen and punched some keys on the computer. The encrypted files appeared almost instantly. "I stayed up most of the night trying to crack this and still didn't get it to open until about an hour ago. Whoever did this knew their stuff."

"Is there a way to find out who these files belonged to?" Barnes asked.

"Hey, pretty lady, I was waiting on the main man over there to arrive for the big reveal. Just give me a second," he said as he punched a few keystrokes. "There it is. Jordan Byrd, that's the guy."

"Jordan Byrd? How do you know that?" Taylor asked him as his heart began to beat faster.

"Well, I could tell you about my magic touch, but it's right here. Dude put his name on things like a good boy."

"Good work Tavon. Can you copy these files for me? Taylor asked.

Tavon handed him a portable hard drive. "Already got you covered. Just finished the download. You can open them, right?"

"I got it figured out, I think. If not, Barnes can do it. She's pretty good with computers herself, you know."

"Really? How sweet is that? Lovely, smart, and talented," Tavon said as he cast his longing gaze back to Barnes.

"We really should be going now. Right Taylor?" she asked as she started toward the door.

"Oh yeah, of course, Detective Barnes. Gotta go, police stuff, you know."

"Well, if you need anything, why don't you send her next time?"

"Okay, sure, Tavon. Thanks again. Just send your bill to the department as usual."

Several minutes later, they were back in Taylor's office going through the files Tavon had decrypted. "Jordan kept all of these files for Lawson Pierson, and Davis killed him for them. What is so important about these that would get him killed? It all looks like old information," Taylor said. "Look, like this one here. We found this information when we were about to bust Leonard Pierson."

Barnes clicked on another file and began to scroll through it. "Maybe there was something else going on. Look, these records talk about shipping information, dates, information on cargo, and recipients. What if Jordan was trying to use this information against some of these people? Like maybe he tried to blackmail some of these low level players."

"Can you run a search on these files? Like a quick, type it in type search?"

Barnes smiled to herself, "Yes, what do you want to look for?"

"Okay, good. Type in the name Edgar Reece."

"Where did you come up with that name?" Barnes asked.

"Oh, I took a little trip yesterday to visit our old friend George Sullivan. He's doing great, by the way. Asked about you too."

"Really?" she asked with skepticism.

"Well, not in so many words, but I'm sure he thought about you at some point in our little conversation. You got anything?"

"Yeah, right here. All kinds of bad stuff in a lot of places. Drug running, guns in the U.S. and Central America. Looks like Lawson kept good notes on him. You think Byrd tried to contact him?"

"I think that is the most logical explanation. Reece must have been this mysterious contact Davis worked for, but according to Sullivan, this Reece guy was a loner and not really part of the Pierson network."

"What if he wanted to be more?" she asked.

"You mean like what?"

"What if he wanted to build his own little network? Like trying to take up with some of Pierson's former clients," Barnes postulated.

"So, Jordan tries to blackmail him, and then this Reece guy

sends Davis after him. Davis kills Jordan and gives the files to Reece, but before he does, he keeps the originals and gives Reece a copy. But how did Davis get the files open?"

"Maybe he forced Jordan to give him access to the encryption before he killed him. That's the only thing that makes sense. Still, how do we know that Reece is the contact?"

"Fits the descriptions we got of the guy that killed Davis. What little we could piece together, at any rate. We know he was keeping tabs on Davis and had access to his home, so he takes one of Davis's uniforms and walks through the front door. Waits for his opportunity to kill Davis and goes right back the way he came, and no one suspects a thing. He knew our procedures and where our blind spots were from Davis. Probably been inside our building dozens of times."

"You're guessing right now, aren't you?" she asked.

"Hypothesizing from what we know and circumstantial evidence," he responded. Taylor began to feel some of the effects of the lack of sleep kicking in again. "Keep digging; see if you can find how Jordan got in touch with him. Find something we can use to get this guy out in the open."

"Wait a minute Taylor, this guy tried to kill you, and you don't even know him? What does he have against you?"

"I don't know. Let's find Reece and ask him."

CHAPTER
FORTY-TWO

It took several days of crawling and scrolling through the multiple files Jordan Byrd kept, but Barnes finally thought she had something worth showing Taylor. She called him over and gave a report of all she had done.

"It's, like you said, mostly stuff we already knew. Most people here are either in jail, out of the game, or dead. But here's the interesting part, right here. It lists Lawson's contacts and how to get in touch with them."

"Okay, so?" he asked.

"Well, look at this one here," she said as Taylor stooped down to better see her screen. "Jordan seemed very interested in this one. It's one he accessed multiple times and one of the last that he ever contacted."

"So, you're saying this is the number we're looking for?" he asked her.

"Only one way to find out," Barnes replied.

Roger grinned as he began to dial the number on his cellphone. Three rings later, a voice greeted him with the usual "Hello?"

It struck Roger as odd that the voice sounded so normal, so

commonplace. He didn't know what he expected the man to sound like, but he imagined it was somehow darker or sinister. It was almost enough to make him forget why he called in the first place.

"Hello, is this Mr. Edgar Reece?" Silence followed. For a moment, Roger thought that the man might hang up. This was a gamble, but he pushed. "Mr. Reece, are you there?" More silence. Roger felt his heart sink just a little.

"Who do I have the pleasure of speaking to?" came the voice on the other end.

"This is Detective Roger Taylor. How are you today, Mr. Reece?"

"Bravo, Detective, bravo indeed. I was beginning to think we'd never speak. Is the lovely Detective Barnes nearby?"

"She's here. We'd both love to meet you in person. Why don't we meet up here at the station? You already know your way around here so well. Come on back; we'll have a snack waiting for you."

"Oh, I'm sure that would be lovely, but I'm afraid I won't be available today. I must say, though, that I hated to kill your man Davis. He was so good at following orders. He told me a lot about you and the lovely Detective Barnes. Sorry about your car."

"Hey, that's alright. Come on over, and we'll exchange insurance information. You, me, Barnes, and a public defender can have a pleasant conversation."

Reece laughed. "I would certainly like that, I'm sure, but I'm afraid not. So many irons in the fire, you know."

"Well, take a break, and let's meet up. Everyone needs a rest now and again. Tell you what, I'll come to you. Just tell me where to come to find you."

"Oh, there's no need for that, Detective. As it happens, I'm coming to see you. I'm patient, but I can't wait to see you again."

"Again? We've never met."

"Oh, but we have, at least from a distance. You don't know how often I've watched your home and observed you at crime scenes.

Even stood not ten feet from you the last time I visited your little station house. Trust me, I know you very well, but I'm afraid our little chess game is almost over now. I'm looking forward to seeing how it ends, aren't you?"

With that, the line went dead. Taylor looked at Barnes with concern all over his face. "Looks like we're going to have company. We need to take precautions. If you've any friends or relatives you're worried about, you might want to call them."

"From the look on your face, you should be the most worried. Do you want someone to stay outside your apartment just in case?" Barnes asked. She knew he would never admit it, but he was afraid. The man they were dealing with was a brazen killer, and while she did have people she was concerned for, she knew Taylor was the primary target.

"No, that won't be necessary. Reece wants a showdown, so he likely won't go after me directly. He'll probably try to force a confrontation on his terms. We need to minimize any collateral damage to those he can use."

"What if you're wrong? What if he's waiting for you outside with a rifle or another bomb?"

"Well, I guess I won't get my security deposit on my rental car then," Roger jokingly answered.

"I'm glad you're taking this so seriously, Taylor. I mean it. I'm requesting that the Chief put a watch on you."

"Dammit, Barnes, it won't do any good. We're stretched too thin as it is. He's going to seek me out—"

"Which is why I'm ordering a protection detail on you round the clock," came the voice of Chief Vanderbeck from just outside his office door.

"Chief, if he sees a uniform, he will not come out of hiding. He's too smart for that," Taylor said in a voice that betrayed his annoyance. This is precisely what he wanted to avoid. Reece had a personal crusade against him, so it was best to keep everyone out of danger.

"We'll make it a plainclothes officer. McClendon will have the first watch since you two seemed to have bonded so well. Barnes, see to the rotation." Turning her attention back to Taylor, "And not another word of protest out of you. Do I make myself clear?"

"Perfectly," he replied. With that, the discussion was over.

Days passed, but there was no sign of Reece. It was as if the man had vanished into the air. Taylor hated to say I told you so, but he still found the occasion to do so. Reece would wait until their guard was down and then strike. He was certain it would not be against him directly, at least not at first.

He tried to keep busy as best he could, but with an entourage following him, it was hard to get much of anything done. The extra attention slowed him down, made him more noticeable than before. Eventually, he knew their guard would come down. In fact, the detail made him a little lax.

Then, he got the call. The game was about to begin at last.

CHAPTER
FORTY-THREE

"Good evening Detective Taylor. I'm glad we finally get to speak again," Reece taunted him. The man's voice grated on Taylor. He sounded like someone trying too hard to sound sophisticated and not doing an excellent job. "I do hope we can finally meet without the escorts you've had these last days."

I tried to tell them, Taylor thought.

"Yeah, sure. Let me know where you want to meet up. You bring your guys, I'll bring mine, and the last man standing wins. How about that?"

"As exciting as that sounds, I'm afraid I must decline. I have something much better in mind."

"Oh really? Sounds like you're going through a lot of trouble. Why don't you make it easy on yourself and surrender?"

"A joker to the end, aren't you? You know a man who just recently lost someone so valuable to him really shouldn't make jokes. Or is that how you deal with your problems? Make light, laugh it off. In some ways, I expected better."

"Tell me, what's this about anyway? Are you mad about the

whole Pierson thing still? Is that it? Be honest, this whole thing is because you had an unhealthy man crush on Leonard Pierson."

"Now there's the bravado. I told my guest here that's probably how you'd react. He told me almost nothing about you, at least not at first. I almost wept when he told me how you and his sister never got the life you wanted. It's a sad story, really. No wonder you make jokes to cover your guilt. Isn't that right, Mr. Lee?"

"Lee? Dylan? Listen, you son of a bitch, if you—"

"Oh, please, let's not resort to threats. We both know how this conversation ends. I want to meet with you tonight. At the place, we first met."

"Place we first met?"

"Yes. Do you remember a small warehouse you raided a while back when you were investigating Mr. Pierson? The one where the reporter, Shelia, that was her name, right? It was the time when she showed up unexpectedly. You don't remember me, but I was there. I managed to slip through your little trap and followed you to her vehicle. I could have ended it all right then, but I deemed the risk too great. Now, it's time to finish our game where we left off. This time all the pawns are gone. It's just the important pieces now, Detective. Time to make your move."

"Yeah, about that. Hope you're ready because this will be anything but a fun game for you."

"Dylan and I look forward to seeing you, Detective. Oh, and leave your friends out of this. Tonight is about you and me. Poor Dylan is counting on you, so don't keep him waiting." Reece ended the call abruptly.

Hanging up the phone, Taylor thought for a moment about his options. If he walked out the front door, Officer McClendon, sitting in the parking lot, would see him and try to stop him. Thinking over his situation, Taylor decided his only option was to escape through his bedroom window.

Taylor was grateful he lived on a ground floor rental. Slipping out a rear window was the easy part. Getting past McClendon was going to be much more challenging. He decided not to go to his car. Instead, he called the only one he knew he could trust.

"Barnes," he said as she answered the phone, "I need a ride." She began to protest almost immediately. "Look, Barnes, I just got off the phone with Reece, and he wants me to come alone."

"Alone? Are you insane?"

"Barnes, he's got Shelia's brother. He's been in town since his father died. Look, if a bunch of uniformed officers shows up, Dylan is dead. I need you on this one."

Dead air followed for what seemed like hours. "Fine," Barnes exclaimed, giving in, "okay, I'll do it. Where do I meet you?"

She didn't like this at all. Every instinct in her said this was a bad idea, and Roger was playing cowboy. Still, she knew if she didn't do this for him, he would find a way to get there. At least now he would have some backup. She just hoped it didn't get them both killed.

CHAPTER
FORTY-FOUR

Reece hung up the phone with a sickening smile across his face. He looked at Dylan, regarding the man with disdain.

"Well, Mr. Lee, your champion is undoubtedly on his way. This seems a fitting place for our final battle, does it not?" Dylan struggled with the ropes that tied him to the chair. "Do save your strength. You will need it once this is over. Assuming, of course, that you survive."

Dylan stopped struggling and stared back at his captor. "What do you want from me? Why are you doing this?" he asked not expecting the man to answer. Dylan was actually surprised when the man gave him an answer.

"From you?" Reese asked. "Nothing. At least, not yet. Believe it or not, I hope you survive this encounter. Your part in this game is twofold. First, as bait to lure Roger Taylor here. The second purpose is to bear witness to what you see take place here tonight."

"Why do you need me to be a witness. Just what am I supposed to see?"

"Must I spell it out for you, Mr. Lee? You are here to witness the death of Roger Taylor. You will live to tell how I was able to kill the man responsible for the death of Leonard Pierson. If, however, the battle should go against me, let's say that a pawn should never survive the death of a king. You and I will die together, and Taylor will know he again failed the woman he loved. So, whether I live or die, I win."

"This is insane," Dylan protested. "Why go through all this trouble? What did he ever do to you?"

"Roger Taylor destroyed my life. When he took down Leonard Pierson's operation, I was left without an organization to protect me. Without the Pierson name, I was vulnerable, weak, and unable to sustain myself. Then I realized that with tragedy comes opportunity. I could rebuild what he destroyed. When I kill Taylor, I will be known as the man who took down Pierson's killer. Then I can return to my interests south of the border triumphally, virtually untouchable."

"It will never work," Dylan protested. "Even if you kill Roger, no one will follow you."

Reece pulled a large knife from a sheath attached to his leg. "A pawn should not speak to his king like that." Taking the knife, he turned the flat side to Dylan's face. "If you forget your place again, I will see just how well this knife cuts." Reece pulled the knife back quickly, opening a small cut on Dylan's face. He put the knife back in its sheath. "When Taylor arrives, you will remain silent. If you speak before he finds you, I will end your life. Then after I finish Taylor, I will visit that family or yours."

Stepping away from his captive, Reece picked up a case with a disassembled scoped rifle. He assembled the pieces carefully, one by one. Satisfied, he made his way to the spot he picked out. There were numerous places to hide in the old warehouse. No one had been here for quite some time, and things were scattered and forgotten.

This will make a most interesting game, Reece thought.

As he waited, his mind drifted back to the day he found out that

Pierson was dead. The cartel captain, Eduardo Luis Delgado, seized and held him somewhere in Mexico for weeks. Reece knew something must have happened because Delgado would never be so bold otherwise. At first, they beat him, deprived him of sleep, and left him lying naked in a dark room for seemingly no other reason than the enjoyment. Then suddenly, nothing. It was as if they had forgotten about him. Reece had long since lost track of time, but he must have gone days without food.

He had nearly given up when one day, the door finally opened. In walked a group of uniformed men that Reece assumed were either Federales or military. He wasn't sure, and he was too weak to care. It was far from a rescue. What followed was a new kind of hell.

He was taken to what, at best, could be described as a prison. There he received what medical attention they had and meager food rations. The Federales subjected Reece to round-the-clock questioning and more sleep deprivation. Day after day, they tried to find out who he was and what he could offer them. He had nothing to give.

Reece thought he would die in Mexico until Ricardo Valenzuela, Pierson's associate, entered the prison. "I heard rumors of some gringo locked up here," he said. "I did not expect it to be you, amigo." Valenzuela took Reece back to his hacienda and began to nurse him back to health. After a month, Reece finally began to feel his strength return.

"You are probably wondering why I saved you," Valenzuela said once Reece had recovered from his ordeal.

"The thought did cross my mind. Not to be ungrateful, but why would you stick yourself out for me?"

"There is an opportunity here I think, amigo. Pierson is dead, but there are enough pieces left for someone to put back together. The way I see it, you seem as likely as anyone to be able to pull it off. I need someone in the Estados to help me expand my operations since my competition here has, how should we say, gone away. Are you that man?"

"I can be."

"Bueno, I have a list of a few people here that can help you get started. I assume you know people in the Estados you can use, si?"

"Oh, indeed I do." A week later, Reece returned to the U.S. to rebuild the Pierson Organization. Once he was established, he began planning his revenge on Roger Taylor. Davis became a valuable tool in getting him closer to Taylor. Then Jordan Byrd nearly ruined the whole thing, so Davis proved his usefulness again. Unfortunately, Davis tried to break free of Reece's influence. He had to be eliminated, but sacrifices had to be made in every game.

Now, at last, the board was set. For a time, Reece actually hated that the game was about to end. There were so few worthy opponents, but every game must eventually conclude. Today would be the day.

CHAPTER
FORTY-FIVE

Barnes picked Taylor up at the agreed upon point several minutes later. McClendon seemed none the wiser that Taylor had slipped out of his apartment.

"This is a terrible idea," she told him. He hardly seemed to take notice of her. He checked his service pistol over and over on the way. "Do you want to get killed? Is that what you think will finally make it up to Shelia? Is that what you think?"

"No, it won't, but if I don't do this and Dylan dies…" he trailed off. "Just drive."

Minutes later, they were at a spot near the warehouse. It all started to come back to him as he surveyed the scene. He had led a team here based on some information he received near the end of the Pierson investigation. They were ready to move in when one of his men spotted movement in the trees. For a moment, Taylor thought it was a lookout and that their cover might be blown. Searching the thin tree line, he spotted Shelia trying to hide among trees too small to conceal even her small frame.

She nearly jumped out of her skin when he confronted her. He told her to stay clear or he would have her arrested. Surprisingly, she stayed put until the raid was all over. He walked her back to the car with the usual "you should be more careful speech" and her usual "I can take care of myself" response. Neither suspected they were being watched as they argued beside her car.

It was getting late in the day, so he decided to take advantage of the last of the daylight to make his move.

"Look, Barnes, I have to go alone. If I'm not back in a half hour, it probably means I'm not coming back. If that happens, bring in as many people as possible and catch this guy."

"Roger, you can't be serious. I'm going—"

"No, you're not. Stay here, and call this in. You can't let Reece escape. That's an order."

He turned to go and started making his way down to the warehouse. He suddenly stopped and turned back to her. "Barnes, you're the best partner I ever had. I," he paused, "I just thought you should know that. Just know that." He gave her a sad smile and made his way to the warehouse.

She wanted more than anything to run after him. Her heart was beating so fast she feared it would erupt out of her chest at any moment. He was right, though. If the worst happened, she couldn't let Reece escape. Picking up her phone, she called the station for backup. Deep down, she knew they would never make it here in time. Whatever happened would be long over by the time help arrived.

As she lowered the phone from her ear, she could see Taylor. He pulled his weapon and leaned against the wall next to the door. Cautiously he tested it, and she could see him slowly open it. Reece would know they were here now for sure. She watched as he took a deep breath and finally made entry into the building. From the moment he stepped inside, near panic filled her. She waited maybe three or four minutes before making her decision.

Orders or not, Taylor was not going in there alone.

CHAPTER
FORTY-SIX

The inside of the warehouse was dark, as expected. Metal shelves with various-sized boxes broke the warehouse into sections. The setting sun shone through here and there from the windows and small holes in the walls. The smell of musk and stagnate water was nearly overpowering at times. Taylor thought that if he was not an allergy sufferer before, he probably would be after leaving here. If he left here alive.

He slowly made his way through the dark space taking cover against the shelves and boxes where he could. The trouble was he couldn't be sure where Reece was located. Slowly he inched forward. Peeking around corners, looking over boxes. Anything to try and stay out of Reece's line of sight. Of course, the man knew he was here. How could he not know? He could have ambushed him at the door or rigged this place to explode, but no, he wanted a game. Reece has made several chess references in his conversations with Taylor. To Reece, this was a game of revenge.

"Oh well done, Detective, well done," came the mocking voice of Reece from somewhere in the darkness. "You remember your military training well, I see." Reece's voice boomed from nowhere and seemingly everywhere simultaneously. "I've had the same train-ing, too, you know." There was a mocking tone in Reece's voice, like what Taylor thought a cat might say to a mouse if it could talk. Then the realization hit Taylor. *I'm the mouse.*

Suddenly a shot rang out. The bullet missed Taylor, but it caused him to take cover.

"I wonder if you can see me, Detective. Because I can see you."

Another shot. This one passed so close Taylor could hear it buzz past. Taylor kept low and switched his position, trying to put as many obstacles between himself and Reece as possible. He thought he knew the general area Reece must be hiding in, but he still could not see him.

"So tell me," Taylor called out, "why go through all this trouble. Was it for Lawson?"

"Lawson?" Reece responded with a sneer in his voice. "Lawson was a petulant child, unworthy of the Pierson name. A spoiled child of a man who defied his father at every turn."

That's it just keep talking, Roger thought as he crept around.

Reece had not fired at him in a while, so that must mean he couldn't see him. He decided to goad him more.

"So what? Lawson paid you well and gave you what you wanted."

"What I wanted?" came the angry reply. "Leonard Pierson was a god among men, and Lawson was too foolish to listen to him. I almost decided to kill the girl that ended Lawson's miserable life myself, but then I realized she really did the world a favor. I hated him. Hated him for the disdain in which he held his father."

Another shot. This one was not close at all.

"Is that what this is really about? Jealousy over Lawson being the chosen one of Leonard Pierson? This whole thing is really nothing more than hero worship?"

"Of course not. I will be the one to carry on the Pierson legacy now. I have contacted many of Mr. Pierson's former associates. I have begun to line them up to be in my organization. Then Jordan Byrd contacted me and tried to rob me of my legacy. He tried to squeeze me for money. Such a small dream."

"So, you had Davis kill Byrd and steal the files so you could continue building this new organization with all of Lawson's information. What you didn't count on was Davis was smart enough to copy the files and keep the originals for himself. How ironic; it's the same trick that eventually brought down Pierson."

Roger kept moving, trying to find any hint of where Reece or Dylan was in the labyrinth. Taylor peeked around the corner toward a small light illuminating what looked like a man bound to a chair. Carefully he made his way there. He was right; Dylan was tied with his hands and feet to the chair with thick ropes. Taylor put his finger to his lips as the two locked eyes. Dylan shook his head, motioning him to look the other way. Taylor raised his weapon and turned.

Reece saw Taylor at the exact moment and matched his speed in raising his weapon. "You give Davis too much credit, Detective. He was simply a pawn who outlived his usefulness."

The man was almost gleeful as he held his weapon to Taylor's head. Both men keenly focused on the other. "And now the final move. One winner and one loser. Which of us shall it be?"

"Drop the gun Reece," came a voice from seemingly nowhere.

"Ah, the beautiful Detective Barnes at last steps from the shadows. Now the game comes to its conclusion."

"Give it up, Reece, you can't win," Taylor ordered.

"Ah, but I can still win. Just simply by removing the queen," he scolded as he turned his weapon on Barnes. Taylor stood there as the world seemed to move slowly all around him. Shots rang out, and the man reeled on his feet. Another shot and then two more, and Reece was on the ground. One more time, Reece tried to aim his weapon, but Barnes's next shot found the right mark, and Reece fell dead.

Taylor ran to Dylan and took the gag off of his mouth. "Roger, I'm sorry. He took me outside of my mother's house. I couldn't…"

"It's okay now, brother. It's over now." Taylor took his pocketknife and cut Dylan loose. The man stood stiffly. "Hold on, I'll get an ambulance."

"Don't worry about me. Check on her," Dylan told him pointing toward Barnes. In his excitement to free Dylan, Taylor had nearly forgotten her.

Barnes stood frozen, still pointing her weapon at the lifeless body of Edgar Reece. Her face was expressionless. Sweat beaded on her brow as her breath went in and out of her body. The smell of burned gunpowder lingered heavily in the air.

"Barnes." Taylor walked toward Reece's body and kicked away the man's gun. He did a quick search and found no other weapons. "Barnes," he said again as he finally made his way to her. "Laura, it's okay now. Laura, it's over. Let me have the gun."

She continued to stare at the lifeless body, mesmerized by the sight and the knowledge of what she had done. "I've never fired it like this before," she said. "All those years in traffic, I hardly ever took it from the holster." Taylor put his hand on the weapon and gently pushed her arms down. She finally let go of the weapon, and Taylor put the gun away. She stood motionless as Taylor took off his jacket and put it around her shoulders.

"Laura," he spoke in a soft, almost whispered tone, "come on. It's over now. You did good."

Taylor tried as best as he could to guide her. In the distance, they heard the sirens blaring. Barnes crossed her arms and held onto the shoulders of Taylor's jacket. "It wasn't like I thought it would be," she said without looking at either Taylor or Dylan.

"It never is," Taylor said. The first cars began to arrive. Barnes walked toward the approaching vehicles. She directed the first officer on the scene toward Taylor, then began to busy herself with her duties, her training snapping her out of her haze.

Taylor supervised the scene as a whirlwind of activity began. Dylan was transported to the hospital for tests and observations. Barnes sat in the passenger seat of a patrol car, staring off into no particular area. Taylor walked over to her, "We'll need to keep your weapon for the shooting investigation. It's just standard procedure for an officer involved shooting. Don't worry; you did everything right."

"Did I?" she asked. She smiled faintly before taking her car fob from her keychain. "Drive yourself home," she said. "McClendon is going to drive me to my place. Just bring it back sometime tomorrow. I've got a few days of vacation, so I may need the car back. Think I might go see my parents or something."

"You do that," he said.

McClendon walked up to drive her home. Taylor extended his hand. "Sorry about leaving like that. No hard feelings, right?"

"We're good, Detective. But next time, ask me to take a lunch break or something."

"I'll do that," Taylor agreed, and soon McClendon and Barnes were on their way. Taylor watched as the car disappeared from sight. He thought about calling her later but decided to let her rest instead. He returned to the crime scene eager to finish processing.

CHAPTER
FORTY-SEVEN

The car pulled into the parking lot of Barnes's apartment complex. She felt tired, more than tired, in fact, as McClendon parked the car. He looked over at her. "You need me to walk you to the door, Detective?" She seemed not to hear him at first because she didn't react. Barnes seemed transfixed as she stared out of the passenger side window. "You all right, Detective?" McClendon asked her again, a little louder this time, which seemed to snap her out of her malaise.

"No, I'm fine. Thank you," came her muffled response.

"Hey, I don't mean any disrespect, Detective, but you look like hell. You want me to call someone for you or maybe run get you a bite to eat?"

"You're a good man McClendon. I'm okay. Really," she said as she opened the car door. "Thanks again for the ride." Barnes shut the door and started to walk toward her apartment. The cat was not there. She couldn't get the door open fast enough.

Walking inside, she flung her things by the door, not stopping to notice where everything fell. Barnes walked straight to her bathroom and ran the water in her sink. Bending down, she started splashing the cold water on her face. She stared into the mirror blankly while a thousand thoughts seemed to rush through her mind.

She stood back up and noticed a sharp pain in her right side. Looking down at her side, she saw a large tear in her shirt. Carefully she moved her hand to her side and winced in pain as she touched the spot where her shirt was torn. Without thinking, she ripped apart the shirt without stopping to unbutton it. She flung the shirt to the bathroom floor as she turned to view her side in the mirror.

Reece's shot must have come much closer than anyone thought. A large red streak resembling a burn mark was located just below her ribcage. The skin was torn in places. It looked like a deep scratch. Barnes knew it was more serious. The pain began to set in, then the burn.

Trembling, she opened her medicine cabinet, grabbed a bottle of hydrogen peroxide and some gauze. She poured peroxide on the gauze and held it to her side, causing excruciating pain. After cleaning the wound, she affixed the remainder of the gauze to her side with some medical tape. Keeping her hands steady enough to apply the cover to the wound was difficult, but somehow, she managed.

Walking into her living room, she retrieved her phone and dialed Skylar's number. It rang several times, and for a second, Barnes thought it would go to voicemail.

Skylar asked, "Laura, what's going on?"

"Sky," she said, doing her best to hold herself together for a little longer. "Can you come over here? I really need someone to talk to."

"Laura, is everything okay?"

"No. No, Sky, it isn't. Do you have any vodka? Or anything really as long as it's strong."

"Okay, tell me what's going on right now, Laura or I'm calling the police and telling them you need help."

"Sky, I am the police. Would you please tell me if you're coming or not?"

"Laura, yes, for god's sake, yes, I am walking out the door right now. Just stay there, alright. Just stay there, and I'll be there as quickly as possible."

Barnes hung up the phone without another word. She sat on the couch, resting her elbows on her knees, replaying the day's events over and over. All she could see in her mind's eye was the cold grin on Reece's face as he aimed his gun at her. The moment replayed over and over as hours seemed to pass. She knew he was dead. She saw his body lying on the warehouse floor, but all she could think about was he had shot her. He tried to kill her, just as he killed Davis.

Then there was Davis. She remembered the last time they were together. Things were going so well between them. As silly as it sounded, she felt like she was falling in love with him, but something went terribly wrong. He lied to her and nearly killed her with a car bomb meant for Taylor. Now he was dead, and her last image of him was his body slumped over the table in the interrogation room. His throat was cut so severely that his head was nearly cut off.

It was all too much for her now. The world seemed to crash in on her, and she felt herself beginning to slip away. Anywhere on the planet would be a better place for her right now. Barnes wanted to sink into a bottle of something for a while. Anything to make her forget what she had been through for a time.

When the knock came on the door, she nearly jumped out of her skin. She tried to stop it, but a shriek came out of her mouth, which caused Sky to knock harder as she called Laura's name. Summoning up the courage to stand, Barnes moved to the door and opened it.

Sky held a bag. She looked worried. "Laura, what's happened? Talk to me," she pleaded with Barnes. "Laura, answer me."

"Come in. Shut the door," Barnes finally managed. When Sky

closed the door, the wall Barnes had built around her emotions finally collapsed. She flung her arms around Sky, holding her so tightly Sky had trouble breathing. Tears flowed from Barnes's eyes.

Dropping the bag with the vodka bottle, Sky put her arms around her friend. "It's okay, Laura. It's going to be okay," she said over and over in a quiet voice. Putting her arm around her friend, Sky led Barnes over to the couch. "Laura, what happened, and why aren't you wearing your shirt?"

Letting go of Sky, Barnes leaned back on the couch. Sky noticed the gauze pad on her friend's side. "Laura, what happened. Are you hurt?"

Barnes wiped her face with her hand. "Sky, I got shot."

Panic rose inside Skylar. "Shot? Laura, we have to get to the hospital. Can you walk? Wait, no, I should call an ambulance."

"No, Sky, you can't. The department can't know about this. Please don't call the ambulance."

"Laura, you just said you've been shot. A doctor needs to look at that. I can see it's still bleeding."

"Sky, it's just a scratch."

"Let me see it then."

"Sky, I'm fine. I just need…."

"Bullshit, you're not fine. You're a wreck. Now let me see it, or I'm calling."

"Fine," Laura said as she carefully removed the bandage, causing her side to throb.

Looking at the wound, Sky gasped. "Laura, that's more than a scratch. I don't think it needs stitches, but you should see a doctor." She said, "Come on, I'm taking you right now."

"Sky, I'm not going to the hospital."

"Yes, you are. Either you're getting in my car, and I'll drive you, or I'm calling an ambulance. Which one do you want?"

"No, I'm not going."

"Fine then," she said as she pulled out her phone. "911 it is."

"No, wait. Okay, okay. I'll go. I'll think of a reason for the hospital not to report it."

An hour later, they were sitting in a curtained area of the emergency room. Skylar could tell Barnes was angry with her, but her friend knew bringing Laura was the right thing to do. The nurse gave Laura some pain medication, which was finally starting to relax her. Just before the doctor came in, Laura looked at Sky and mouthed the words, "thank you." Sky smiled back at Barnes and took her hand gently.

The doctor walked in a few minutes later. "Well, Mrs. Barnes…"

"Detective Barnes," Skylar interjected.

"Sorry, Detective Barnes, then. The good news is there doesn't appear to be any internal damage, and we've stopped the bleeding. I want you to stay off your feet for a couple of days, just in case. I've also filed the report with the Police Department. I know that's not what you want to hear, but I have no choice. Just keep it clean. No heavy lifting or strenuous activity for at least a week."

She thanked him and promised to take it easy for a few days. Before he turned to go, he told her, "By the way, your friend did the right thing by bringing you in. If the wound had become infected, it would have been bad news. I'll have the nurse bring your discharge papers."

He disappeared behind the curtain, leaving the two women alone. Forty-five minutes later, she was being wheeled out to Sky's car. When they arrived back at the apartment, Sky insisted on staying the night with her. As they came through the door, Sky moved her toward the bedroom.

"No, put me on the couch," Barnes said in a weary voice.

"Laura, you need to go to bed."

"I'm not sleepy. Just let me sit up for a while. Not long, I promise."

"Alright, but you are not staying up all night. Do you hear me?"

"Fine. Did you bring the vodka bottle?"

"Laura, no. You have painkillers in your system."

"Sky, they're not that strong. Just one drink. Big enough to take the edge off."

"I give up. One drink, then you go to bed," Sky told her as she walked to the kitchen to get a glass. She returned with two glasses and a bottle of orange juice. Sitting down the glasses, Sky opened the orange juice and poured the glasses about two-thirds of the way full. Next, she retrieved the vodka bottle from the bag and poured a small amount into both glasses. Laura protested, but Sky was adamant about not overdoing it.

The two sat and chatted for several minutes. Barnes thanked Sky for everything she did for her and then disappeared into her bedroom. A minute or two later, she returned with a couple of extra blankets and a pillow for Sky. They said goodnight, and Laura went to lie down. Surprisingly, sleep took her quickly.

CHAPTER
FORTY-EIGHT

Barnes woke up about three in the morning. The pain in her side was not as bad as yesterday, but she felt stiff in all the wrong places. Quietly she opened the door to her bedroom and spotted Sky still asleep on the couch. Laura slowly moved from the bedroom to the coffee table where the vodka bottle sat. She picked up one of the glasses and poured it nearly full.

Laura felt bad about lying to Sky regarding the vodka, but she just wanted to drink away her concerns. Making her way back to the bedroom, she began to sip from the glass. The strong taste unsettled her more than she thought that it would. Laura was not a heavy drinker, and she knew she had more than enough in the glass to get drunk.

Back in the bedroom, she sat down on the bed. Almost by force, she filled her mouth with the clear liquid, feeling the burn as she swallowed it. She nearly retched but somehow managed to hold it down. Then she followed it with another, quicker sip from the glass. Feeling emotion hitting her again, she crawled into a ball and began to weep.

"You're not very slick, you know," Skylar said as she stood in the doorway.

Without waiting for Laura to respond, she walked over and sat next to her on the bed. "Might as well finish it."

Barnes did and shivered. Sky put her arm around Barnes and stayed with her until daybreak.

By 7:00 am Barnes was as sick as she ever remembered. "I think I drank half the bottle," she confessed as the buzz from the alcohol began to fade. Within an hour, Sky was holding her hair while she vomited. She thought she would feel better, but now Laura felt much worse.

Breakfast consisted of toast and coffee; it was the only thing she thought she could stomach. To her credit, Sky didn't criticize her friend or get preachy. She sat and let Laura go through whatever she needed without criticism or judgment.

"I guess I should tell you about what happened, shouldn't I?" Barnes finally managed to say. "I think I want a shower first, though. Is that okay with you?" Laura picked up her coffee cup, taking small sips of the warm liquid.

"Whenever you're ready, Laura," Sky said.

Barnes nodded and excused herself to the bathroom. She disrobed and stepped into the shower without letting the water warm up first. For the most part, she stood weakly and tried to keep her feet under her. The cold water snapped her into a greater aware-ness, which was starting to be bad because her head was beginning to pound. She found the strength to wash her hair and body, careful not to aggravate her injury. When she shut off the shower, the water had grown cold again.

She dried off and dressed before returning to Sky. It took time, but she recounted the events leading up to the gun battle. She recounted how Davis betrayed her and his death at Reece's hands. Then, Laura told how she got the gunshot wound. Sky listened to the whole story, trying to understand what her friend was going through.

Around lunchtime, Sky made ready to leave. She offered to buy Laura's lunch but Barnes doubted she could eat much. They embraced again; Sky promised to call and check on her later. Barnes thanked her again and waved goodbye.

Barnes shut the door and exhaled aloud. Her headache was not improving, and the bright sunshine outside didn't help much. Checking the clock on her cellphone, she saw that the early games were already underway. She decided to watch one of them no matter who was playing.

CHAPTER
FORTY-NINE

Roger arrived at Barnes's apartment sometime after lunch Sunday afternoon. Taylor thought about getting there earlier but decided to give her some space to process the previous day's events. As he knocked on the door, he reflected on the past several days. She, of course, would not admit it, but she had held high hopes for her relationship with Davis. Then, everything turned around and someone shot at her. She'd been grazed by the bullet then forced to kill someone for the first time. True, he was a worthless bastard, but it was never easy to take a life.

When she answered the door, Barnes had a disheveled look. Her hair hung partly in her face, and she wore a t-shirt and pair of shorts without shoes. Though he could tell she had showered, Laura otherwise looked like it was a long night. Her eyes squinted the sunlight, and she used her left hand to shield her eyes.

"Hey, Barnes, I uh…brought your car back. How are you feeling?"

"Yeah, I look and feel like hell. But the game is on, so I'll be fine," she told him, hoping she was telling the truth. "You want to come in and watch the game? The place is a mess right now."

"No, I can't stay," he said. "Listen, why didn't you call me last night? I could have gotten you to the hospital a lot quicker."

"I'm fine, Roger. Really I am. I threw a little pity party for myself last night with my friend Sky. She hasn't been gone long, so I haven't been alone for long. I swear I'm fine now. Except for a headache that won't go away."

It was hard for Taylor to see her like this. "Are you sure? I can call someone if you need me to. Maybe get you something to eat."

"No, I'm not thinking I'll be eating anything today." She stood at the door, not really knowing what more to say. "Don't you need the car? How are you going to get back to your place? I probably won't need it for a day or two."

"I'm good. Eddie's picking me up here in a bit. I'm going to hang out at the restaurant for the afternoon, and then he will take me home. I've got my rental car for a few more days, and I'll get my new one."

"Need I ask what you're getting?"

"A Charger, of course. All shiny and new." They both laughed softly. "So, what are you going to do for the next few days?" he asked her. "Got any plans?"

"I have some vacation time saved, so I'm going to see my parents. My Dad is in another fishing tournament and wants me to go with him. Other than that, I want to get out of town for a while. Get my mind back in order."

"Get some rest. You deserve it. We'll talk when you get back." Looking at the parking lot, he saw Eddie's car pulling into a parking spot. "My ride's here, so…" he trailed off. "Are you sure you don't need anything?"

"Thanks, no, I'm fine. At least, I will be. Do me a favor, and don't catch all the bad guys while I'm gone, okay?"

"No promises," he said. "See you when you get back." She smiled and shut the door as he turned to leave. Slowly, he walked to Eddie's car. He opened the door and sat in the passenger seat.

Eddie looked at him quizzically. "Everything alright?" he asked as he brought the car to life.

"It will be," Roger told him as he put his seatbelt on.

Eddie nodded and put the car in gear. "So, when we get there, should I get some onion rings ready for you?"

"Yeah," Roger said. "Today feels like an onion rings kind of day.

EPILOGUE

A month had passed since his showdown with Edgar Reece. Since then, life in Warrenton had slowed down to a more normal pace. It was late December, and the Christmas season was fully underway. Taylor drove his new Charger to a local hobby store. Before walking through the door, he stopped long enough to drop a couple of dollars in the bell ringer's bucket outside. Inside he greeted a couple of people who recognized him.

He reached the pick-up window at the back of the store. The man on duty was the same guy who had taken his order a couple of weeks before. He was on the phone with a customer. A minute or two passed before he hung up.

"Mr. Taylor, I have you ready to go. Take a look and see if you approve of my handiwork."

The piece was magnificent, better than he could have hoped.

"It looks amazing," Taylor said.

Satisfied, the man took the piece to the back and wrapped it in bubble wrap before cradling it in a cardboard box. He handed it across the counter.

Taylor got in his car. His thoughts turned to the Christmas

season. Shelia had loved this time of year. She often talked about how she would like to go somewhere and experience a white Christmas. He teased her that he'd seen a few too many white Christmases and was fine with never seeing another one. The look on her face had made him laugh, and he smiled at the thought.

On the way home he decided to stop by the fountain where he had proposed to her all those years ago. There were people everywhere. There were a few people around the fountain but not enough to interfere with his memories. He went back in time…imagined it was night…he was holding hands with a beautiful young woman and they were starting to plan a life together. He clung to the fading moment as long as he could before it slipped out of his mind like smoke through a clenched fist. He looked at the fountain, had one more thought for what might have been, then returned to his car and drove home.

When he got home he flung his things on the chair by the door. He was still carrying the package. One more time, a beer bottle minus one sip winked at him from the coffee table. He picked it up and poured the remainder down the kitchen sink before he plopped the bottle into the garbage can.

In the bedroom, he unwrapped the package with the care of a surgeon performing a delicate operation. He lifted the contents and admired it at arm's length for a while. The craftwork on the frame was perfect – a fitting tribute indeed.

He hung the frame on the nail he'd placed the night before. He spent a while adjusting it before he was convinced it was perfect and level. He stared at it for a while before he wandered back into the den.

He'd ordered the gold chain three weeks earlier. The saleswoman had tried her best to convince him to buy a charm to go with it, but the chain was all he wanted. Taylor took the chain to the hobby store and explained when he wanted. The frame was ready on time – and the setup was exactly what he'd requested: On the left of the frame a diamond engagement ring dangled from the chain. To the right stood a photo of a young man and a young woman. The woman was beaming almost as brightly as the dazzling ring on her left hand.

The display was a tribute of sorts – a memorial to a woman who now lived exclusively in the bittersweet Land of Memory.

ABOUT THE AUTHOR

Chad Spradley, who resides in Alabama, is an author and teacher of US History, Government, and Sociology in both high school and college. Along with his passion for teaching, Spradley is an enthusiastic sports fan and enjoys exploring various genres such as mysteries, science fiction, horror, and westerns. He likes to travel around the US and play electric guitar when not writing or teaching. Spradley has written two novels including A Long Road To Redemption, with Memories and Remorse being his second publication.